COPYRIGHT

REVIEWS

He Completes Me by Cardeno C.: Watching them find and make their own family was such fun for me... Thank you, Cardeno, for another insanely wonderful story that reminded me of the important things in life.

— Rainbow Book Reviews

Home Again by Cardeno C.: I was immediately swept up in the fast-paced storyline and captivated by the well-written and unique characters. ...Between the laugh out loud moments and the bittersweet-tearjerker ones, I was highly entertained throughout the book, and I truly hated to see it come to an end.

— Night Owl Reviews (Top Pick)

Just What the Truth Is by Cardeno C.: The narrative of this story was wonderfully engaging, providing the reader with the sense that they are living the story. I loved this book and highly recommend it to those who enjoy character-driven romances.

— The Romance Reviews

The One Who Saves Me by Cardeno C.: Cardeno C, once again, did a splendid job in bringing this story to the page. ...To see them growing from teenagers to wonderful men was a joy to me. Their friendship and devotion, Andrew's struggles, their lust, emotions and acceptance of each other was beautifully weaved together in a way that truly made this story real for me. The dialog was both entertaining and revealing. The events that took place throughout the story were perfectly placed to have their proper impact on the reader. I was grinning with happiness each and every time they got together, screaming at them to get their heads on straight and crying my eyes out with each betrayal and each painful thought.

— *LeAnn's Book Reviews*

Where He Ends and I Begin by Cardeno C.: Emotionally laden romance with excellent alternating dual first-person narration that I devoured.... I'm a sucker for the friends to lovers romance trope and I got that here but without a lot of angst that usually happens for the previously "straight" lead. Jake's total acceptance of his love for Nate had a simplicity that is rarely found in gay-for-you books and I ate it with a spoon! This book is emotionally intense where every sex scene is steeped in the men's grandiose feelings for each other and I loved this huge romantic relationship.... I loved how this romance was told as well as the huge, idealistic relationship between two nearly perfect men.

— *The Book Vixen*

Walk With Me by Cardeno C.: This book is everything that the Home series means to me. Love, friendship, family, growth, relationships, dreams, romance, hot sex, faith, hope, beauty and a delicious kiss of angst. ... This book made me laugh, frequently out loud, there were looks. There are some of the funniest scenes I have ever read in a romance.

— *Gay Listed Book Reviews*

DEDICATION

To Tisha Barcus, thanks for pushing me to publish my work—you're a doll.

CHAPTER ONE

DO YOU believe in love at first sight?

Jonathan Doyle sure did. Oh, he knew it was silly and naïve, but deep down he believed. He wanted to believe. Jonathan was a dyed-in-the-wool hopeless romantic. He always had been.

As a teenager, Jonathan spent hours watching old black-and-white movies on television. He was mesmerized by the chivalrous men holding doors open for their dates, taking their coats, pulling their chairs out, and all the rest of it. When other boys dreamt of growing up to be basketball players, rock stars, or firefighters, all Jonathan wanted was that head-over-heels, traditional love story. Well, almost traditional, because in his daydreams Jonathan—and not a woman—was the person sharing that endless love with Mr. Chivalrous. None of those old black-and-white movies covered that territory.

Though he was amiable and good-natured, Jonathan never could seem to keep things together. Somehow, no matter how hard he tried to stay out of trouble, trouble found him. He had a scar on the tip of his right elbow from the huge picture window he'd broken when he was learning to ride a bike and lost control. He'd put his father's car in drive instead of reverse when he was learning to drive and ended up taking down the neighbor's entire front fence and landing in their swimming pool. And, in an attempt to make his best friend happy, Jonathan had lost his virginity in a blaze of... disappointment and life-altering consequences.

"Is he looking at us now?"

Brown-haired, blue-eyed, petite Kathy Gromley twirled her curls around her finger and forced her eyes to remain glued to Jonathan even as her mind concentrated on her boyfriend, George Rodriguez, who was standing behind her and across the room. Technically, he had been her ex-boyfriend for about a month, but nobody thought the "ex" would stick for long. Jonathan had started to look over at George when Kathy regained his attention by clutching his arm and digging her nails into his skin.

"Don't look at George! He'll know we're talking about him."

Jonathan rubbed his sore skin and frowned at Kathy. He was frustrated with the conversation and the entire evening, frankly. Kathy was his best friend. Actually, she was one of his only friends. So he had joined her at a party to celebrate the end of high school, even though he was painfully shy and more than a little uncomfortable in social settings.

"I thought you just asked me if he was looking at us."

Kathy kept a fake smile plastered to her face, threw her head back and let out a loud laugh, then answered Jonathan's question in a whisper.

"I did ask you to tell me if he's looking at us. But you need to check without him noticing that you're checking, you know?"

Jonathan was frustrated, tired, and done with that party. He had no idea how to check whether Kathy's boyfriend was looking at them without, well, checking.

"Kath, I want to go home. I'm tired. Why don't you just talk to him? You've been with the guy since freshman year. Surely you can have a conversation with him."

At that very moment, a pretty sophomore approached George and stroked his arm as they spoke. Being across the room, Jonathan couldn't hear what they were saying, but when George put his arm around the girl and led her toward the door, some of Jonathan's shock must have shown on his face, because Kathy forgot all about checking without checking and spun around just in time to see her boyfriend leaving the party with another girl. Ex-boyfriend. Whatever.

"Oh, Kath, I...I'm sure there's a good explanation. Maybe he's..."

Damn. Jonathan had no idea how to end that sentence. He knew nothing about relationships and he didn't know much about George. Yeah, Kathy was Jonathan's friend and she'd been George's girlfriend for almost four years, but the two of them didn't have anything in common, so they rarely spent time together.

George was a popular athlete, social, friendly, and

outgoing. Jonathan was quiet, kept to himself, and hoped to get through the day avoiding taunts from classmates. He often heard people mutter that he was weird or strange under their breath. Clumsy and uncoordinated were also fan favorites. But there was one genre of taunt they liked to use most of all: queer, fag, homo, and, on a good day, gay.

Those words had trailed Jonathan down the hallways at school and in the playground since middle school. He'd never been with another guy, never even outwardly expressed an interest in another guy. But it was true. Jonathan knew it was true. He was terrified about how his family would feel about it, though, so he kept the information to himself.

"I can't believe he just left with that slut! That cheating asshole! I knew it! I just knew it."

Kathy was steaming mad, her fists clenched at her sides as she stomped her pink, glittery boots.

"Fine. He wants to play this game with me. I can find another guy too."

She flicked her long hair behind her shoulder and looked around the room with a determined glint in her eyes. Jonathan had to stop her before she did something she'd regret.

"Kathy, come on. I'll take you home and you can call him and talk. Let's go."

As soon as she felt Jonathan's hand on her arm, Kathy turned on him. She opened her mouth to yell, but then her rage twisted into a frightening grin.

"Oh, this is just too perfect. Let's go, Jon."

Jonathan started walking toward the door, but Kathy grabbed his hand and hauled him in the opposite direction.

"Where are we going? Front door's that way, Kath." Jonathan pointed toward the exit.

"We're not leaving this party. We're going into the bedroom, we're leaving the door open a crack, and we're making enough damn noise that George's boys will be sure to tell him that he's not the only one who can have some extracurricular fun. Come on, Jonathan."

Ten minutes later it was over. Jonathan was lying on the guest room bed with his pants and underwear shoved down to his knees, but otherwise still completely dressed. He was even wearing his shoes. Kathy climbed off him and pulled her underwear back on under her skirt. He came, so that should mean he'd enjoyed it, right? But he hadn't. Hell, Jonathan wasn't even sure what "it" was. Kathy had just pushed him down on the bed, ripped down his jeans and briefs, stroked his dick until it got hard, and rode him to completion.

"Pull your pants up, Jon. We can go now."

Kathy turned to him and looked at his face. Jonathan wasn't sure what she saw there, but for the first time, she seemed to realize that her advances might not have been welcome.

"Oh, shit. Are you okay, Jon? I didn't think you'd mind. I mean, you're a guy and everything. You're all about sex, right?"

He raised his hips, pulled his underwear and pants up, and sat on the bed, cross-legged. Then Jonathan looked at his friend, cleared his throat, and spoke in a whisper.

"I, umm, I've never done that before, Kathy."

He'd actually never done *anything* before. No sex, no hand jobs, not even a kiss. Well, the kiss hadn't happened with Kathy, but the rest was all brand-new.

She looked shocked. Probably because she'd been having sex since she was fourteen.

"Seriously?"

Understanding and then regret passed over her pretty face. She walked over to Jonathan, sat next to him on the bed, and put her hand on his knee.

"Jon, are you...I mean, ehm, those things they say, I thought it was just because you're so pretty, you know. But are you..."

Pretty? Guys aren't pretty. Yeah, he had delicate features, long eyelashes, and a slender build. But still.

"Hey, I don't look like a girl!"

Kathy giggled and looked down at her friend's lap.

"Oh, I *know* you're not a girl, Jonathan. I just experienced the evidence firsthand."

Jonathan chuckled.

"Yeah, no kidding. I think you just scared me gay, Kath."

Somehow that lightened the mood and Kathy laughed.

Unshed tears glistened in her eyes.

"You're not mad at me?"

Was he mad? Jonathan thought about it. No, he couldn't be mad at Kathy. Hell, he had a hard time staying mad at anyone. He just didn't have it in him.

"Nah, I'm not mad. At least now I can say I've tried to screw myself straight. I'll add it to my list of failures. Like when I played Little League and didn't hit the ball a single time the entire season, even in practice. Or the time I entered the science fair in fifth grade and started a fire, so the sprinklers drenched everyone."

Kathy put a hand on each of her friend's cheeks and caught his eyes. Her voice was serious.

"Jonathan, there is nothing wrong with being gay. *Nothing.* Don't you dare call it a failure."

And that was just one reason she was his best friend. Even if she had mauled him in their classmate's guest room.

"Do you think my parents will be disappointed in me?" Jonathan chewed on his bottom lip and played with a loose thread in his shirt. He didn't want to sound like a little kid, but he hated the idea of upsetting his parents. He hated the idea of upsetting anyone.

"Nope. I really don't think they'll be disappointed. If you want, I'll come over and sit with you when you tell them."

"Thanks, Kath. I'm not ready yet, but I'll let you know."

Kathy scooted off the bed and walked toward the open door.

"'Kay. Let's go, Jonny boy. We have to get up early tomorrow for the trip."

The next day Kathy's mother picked Jonathan up and dropped both of them off at the airport. Their theater teacher was taking the graduating seniors on a three-day trip to Broadway. Kathy had been the lead in a couple of plays and she'd played important characters in a few others. Jonathan had helped build sets.

New York was fun and Jonathan managed to steer relatively clear of trouble for almost the entire trip. On the last day, he and Kathy were sitting on the floor in her hotel room, trying to decide how to end their visit.

"We have a free morning for our last day, Jonathan. What do you wanna do? Maybe we can get into some of those crazy New York bars!"

Jonathan rolled his eyes and looked at the brochures of museums and monuments strewn all around him, flipping through each one in turn and studying it intently.

"Kathy, it's eight o'clock in the morning. Bars probably aren't open yet, even in New York. Besides, neither of us is old enough to get in."

Kathy pouted and opened her mouth to answer when they both heard Miranda Lambert's "Kerosene" playing from across the room.

Well, I'm giving up on love, hey, love's given up on me.

Jonathan raised his eyebrows at Kathy. "You changed George's ringtone?"

She flushed. "Why's the asshole calling me?"

Jonathan gave her an understanding smile. "He's not an asshole, Kath. And you still love him. I'll go see the Statute of Liberty and give you some privacy so you two can talk."

Kathy didn't argue. She stalked over to her phone and looked at it like a snake that might bite her. After a few seconds, she steeled her body, put on her toughest frown, and answered.

"Wadda you want?"

Jonathan walked out of the room with a few brochures clutched in his hand and waited until the door was closed before he started laughing. He didn't understand what had been going on between his friend and her boyfriend, but he knew George loved her. Frankly, he was surprised it had taken this long for the guy to call. The only question now was how long Kathy would make him suffer before she'd let him off the hook for whatever it was he'd done wrong.

Jonathan stepped out of the hotel and made his way through the crowded New York streets. That was when his life turned upside down. Well, technically, his body turned upside down when he tripped walking down the stairs to the subway. He wasn't seriously injured, but he had sprained his wrist, so the paramedics took him to the hospital for an X-ray. The doctor confirmed that nothing was broken, put Jonathan's wrist in a brace, and discharged him.

Because he was already eighteen and legally an adult, the hospital didn't need to call anybody before treating

Jonathan, but he didn't want his teacher to worry, so he called her to explain where he was. Once the sling was in place, he got into the elevator to make his way out of the hospital and back to the hotel. No surprise here, he hit the wrong button and got off on the wrong floor. By the time he realized he was in the maternity wing instead of the lobby, Jonathan was standing in front of the baby nursery, mesmerized by a man behind the glass.

The man was wearing one of those blue hospital-issued covers over his street clothes and was sitting in a rocker, holding a tiny baby wrapped in a blue-and-pink-striped blanket. His hair was a deep black color, his skin fair, and his eyes...wow, those eyes. They were beautiful, a sparkling navy-blue color that Jonathan had never before seen, never even imagined. Jonathan could drown in those eyes.

Jonathan was frozen in the hospital hallway, staring at the gorgeous man. He couldn't hear through the glass, but it looked like the man was singing to the baby he was rocking. And there were tears streaming down that perfect, chiseled face. Jonathan wanted to walk over to the blue-eyed man, crawl into his lap, and wipe away his tears. He wanted to feel that soft black hair, lay his head on that broad chest, and hear the man's heart beat. He wanted to take care of that man so he'd never cry again. Time stood still as Jonathan saw his future with the blue-eyed man behind the nursery window.

"Jonathan Doyle! There you are."

Jonathan turned his head toward the elevator and saw his teacher racing toward him in a panic.

"You said you were coming right back to the hotel. When you didn't arrive, I called the hospital, and they said you'd been discharged hours ago. Thank goodness you're okay. What did you get yourself into this time, dear?"

His teacher looked at his arm and touched the sling tenderly. Jonathan looked up at the clock on the hospital wall and realized that three hours had passed. It'd felt like only a few seconds, but he'd been staring at his dream man for over three hours. When he looked back through the nursery window, the man was gone. It was like he had vanished into thin air. Jonathan's heart stung with the loss, and he had trouble getting air into his lungs. Forcing himself to calm down, he answered his teacher, "Oh, sorry, Mrs. Burns. I didn't mean to worry you. I got off on the wrong floor and I lost track of time."

"It's okay, dear. I understand."

Mrs. Burns had known Jonathan since he was a freshman, so she no longer asked questions when he got himself into yet another predicament. She just took his uninjured arm and walked him into the elevator, out of the hospital, and to a cab waiting outside.

"Kathy packed your bag, Jonathan. We need to go straight to the airport to make our flight."

He nodded, but all he could think about was that man. The one behind the nursery glass. The man with those amazing navy-blue eyes.

By the time Jonathan got back home to Emile City, he'd come up with some justification for why he should move to New York after graduation. His reasoning had something to do with finding his life's calling in the city where anything was possible, exploring the music scene, because Jonathan loved music. Who cares? It was baloney and Jonathan knew it. He had no calling. He'd never had an interest in any particular thing. He'd always been decidedly average in every subject and every activity.

The truth was, Jonathan wanted to move to New York because that was where *he* lived. Jonathan wanted to meet *him*. He needed to know *him*. That lovely, striking man with the navy-blue eyes. That very clearly straight man who had just had a baby. The man whom Jonathan had fallen in love with at first sight.

CHAPTER TWO

AFTER GRADUATION the following week, Jonathan packed up his belongings, gathered the money he'd saved working at his family's restaurant, and left for his new life in New York City. He got a room in a cheap hostel and found a job washing dishes. Between work and his attempts to find his dream man, Jonathan was exhausted. On the plus side, he was too tired to be depressed about the fact that he hadn't seen *him* and really didn't know where to find *him*—the lovely man with the intense blue eyes whose image was burned into Jonathan's mind. The downside was that Jonathan was lonely. Deeply lonely.

Days turned into weeks and weeks turned into months, but no matter how hard he looked, Jonathan never could find that man. As with everything else in his life, Jonathan's plan of finding Mr. Right and riding off into the sunset together didn't quite work out. And then he managed to mess things up even further.

It started with a telephone call in the middle of the night.

"Jonathan?"

Her voice was barely a whisper, but Jonathan still

recognized it.

"Yeah, Kathy. What's wrong?"

He tried to rub the sleep from his eyes with his free hand while he sat up on the thin mattress, winced when a spring poked his leg, then leaned back against the crumbling wall. A quick glance at his alarm clock told him it was almost midnight. Why would Kathy be calling?

"Did something happen with George again?"

Kathy and George had gotten back together about a month earlier. He'd enlisted in the army and shown up at Kathy's door with an engagement ring. She'd accepted. Jonathan hadn't ever figured out what'd caused their breakup in the first place.

"No, George is fine. We're good."

There was an eerie silence on the line and then the whispered voice again.

"Jonathan, I'm so sorry. It's all my fault. I didn't mean to, but...shit, this is hard."

"Kathy? Are you okay? What's going on?"

A long sigh and then, "I'm pregnant and you're the father."

Now it was Jonathan's turn to be silent. His mouth dropped open and his brain froze.

"Shit. I'm sorry, Jonathan. That wasn't how I planned to tell you. I was going to work up to it, but then I figured maybe the Band-Aid method was best. You know, just rip it off."

Still no response from Jonathan. His brain was waking up and just starting to process the enormity of what Kathy was telling him.

"Look, you don't need to do anything. I was an idiot and I didn't even think about what was happening until I went to the doctor for my annual and she asked me when my last period was. I peed on a stick and voila! Baby on the way. George and I are getting married, and we're moving to Kentucky for his basic training. He doesn't want to take another guy's baby with him, which I totally understand. Too late to do anything about it now, though, so I'm giving it up for adoption. Anyway, I'll send you some paperwork, you sign it, and in about four months we can forget any of this ever happened."

That entire speech was given in about thirty seconds, which was about as long as Kathy gave him to react.

"Jonathan? Say something."

His mouth was still hanging open but no words were coming out.

"Look, Jonathan, I know you're there. I can hear you breathing."

Really? He was still breathing? Well, that was a good sign. He cleared his throat and managed to push a few words out.

"I need to think about this, Kathy."

"Yeah, I know. It'll take time for the stuff to get to you anyway. There are lots of papers, and I don't have them electronically, so I'll need to use snail mail. What's your address?"

Jonathan tried to be clearer.

"That's not what I meant. Kathy, I need to think about whether or not I'm willing to give the baby up for adoption. I...I don't know if I can do that."

A loud sigh from Kathy followed by long, awkward moments of silence stretched between them.

"If you keep the baby, Jonathan, it'll be on your own. I'm relinquishing my rights. That's what they call it when you sign these papers. It'll be like I'm not the mother at all. I'm sorry. I know it sounds heartless, but that whole night was a stupid mistake. George is my life. We're getting married. We're going to have our own children. And he doesn't want a kid around to remind him of that time."

"I understand, Kath. I don't blame George. And I don't think you're heartless. I just need a little time to process all of this."

It was funny, but when Jonathan hung up the phone, the anxiety and heartbreak that filled him had nothing to do with a fear that he'd disappoint his parents or that he was too young and unsettled to have a baby. No. The only thing on Jonathan's mind was that those beautiful navy-blue eyes would never be his.

Finding the man from the hospital had been a long shot, and he probably wasn't gay anyway, or, if he was, he was probably already with someone else. But a guy with a baby... Who'd want that? It was the final nail in the coffin, burying any hope Jonathan had of connecting with his dream guy.

It was that loss and sorrow, mixed with the ever-present loneliness that had surrounded Jonathan since he'd moved to New York—or, if he were really being honest, the loneliness that had been with him his entire life—that motivated him to throw on some clothes, leave the seedy hostel, and walk into the first gay bar he could find. He hadn't been in the place two minutes when a decent-looking, if smarmy, guy strutted up.

"I'm Ray and you're beautiful."

That kind of cheesiness should make a person want to vomit. But Jonathan, who hadn't ever understood how exceptionally attractive he was, felt flattered that someone would think he was worth a second look, let alone a conversation, so he talked with Ray. After twenty minutes, Ray invited Jonathan to his place so they could talk in a quieter setting. It seems like a really obvious line, right? Well, Jonathan didn't catch it.

Jonathan couldn't figure out what happened after he got to Ray's apartment. It was all a blur of loneliness and sadness over losing hope of ever being with *him*. And it felt so good to have a man touch him, rub him, and want him. So Jonathan just went with it. He had been waiting for so long, or at least that was how it seemed to his eighteen-year-old mind. He was tired of being lonely, he hadn't found the man with the navy-blue eyes, and the dream man would never want him now anyway.

So Jonathan had sex with the stranger. Even without kisses and words of devotion, the act itself felt good. At least, the during part felt good. But after they were done, Ray hurried Jonathan out the door without even bothering to come up with an excuse. Then he didn't call Jonathan for several days, and when he finally did, it wasn't to ask for a date.

"I need you to come over. Remember where I live?"

Jonathan wanted to refuse the offer, but Ray was insistent and Jonathan didn't want to upset him. He knocked on the door to Ray's apartment, knowing he'd been invited over for nothing more than a quick fuck. He wasn't kidding himself that there could ever actually be more between them. The thing was, Jonathan didn't care anymore. It seemed that his life was over as it was; he was never going to have the fairy tale. He'd have to explain being gay *and* being a single, unwed, teenage father to his parents. And he'd never be with *him*, so he might as well have sex with Ray. At least that let him feel something other than emptiness and despair. For the moment, anyway.

"Hey, James."

Ray's slick smile greeted Jonathan and his stomach heaved.

"It's Jonathan."

"Right. Jonathan. Whatever. Come on in."

Jonathan thought about turning around and going back to the hostel. What was he doing there? But he didn't want to be rude, so he followed Ray into the tiny apartment.

"I have exciting news! Sit down on the couch."

Jonathan shuffled over to the stained couch and furrowed his brow in confusion as Ray sat next to him with a laptop, pressed a few buttons, and pointed at the screen. There they were, naked as the day they were born, Jonathan on his hands and knees and Ray behind him.

"You...you filmed us having sex?" he shouted in horror.

"Yeah, I thought it would be just for me later. But I showed it to my buddy and he noticed how hot you are so he said he'd pay us for it. I just need you to sign a release. Easiest way to make a hundred bucks ever!"

Jonathan was appalled. He wasn't sure if it was with himself or with Ray.

"No! I can't do that. What if someone I know finds out? What if my parents see it?"

Ray rolled his eyes.

"Oh, come on. Are your parents into amateur gay porn? How would they ever find out? We'll just make up a name for you and tell my buddy to use that for the movie. No harm, no foul."

"I..." Jonathan shook his head furiously and tried to get control over his emotions and the situation. This was bad. Really, really bad. "Ray, I can't do that."

Ray's excitement turned to anger and he scowled at

Jonathan.

"Look, you might be some rich kid, but I need the money. I'll give you a hundred and fifty. That's half, so I don't even get paid for doing all the filming work."

Right, because hiding a camera in his bedroom consisted of work. Jonathan knew that agreeing with Ray was a bad idea, but he couldn't bring himself to fight with the bigger, older, more confident man. So when Ray handed him a pen and shoved the release at him, Jonathan reluctantly signed it.

"You'll make up a fake name?"

Ray walked across the room to get his phone.

"Yeah, sure. We'll use your porn name. What is it?"

"My porn name?"

An annoyed eye roll from Ray.

"Yeah, you know, your middle name and the name of your first pet. Your porn name."

Did everyone know that? Was Jonathan really that socially inept? Probably.

"Umm. My middle name is William. And my first pet was a bluebird named Dragon."

Ray pressed the buttons on his phone, paying only minimal attention to what Jonathan was saying.

"Great. Will Dragon. Perfect porn name."

He held his pointer finger up in the air and concentrated on the phone.

"Hey, man. He signed the paper. When can we get our

check?" A pause while Ray nodded his head toward nobody in particular. "Cool. We're here now. I'll just tell him to wait."

He ended the call and turned to Jonathan.

"Wait here and we'll get our money."

Jonathan wanted to leave. Yeah, he could use a hundred and fifty dollars, especially with the whole fatherhood thing hanging over him. But his gut told him to cut his losses and walk away. He got up from the couch.

"I'm just going to take off, Ray. I'll call you about the money later."

It was just something to say. The truth was, he'd never call because he wanted to leave that apartment and pretend he'd never met Ray.

"No, don't go. My buddy said that he wants to talk to you. Just hang out for a few. He's right down the street."

Ray was so insistent and, really, what did Jonathan's gut know? Wasn't it his gut that'd told him the blue-eyed man was *the one*? It now seemed pretty clear what a flop that was. So Jonathan relented in the face of Ray's demand that he stay and wait. He sat back down on the couch.

"Oh, okay."

What could it hurt to meet his friend? Jonathan thought, as he nervously tapped his foot and chewed on his bottom lip.

An hour later, Jonathan had met Ray's friend and agreed to take part in another movie. Higher production values this time, good money. He was out of the apartment and in some makeshift studio, stripped and lying on his back with his ankles pinned by his ears before he knew what'd happened.

Somehow, having sex with some stranger while a few other guys stood around and filmed it wasn't any worse than having sex with Ray. The act still felt good. Jonathan couldn't deny how much he enjoyed getting fucked. And if he had to shut down his heart and force his brain to stop thinking, well, he could do that. Or at least he could try.

After that day, agreeing to have sex on camera didn't seem to matter. He'd already done it once, what did twice matter? Or three times? Or four? He'd been in bed with one guy, what did two guys matter? Or three? Or more?

Two months later, Jonathan was almost numb. He'd quit his job at the restaurant and had stopped spending his days looking for Mr. Right, knowing that the blue-eyed man wouldn't want him anyway. Instead, he devoted his time to having sex with strangers while other strangers filmed him. And he hated himself for finding some enjoyment in the act, in spite of the fact that he knew it was an empty life.

Then one day, in what he considered to be the first stroke of luck in his entire existence, Jonathan was at work, hanging in a sling, surrounded by men taking turns with his mouth and his ass, when a loud noise startled everyone. Police officers invaded the studio space, and Jonathan didn't even grimace as they looked at his cum-covered body in disgust. *Typical,* he thought. *Of course a bunch of alpha males would barge in at just that moment.*

Jonathan closed his eyes to shut out the sneers and smirks surrounding him. There was no way to ignore some of the nasty comments directed his way, but really, Jonathan didn't expect anything else. Just one more way he'd managed to embarrass himself. At least he hadn't been doing anything illegal. Wait, making those movies wasn't illegal, was it?

CHAPTER THREE

WHEN JONATHAN opened his eyes, there was a gorgeous guy towering over him. Piercing green eyes studied him from a fierce but strikingly handsome face, topping off what had to be one of the best bodies Jonathan had ever seen. Jonathan scrambled out of the sling and found a bathroom. He was wiping the last bit of cum from his hair when Officer Hottie walked in and dropped a pile of clothes on the floor.

"Get dressed and then we can talk. What's your name, bud?"

Oh, no! Jonathan panicked. If he gave his name to a police officer, it'd all be official and his parents were bound to find out.

"Will Dragon?"

Maybe he'd buy it. It sort of sounded like a regular name. And it was the one listed on all the movies.

"Give me a break. I want your real name."

Darn. Well, Jonathan hadn't actually thought that'd work. He sighed and slumped his shoulders.

"Jonathan. My name is Jonathan Doyle."

Instead of writing down his name and handcuffing him or something, the police officer smiled and wrapped his arm protectively around Jonathan's shoulder.

"Nice to meet you, Jonathan. I'm Detective Owens. Get dressed and I'm going to buy you lunch as an apology for that asshole's behavior."

Jonathan was confused. What asshole? The other police officer? Sure, he hadn't been very nice. Well, he'd been rude, if Jonathan were being honest, but so what? It wasn't as if it was the first time a guy had made fun of him, and it surely wouldn't be the last.

"Cops aren't the bad guys, bud. I'll wait for you out here."

As Jonathan slipped on his pants and shrugged into his shirt, he wondered what the detective wanted from him. He clearly wasn't gay, so it couldn't be sex. Oh well, lunch sounded good. Jonathan hadn't eaten anything all day.

As it turned out, Jonathan got a lot more than lunch from Detective Owens. The gorgeous guy was a great listener. Jonathan told him how long he'd lived in New York, why he'd moved there, how long he'd been doing porn, and that he was about to become a father. It felt good to talk to someone who really listened and didn't seem to judge. Jonathan was so comfortable with Detective Owens that, when he offered to help Jonathan get his life together and become a person worthy of the baby on the way, Jonathan took him up on the offer. The first step was to stop working for the studio, because whether he liked it or not, he was going to be a father.

After Samuel was born, Jonathan spent a week in Emile

City. His parents practically begged him to stay, but Jonathan was reinspired to follow his dream and find the man with the navy-blue eyes. So he returned to New York City, with his son in tow and renewed hope that he'd find his soul mate.

His life was different than the previous time he'd embarked on this journey. The loneliness was still there, but it was no longer tinged by recklessness. He'd finally caught a break—he had a son, a wonderful, beautiful son whom Jonathan adored. And he was good at something for the first time in his life. He was a good father. Everyone who saw Jonathan with Sam said so. And the smile on his baby's face whenever his papa walked into the room didn't lie.

So Jonathan worked hard—with his clothes on—and raised his boy. And he resurrected his search for *the one*. He also made himself follow certain rules. He didn't go to bars to meet men. Women and men alike often tried to pick him up, but he refused to go home with a guy he'd just met. And he refused to have sex with someone just because he fed Jonathan a good line and a temporary cure for loneliness. Jonathan was waiting for Mr. Right, and whenever he imagined him and their perfect, romantic life together, Mr. Right had those beautiful navy-blue eyes that Jonathan had seen through the hospital nursery window.

ALMOST THREE years later, Jonathan was ready to give up.

He was tired of being alone. He had left his family to move across the country, hoping to find his soul mate, and instead he'd had a short stint as an adult film actor followed by two and a half years of celibacy. It seemed like there was no point. Jonathan figured that if he was going to be alone anyway, he might as well go home, where he and Samuel had family. And if he packed up their meager belongings soon, he'd be back in time for Thanksgiving.

So Jonathan moved himself and Sam back to Emile City, and into his old bedroom in his parents' house. He promised himself and his folks that it was only temporary, that he'd move out as soon as he saved a little money. The best way to do that was to go back to his old job, working in the kitchen of his family's restaurant, so that was what he did. And just like that, Jonathan was settled into an only slightly less lonely life. Oh well...at least his son was around family. That was an improvement over New York.

On the evening of his twenty-second birthday, Jonathan's parents offered to babysit Sam so he could go out with friends to celebrate.

"We'll watch Samuel tonight, honey. You haven't had a night to yourself in years. Go on and have a good time and let us be grandparents. You can use my car."

Jonathan's mom dangled her car keys in front of him. Her warm voice was laced with concern.

He didn't want to worry his parents and he didn't have the heart to tell them that he didn't have any friends, so Jonathan borrowed their car and drove to downtown EC West. It was a part of town he'd always enjoyed, full of big trees, brick sidewalks, and same-sex couples walking around holding hands. Being there gave Jonathan hope that someday he could be that lucky. That maybe he wouldn't always be alone.

He wandered through some shops to kill time, but he didn't have any spare money to spend, so that didn't last long. Then Jonathan walked by a red brick building with a hand-stenciled sign reading "Where Cowboys Dream." He hadn't been in a bar since that fateful night in New York, but something in Jonathan's gut, or maybe it was his heart, told him to go inside. That gut had been quiet since he'd ignored it that tragic day in New York when he'd embarked on his former "career," so Jonathan thought maybe this time he should listen.

The bar was quaint and comfortable. It had exposed brick walls, thick drapes, and old leather benches. Jonathan slipped off his coat, slid into a well-worn booth, and ran his hands over the wood table, taking in the ridges and scars. There was something remarkably calming about that table, or maybe it was the whole bar. A sense of peace settled over Jonathan that he hadn't felt since that day in the hospital when he'd lost time staring through the nursery glass.

"Hey there. Thought you could use a drink. I'm Nick."

Jonathan glanced up to see a tall man with a ridiculously broad chest trying to rip its way out of a too-tight shirt suspended over toothpick legs. The man pushed a beer in front of Jonathan and then squeezed himself into the booth. He scooted in right next to Jonathan and left no room for personal space. Jonathan moved his body as far as he could toward the wall.

"Oh, umm, thank you. I'm Jonathan."

Jonathan held out his hand, creating a small space between their bodies. He hoped Nick would take the hint and stay on his side of the bench.

"Jonathan, huh? Fine."

He smirked as he said it, which Jonathan didn't understand. The whole situation made him nervous, so he picked up the beer, raised it to his mouth, and drank it down. The taste was bitter and unfamiliar, but at least it occupied him for a few minutes. Jonathan noticed Nick's heated eyes on his body and fidgeted uncomfortably.

"Look, umm, thanks for the beer, but I'm not, umm..."

Wow. What could he say to get rid of the guy without hurting his feelings? Jonathan felt slightly panicked from being pinned in that booth, and his face reddened with anxiety.

Nick rubbed his hand roughly up and down Jonathan's arm, then moved down to his knee, his thigh, and crept higher. Jonathan clutched Nick's hand, stopping the upward trajectory.

"Please don't. Look, I don't know you and I have no interest in, umm, fooling around with you. I don't do this, umm, don't do pickups, okay? I'm sort of waiting for a certain guy."

That didn't work.

"Yeah, right!" Nick laughed and kept touching Jonathan.

Never having enjoyed conflict and feeling deeply uncomfortable in the face of the persistence Nick exhibited, Jonathan had to gather all his inner strength just to plant his hands on Nick's chest and push forward, hoping Nick would move so he could get out of the booth. That was when things really turned ugly. Nick wouldn't budge. He glared at Jonathan and hissed under his breath in a menacing voice.

"Oh come on, *Will Dragon*." Jonathan's mouth dropped open in shock, but Nick was completely undeterred, and kept taunting him. "That's right, I know who you are. Don't be such a cock tease! We both know what you want." Nick grabbed his own dick and crudely shook it through his pants at Jonathan. "And I can give it to you."

Jonathan's arms dropped from Nick's chest down to his sides. He sat, paralyzed, in the booth, blinking back tears at the realization that his old life in New York had caught up with him at home in Emile City. Would his parents find out? Would they be as disappointed with him as he'd become with himself? Nick took advantage of Jonathan's frazzled state and moved his hand back into Jonathan's lap. Jonathan gasped and once again tried unsuccessfully to push the larger man back. Suddenly, someone came over and hauled Nick away from the table and onto his feet.

"I think the gentleman said no. We all heard him and none of us were as close to his face as you. Now get the hell out of this bar and don't come back, asshole!"

The voice was deep and strong. It made Jonathan's skin shiver, and he could feel goose bumps running up his spine. Jonathan couldn't see his hero's face because his back was turned, but Jonathan was still enjoying the view. The man was taller than Jonathan's five foot ten inches by about five inches. He had silky black hair and a broad, muscular build with shoulders that were at least twice as wide as Jonathan's. He was wearing a collared shirt under a thin sweater and dark jeans that showed off his thick legs and firm ass.

Jonathan started fantasizing about what that body would look like naked, wrapped around his own, how it'd feel to be surrounded by all that muscle and strength, when he was interrupted by the sound of Nick screaming obscenities.

"Fuck off, man. I saw him first and I can handle him just fine. Mind your own business!"

"It's my bar, so this is my business. You need to leave right now."

The voice was calm but laced with steel. None of that registered with Nick, who ignored the command and, instead of leaving, took a swing at the guy who'd helped Jonathan. Jonathan got up to try to defuse the situation, but that was a mistake. Nick spun around and hissed at him.

"Come here, *Will Dragon*." He sneered as he spat out

the painfully resurrected name into Jonathan's ear. "I bought you a drink. I saw you eyeing my package. Don't act like you don't want this. You're coming with me."

Nick reached over to seize Jonathan's arm but the tall, dark-haired man stepped in, blocked his reach, and shoved Nick away. He was incredibly strong, which made Jonathan's dick take interest.

"Get out of my bar. *Now!*"

And with that, Jonathan's protector took Nick's arm, twisted it behind his back, and pushed him out the door. Jonathan was startled, a little drunk from having consumed the first beer in his life in a matter of minutes, and distracted by the sexy, dark-haired hero, but he was holding it together pretty well. He got up to thank his savior as he walked back to the table. That was when Jonathan saw the face attached to that gorgeous body for the first time.

Oh my God, those eyes. Those navy-blue eyes.

"Are you all right, buddy? He didn't hurt you, did he?"

"It's you," Jonathan muttered as he fell to the floor.

CHAPTER FOUR

WHEN JONATHAN woke up, he was lying on the floor with a jacket folded under his head, his coat covering his body, and the most amazing eyes he'd ever seen looking deeply into his. There was so much to take in at once. Those navy eyes had twinkles of aqua and turquoise running through them, which Jonathan hadn't noticed when he'd seen his dream man from across the room. The face that had been smooth a few years prior now had a rough covering of hair—not a thick beard, but more than just not shaving for a day, like a sexy-as-hell heavy stubble. And the broad body was covered in bulging muscles.

"Welcome back, Jonathan. You scared the shit out of us, passing out like that. I don't think I served you enough to make you pass out. I only gave that asshole two beers."

"How…how do you know my name?"

The blue-eyed man laughed a deep laugh and smiled widely, showing perfectly straight, sparkling white teeth. Jonathan wondered if he was going to hear a "ping" noise and see a burst of light, like in a toothpaste commercial.

"I looked through your wallet and found your driver's license. We were about thirty seconds away from calling an ambulance. Come on, man, you're pretty toasted. Let's get you home. I can call you a cab."

Jonathan didn't want to leave. He had found him! He had finally found him.

"Uhh. No, that's okay." Jonathan searched his mind for any possible excuse to stay and get to know his dream man. "I don't want to leave my car here. I'll just stay for a bit and sober up. Do you guys have any coffee?"

Jonathan scrambled up and swayed a bit, but managed to stay on his feet.

"No, man. We bought one of those do-it-all fancy-shmancy machines and it broke. The repair guy they use is booked like two weeks out. I should probably just return the damn thing and buy a twenty-dollar coffeepot." He shook his head and rolled his eyes. "Anyway, we're in a safe neighborhood. Your car should be fine."

The taller man looked at Jonathan's face, met his gaze, and his expression softened.

"Listen, I'm not actually working, just covering for the bartender while he runs an errand. He should be back in about twenty minutes. If you don't mind waiting, I'll drive your car home for you. You really shouldn't be driving right now. It looks to me like you're still having trouble standing."

Jonathan was having trouble standing, but it wasn't because of the alcohol he'd consumed. It was because of him. Being that close to the blue-eyed man made Jonathan weak in the knees.

"I don't mind waiting for you. Thanks for the offer."

Jonathan sat back down on the bench, propped his elbows on the table, held his chin in his hands, and tried to process what he was doing. Why was he sitting at that bar, waiting for a straight guy to drive him home? What could possibly come of this? And how ironic was it that he'd promised himself not to meet men at bars and not to go home with a guy he'd just met and here he was, about to do both? Of course his last promise was that he wouldn't have sex with a guy just because he fed Jonathan a good line. Jonathan wasn't going to break that promise, he knew that. But it wasn't because of his self-restraint. His dream man wasn't going to feed Jonathan a line because he had no interest in having sex with Jonathan.

But no matter how silly and self-destructive Jonathan knew he was being, he couldn't get up to leave. He couldn't walk away from the man with the navy-blue eyes. He was powerfully drawn to him. He was in love with him and had been since the first day he'd seen him over three years earlier, holding his baby in the hospital nursery.

After about fifteen minutes, the impossibly handsome man with the captivating eyes walked back to the booth where Jonathan was sitting.

"How're you doing, Jonathan?"

Jonathan heard the kind voice, looked up into those warm, blue eyes, and felt his stomach flutter and his heart clench.

"I'm fine. I'm good. I, umm, I didn't catch your name?"

Jonathan held out his only slightly shaking hand as he nervously asked for his dream man's name and mentally patted himself on the back for sounding suave. Well, as close to suave as Jonathan had managed to sound at any point in his life.

"Name's David. Nice to meet you, guy."

David shook Jonathan's hand and slid into the booth across from him. His gaze met Jonathan's and a kind smile took over his amazing face. Seriously, the guy looked like he'd just walked off the cover of a magazine.

"David, can I go home now, or do you still need me here tonight?"

A pretty brunette had made her way to the table without Jonathan noticing. Not a surprise considering the fact that he was spellbound by his dream man. The brunette had large breasts, perfect lips, and she was eyeing David with a hungry look that Jonathan recognized. It was the same look that met him in the mirror every time he thought of those blue eyes.

"No, I'm good, Denise. I can man the ship until Eric gets back and Raquel will be here soon. You go on and head home."

David answered her without his eyes ever leaving Jonathan's. Denise leaned down and kissed David's cheek.

"Okay, see you later, handsome."

Jonathan felt an overwhelming sadness overtake him.

He wanted to be the one who'd get to see David at home later. Their home. Where they could cook dinner together, watch television with Sam, go to bed together, and…

"Are you okay? You just got really pale."

David's hand reached for Jonathan's face and cupped his cheek.

"Is she your girlfriend?"

Jonathan squeezed his eyes shut in horror after the question slipped out of his mouth. It was none of his business and it was a *weird* thing to ask. Why couldn't he be normal just this once?

David chuckled. His left hand was still on Jonathan's cheek and, for the first time, Jonathan noticed that his right hand was still holding Jonathan's. They hadn't let each other go after the introductory handshake.

"Nope."

Jonathan swallowed hard and his voice shook as he asked the next question, knowing he shouldn't, but completely unable to restrain himself.

"Why not?"

David's thumb rubbed circles over the back of Jonathan's hand.

"She's not my type. A little too much up top and not enough down below. I don't waste my time pretending."

Oh God, that tender touch combined with the velvet voice and the beautiful eyes trained on him were too much. Jonathan's brain was melting and he couldn't comprehend the meaning of David's words.

"Your time? You...you're too busy for a girlfriend?"

The hand on Jonathan's cheek made its way to his ear, lightly trailed over the edge, and massaged the back of his neck.

"Not too busy. Too gay."

Hope filled every part of Jonathan's body. Gay. The man with the navy-blue eyes was gay, sitting across from him, *and* touching him. Was this real? It couldn't be. It had to be a dream, right? Some pathetic fantasy created by Jonathan's desperately lonely brain.

"Shhh, baby, don't cry. Do you want me to take you home now? I just saw Eric, my bartender, come in, so I can leave."

A warm thumb swiped across Jonathan's cheek, drying his tears. Was he crying? Oh, how embarrassing. Wait, did David just call him "baby"? Oh, please let this be real.

"I don't want to go home."

Jonathan's voice was soft, but he hoped his meaning was clear, because he really couldn't find the courage to say more. Was it actually possible that this beautiful man could want to be with him? And, again, had he called Jonathan "baby"?

David nodded in understanding, a tender look in those beautiful eyes.

"Do you want to come home with me, Jonathan?"

"P-p-please."

Those eyes, so soft and caring, gazed at Jonathan from the handsome, kind face.

"Okay, Jonathan. Don't be scared of me. I won't hurt you."

Jonathan shook his head from side to side.

"Not scared of you."

Of everything and everyone else, maybe. Of messing up yet another part of his life. Of breaking yet another of his brother's tools or his sister's prized ceramic collectible snow globes. Of disappointing his parents because he was gay, not smart enough, not strong enough, or not driven enough. Of never earning as much money as he'd need to give Sam a good life. Yes, he was afraid of all of those things. But not of David. He could never be scared of the man with those warm, caring, navy-blue eyes.

Slowly, oh so slowly, David scooted out of the booth and took a step in Jonathan's direction, never letting go of his hand. Jonathan raised his body out from behind the table and found himself chest to chest with David. The hand that had been holding his let go and made its way to his hair, petting him, while David's left hand wrapped possessively around Jonathan's waist.

"I have no idea what's happening here, but..." David licked his plump, red lips and swallowed, the movement of his Adam's apple taking Jonathan's breath away. "Can I kiss you, Jonathan? I need to kiss you."

Jonathan must have been nodding because things in

his line of sight moved up and down, but his brain seemed to have shut down. He was rigid as David leaned toward him and those warm lips—so soft, so tender—met his own. And then Jonathan opened his mouth and tasted David's flavor for the first time. He whimpered and melted against that hard body. His arms wrapped around the flat waist, his fingers dug into the hard muscles, and his tongue met David's and danced.

Jonathan moaned when David's hard length pressed insistently against his waist. The moan turned into a whimper when David's knee edged its way in between Jonathan's and pushed until Jonathan's cock was pressed against David's thigh. A big hand tickled its way across Jonathan's back and down to his ass. David clutched him and pulled him forward, urging Jonathan to rock against his leg while David plundered his mouth.

Jonathan's hips thrust forward and back, his whimpers and moans flowing into David's hot mouth. Though he feared that he'd come right there in the bar, Jonathan couldn't stop himself. It felt so good. David's taste, his flavor, his scent. Just as Jonathan neared the edge of the precipice, David stopped his rocking motion with a firm grip on his hip and spoke into his mouth.

"Can you wait, baby? I want to taste you when you come and I can't do that here."

That endearment, flowing from David's lips and aimed at him. The thought of David's mouth on his cock, something no one had ever done, of David wanting to taste his cum, something he hadn't ever considered someone wanting to do. Oh, just that word and those thoughts were all it took for Jonathan to explode.

"Oh, God!"

He threw his forehead against David's chest and whimpered as he climaxed.

"Holy shit. You weren't even moving and you just came."

David's deep voice rolled over him, but Jonathan kept his head ducked down, eyes averted. He was mortified. He'd just creamed his pants in front of his dream man. In a bar. Yes, it was early, so the bar was essentially empty, and they were in a dark corner where nobody could see them. But David knew, and that was all that mattered.

Jonathan steeled himself for rejection and opened his mouth to apologize, but David's lips descended on his, tongue demanding entrance, and he lost the power of speech. David licked and nibbled, sucked and moaned, and by the time he pulled his mouth away, Jonathan's lips were swollen and he was gasping for air. David held Jonathan's face between his large, warm hands and peered into his eyes.

"You are the single hottest thing I have ever seen in my entire life. I don't know where you came from, but I am *never* letting you go. I'm going to tell Eric I'm taking off. You can clean up if you want, bathroom's that way."

David tipped his head toward an area behind

Jonathan's left shoulder. Jonathan stood still and blinked his eyes, trying to get his spinning head under control and calm his racing heart. He hadn't blown it. He didn't know why or how, but David still seemed interested. David looked at Jonathan in wonder for several long moments. Eventually, he dropped his hands from Jonathan's face, and started walking toward the bar, where a tall man was wiping a spot on the section farthest from them. But after taking only a few steps, David flipped around, strode back over to Jonathan, and pulled him into his arms for another full-body kiss.

"Hottest thing ever. Seriously. Where have you been all my life?"

And with those words, David really did walk away and head toward to the bar.

CHAPTER FIVE

THE ITCH from the cum drying on his skin jolted Jonathan from his David-induced stupor, and he stumbled into the bathroom. He leaned against the sink and gulped air into his lungs. Once he was able to catch his breath and clear his mind, Jonathan looked down at his jeans and was happy to notice only a small wet spot. Thankfully, his briefs had caught most of his seed. He toed off his shoes, stripped down, then chucked his underwear in the trash bin, deciding that going commando was preferable to walking around feeling wet and sticky.

He smiled at his luck in finding David in EC West of all places. It turned out he shouldn't have fled to New York all those years ago. Oh well, no reason to dwell on past mistakes; it'd take too long and the man with the navy-blue eyes was waiting for him. Plus he finally had a name to go with the eyes. David. David and Jonathan. That sounded good. It sounded right.

Jonathan turned on the faucet, wet a few paper towels, and wiped his body down. He was mostly hairless, so the cum came off his lower belly easily. He concentrated on his short pubic bush. Some scrubs with his wet hand and a few paper towels to dry him off, and he was done cleaning up. He stepped back into his jeans and pushed his feet into his shoes. Jonathan was bent over, tying his laces, when he heard a moan from behind him. He turned quickly and tried to raise his body at the same time, a combination that resulted in an unfortunate head-to-sink collision.

"Ow!"

David was next to him before Jonathan's hand made it to the side of his head, where he rubbed at the bruise.

"I'm sorry. I didn't mean to startle you. I was just coming in to see if you were ready to go and you were bent over, and, oh man, you have to know that you have the best ass, and…"

The pain in his head disappeared, and Jonathan moved his hands to the back of David's head and pulled him down for another drugging kiss. Damn, but Jonathan loved those kisses. The man could melt him to his core with his lips, and his tongue, and his taste. He'd always imagined kissing would feel good, but he hadn't realized just how good.

"Oh, I love kissing you. Never done this before. It feels so right."

Jonathan was mumbling into David's mouth, not aware that he was speaking out loud, just feeling and sharing. David groaned, dropped the coats he held, cupped his hands around Jonathan's ass, and picked him up off the ground. Jonathan gasped at how easily David was able to lift him. Damn, he was strong. Jonathan wrapped his legs around David's waist, continued the kiss, and twined his hands in David's hair.

David clutched Jonathan's tight little globes, and Jonathan felt his pucker twitch with the memory of how good it could feel to be touched there. He'd really enjoyed being penetrated, even by strangers who he didn't know and didn't like. What would it be like with David? The bigger man moved them toward the wall, pinned Jonathan against it, and pumped his hips. Jonathan whimpered and met each thrust, his cock hard again, while David moved his lips down Jonathan's neck, sucking and biting as he went.

"We have to get out of here. The bathroom door doesn't lock, and I'm about two seconds away from bending you over the sink."

It had been so long since he'd had another man inside him, and to have *this man* suggest it was not something Jonathan's lust-addled brain could decline.

"Over the sink? Okay. Please."

Jonathan nodded against David's mouth, ready to do anything to get closer to him and wanting to experience that full feeling again, hoping it'd be as good as he remembered.

"Oh, damn, you're so eager. Fuck if you didn't just manage to get hotter. Didn't think that was possible."

David set Jonathan down on the ground, and he just about whined in protest. But David pulled him against his strong chest, caressed his back, and reassured him with his deep voice.

"I'll give you what you want. But I need to get us out of

here, Jonathan."

David squatted down, scooped up their coats, then raised himself back up and led Jonathan out of the bar, keeping his arm around Jonathan's shoulders. It felt to Jonathan as if he was making sure everyone knew they were together, and that possessiveness thrilled Jonathan to no end. Nobody had ever wanted to claim him. Of course, he hadn't ever wanted to belong to anybody other than the man with the navy-blue eyes, so he'd never given any other guy a chance, let alone a second look.

When they got to David's car, he opened Jonathan's door and kissed him yet again, then waited for him to sit down before closing his door. Jonathan leaned back against the headrest and closed his eyes. This was all much too close to every fantasy he'd ever had to be real. No way was the man he'd been dreaming about for three and a half years calling him baby and taking him home. He'd wake up soon and it'd be over. Oh well...he might as well enjoy the dream while it lasted.

Jonathan felt a hand cover his knee and give him a soft squeeze. He rolled his head to face David and opened his eyes. That kind blue gaze met his, and a deep sense of contentment washed over him.

"You doing okay, Jonathan?"

"Mmm hmm."

"Good. I live right down the street. We just need to make a quick stop on the way. So, tell me about yourself. I know I'd have noticed you if you lived here, and I'm guessing you didn't actually come down from heaven, so tell me where you're from." David groaned right after he finished his sentence. "I can't believe I just said that. Strike the cheesy heaven bit, okay? I swear I'm normally way smoother than this."

Jonathan laughed out loud, feeling relaxed and happy with this attentive man who was incredibly handsome, yet self-effacing.

"I grew up here in EC West, but I moved to New York City a few years ago. Just got back into town a couple of weeks back."

"New York, huh? I used to have family there, but..."

David's voice trailed off and Jonathan wondered why. He knew the man was about to tell him about the baby he'd been holding when Jonathan had first seen him in the hospital, but then he stopped. Maybe there had been a custody issue when the mother realized David was gay. Of course, the idea that David would have hidden that information was completely incongruous with what he'd previously said about not pretending.

"Okay, just sit tight for a minute. I'll be right back."

David put the car in park, unbuckled his seat belt, leaned over to Jonathan for a quick kiss then opened his door and unfolded his tall frame out of the car. It was all done with such a casual comfort that it felt to Jonathan as if they'd been together for years instead of minutes. He peered through the windshield and saw they were parked in front of an Italian restaurant. It wasn't long before David came back, carrying two overflowing bags. He placed the bags in the backseat, but the delicious smells filled the entire car.

"Have you ever had Magiano's? It's the best Italian in EC West."

Jonathan's stomach growled, reminding him that he'd skipped lunch and hadn't eaten dinner. David chuckled.

"I'm glad you're hungry. I got vegetable lasagna, lobster ravioli, and chicken cacciatore. Oh, and a caprese salad."

David pulled out of the parking lot and stole quick glances at Jonathan as he drove.

"What?" He smiled at his passenger, then moved his hand back to Jonathan's knee and squeezed. "Seriously, what's up? You've got a funny look on your face."

The look was more "dreamy" than "funny," but David didn't know how to say that without causing yet another blush to creep onto his companion's face, and making himself sound arrogant to boot.

"You bought me dinner. Nobody's ever bought me dinner."

David's heart broke a little at the confession, but he schooled his features and made sure that his expression remained outwardly neutral.

Jonathan bit his tongue and forced himself to stop talking before he admitted that he'd never been on a date.

That this time with David was already the longest relationship he'd ever had. That is, assuming letting Ray fuck him after having known the man for all of thirty minutes constituted a relationship. He really couldn't count any of the other men, because he hadn't so much as said two words to them during the couple of months he'd worked for the studio. Well, other than "harder," "deeper," and "oh, yeah," but that probably didn't constitute conversation. Jesus, was he ever pathetic. He had to make sure David never found out about his past.

"I'm honored to be the first, Jonathan."

He looked closely, but Jonathan didn't see anything but sincerity in David's eyes. He relaxed and returned David's smile.

"Here we are. See, I told you it wasn't far. I can actually walk from here to Where Cowboys Dream, but I was at a friend's house tonight when Eric called to tell me he needed to run a quick errand, so I stopped by on my way home to help him out."

Jonathan got out of the car and looked at the most beautiful house he'd ever seen. It was dark out, so he couldn't make out the details, but he could clearly see a sloped, Tudor-style roof, diamond-shaped windows, a brick chimney, and stone facing. The yard was huge, with enough room to fit another couple of houses if it wasn't for the mature trees filling the space. The entire place looked like a fairy-tale cottage in the woods.

He followed David onto the front porch and walked

inside while David held the door open. The building was probably at least a hundred years old, but it had obviously been remodeled. The wood floors were gleaming, and the plaster walls were free of cracks. Not an easy feat in a house that age. They were standing in a nice-sized entryway. There was a walnut console table holding a red ceramic lamp against one wall with a gilded mirror hanging above it, an antique coat rack stood in the corner, and an upholstered platform bench took up the opposite wall.

To their right was a huge, beautiful living room, furnished with a tan sectional scattered with silk and velvet throw pillows in shades of dark brown and red. The wall behind one leg of the couch held the diamond-shaped windows Jonathan had noticed when he was outside the house, and they were covered with a sheer fabric flanked by heavy, raw silk drapes. The other leg of the couch was facing Jonathan, so he couldn't see exactly what was pressed against its back, but he guessed it was some sort of a table because there was an antique-looking vase and a beautiful ceramic bowl sitting on it. Two mismatched but perfectly coordinated end tables flanked the sectional and an octagonal-shaped coffee table made of copper sat in front of it. A leather armchair and ottoman were placed beside one of the end tables at a carefully calculated angle. A large flat-screen television mounted over the fireplace and directly in front of the sofa completed the space.

The dining room was to their left. A square, dark wood

table sat in the middle of the room with two leather-padded chairs on each of its four sides. A retro chrome chandelier hung above the table. The windowed wall facing the front of the house was covered in the same heavy drapes that adorned the living room. The opposite wall held a three-door credenza, and above it hung an abstract oil painting with streaks of red, purple, and black combining in a shape that looked to Jonathan like a cyclone. Built-in, lighted glass-front cabinets flanking an arched doorway took up the final wall.

Jonathan had never been in such a richly appointed space. His parents' house was furnished with beat-up, mismatched items they'd inherited from family or picked up at yard sales or thrift shops over the years. His own one-room apartment in New York had been even more run-down. Trying to push away a sudden anxiety attack, fearing he couldn't possibly fit into David's life, Jonathan closed his eyes and leaned his head back. When he was sure he wouldn't lose his breath, he opened his eyes and noticed that the plaster ceilings had an incredible diamond pattern.

David dropped the bags of food, pressed his chest against Jonathan's back, and wrapped his arms around Jonathan's waist. He was amazed at how natural that closeness felt with a man he'd just met. Especially since David wasn't a touchy-feely kind of guy. He followed Jonathan's gaze up to the ceiling.

"That was hand done when the place was built. It's one of the reasons I bought this house. You can't find detail work like that in new builds. Plus it was a good investment— bank repo with a rock-bottom price. I scooped it up before the sign went into the ground. Had to redo the bathrooms, and the kitchen's a disaster, but otherwise it's in great shape. The previous owners had already put in copper plumbing and rewired."

He kissed Jonathan's neck, nuzzled against him, and gave a final squeeze before pulling away with a regretful sigh.

"I have to feed you before I completely lose control over my body. Once the little bit I'm hanging on to goes, I'm going to drag you to bed. And I don't plan on letting you out for a very long time. You need your energy before that happens, so let's eat."

CHAPTER SIX

DAVID WAS just starting to lean down to pick up the bags of food he'd dropped in the entryway when Jonathan turned and leaped against him. Suddenly, David found himself holding an armful of hot, horny man. While peppering kisses over David's cheeks, chin, and neck, Jonathan ran his hands all over David's body.

Jonathan was doing everything possible to prove to himself that the moment was real, that he was actually with David, and that the man with the navy-blue eyes wanted him. He needed to fill every one of his senses with his dream man.

"Jesus, fuck, Jonathan, if you don't stop, I—"

"Not gonna stop. Not that hungry for food," Jonathan mumbled into David's ear. Then he dropped to his knees, unbuttoned and unzipped the David's jeans, and pulled them down to his ankles. He took a few moments to nuzzle his prize through the sexy black briefs David wore, feeling them get completely wet before pulling down the fabric and exposing what had to be the most enticing cock he'd ever seen. It was slightly darker in color than the rest of David's fair body, with pulsing veins running up from the base to the perfectly shaped crown. Well above average in length and very thick around, Jonathan knew it'd take all the skill he'd mastered in his old profession to be able to go down on the man.

He wanted to savor the moment, go slow and enjoy every second. But as soon as Jonathan's tongue took its first swipe of David's dick, he knew he'd never be able to wait. One of the best things about the studio where Jonathan had worked was their strict safety policy, which meant condoms absolutely every time. So despite his vast experience sucking cock, Jonathan had always tasted latex. He lapped at David's member and was incredibly aroused by the unexpected flavor and feel of David's skin. There was a hint of sweat, the smell of sex from the drops of pre-ejaculate that had been dripping down the shaft, and the silky texture of that soft skin covering the thick pole. Jonathan moaned in pleasure at the taste and smell of his dream man and forgot all about taking it slow. He plunged down and took David into his throat, covering his cock in moist heat down to the root.

"Oh my God! Jesus, Jonathan. How...how...oh, God. That's so good," David groaned.

A shiver of satisfaction ran through Jonathan's body at the awe and joy in David's voice. And damn, did he ever enjoy having a cock in his mouth. He'd missed it, missed the hardness stretching his lips, pushing across his tongue and into his throat. He sucked desperately, swallowed around the head, then raised his mouth up with the tightest seal he could muster and plunged back down again. He kept up that attention, sucking, swallowing, bobbing his head up and down while David continued moaning and uttering words of shock and pleasure.

"I'm gonna come, baby. Can't hold back, you're so good at that. So, so good."

David tried to warn Jonathan so he could remove his mouth in time, but Jonathan just made a "mmm" sound and increased his suction and the speed of those up-and-down motions. David lovingly stroked Jonathan's hair, then pushed his fingers into it and held his head as he gave a few short thrusts into the willing mouth in front of him. Waves of ecstasy slammed through David's body and moans left his mouth in an expression of pure pleasure as he released inside Jonathan.

David dropped his head back against the door, closed his eyes, and caught his breath. When he opened his eyes, he looked down and saw Jonathan, still on the floor, licking his cock reverently. Oh, that was just too much for any man to resist.

"Too sensitive. Come up here, baby."

David bent down and lifted Jonathan to his feet. He whimpered when he was taken from David's cock. And didn't that give a guy an ego boost? David didn't know what he'd done to earn this doting, gorgeous, kind person in his life, but he was going to be damn sure to show his appreciation. He kissed Jonathan soundly, pressing his tongue into Jonathan's mouth and wrapping his arms around Jonathan's narrow waist.

"Living room."

He raised and zipped his jeans, then lifted Jonathan, who locked his ankles behind David's waist and thrust his hard dick against David, seemingly on instinct. David carried Jonathan into the living room, kicked the ottoman aside, and lowered Jonathan onto the armchair. He looked down and readied himself to take his turn worshiping the beautiful man in front of him. Jonathan's lips were swollen, his skin flushed with arousal, and his hard dick was desperately trying to make its way out of the confinement of those pants. David unfastened the button, lowered the zipper, and gasped when he realized Jonathan wasn't wearing any underwear. That was all it took for David's cock to twitch in an attempt to wake back up. He moaned and dropped to his knees between Jonathan's spread legs.

"Lift your hips, baby."

Jonathan whimpered and raised his ass up off the chair so David could pull down his pants. Those big hands caressed Jonathan's balls, cupping and rolling them gently. David then alternated the texture against the sensitive orbs from his smooth hands to his rough beard by tenderly rubbing his cheek over the testicles, and enjoying Jonathan's responding groan. David followed the rough stubble with swipes from his wet tongue, and finished the varied sensations by sucking each testicle into his warm mouth. After paying attention to Jonathan's balls, David moved up to his cock, again sliding the stubble on his cheek against it, then licking it from base to tip, giving a nuzzle to the crown, and licking his way back down in a swirling pattern.

Jonathan was sitting on the armchair, his head thrown back and his hands in tight fists at his sides, making strangled noises that were getting increasingly louder. After a few minutes of David's ministrations, Jonathan's mewls began to sound more like cries, and David took pity on the man and decided to let him out of his misery. He made a final swipe over Jonathan's dick with his tongue, then plunged down and took Jonathan's entire length into his mouth with a firm suck.

"Oh! David, yes!"

Jonathan cried out and came, his whole body shivering. David groaned in appreciation and swallowed down every last drop, before giving a few more licks to his nuts, then tucking him back into his pants. When he raised himself off his knees and leaned down to kiss Jonathan, he saw tears streaming down his handsome face and noticed that his entire body was shaking. David's chest spasmed, and he knew he'd do anything to make whatever was upsetting Jonathan better.

"Jonathan? Baby, what's wrong? Did I hurt you?"

Jonathan shook his head and reached a shaky hand out for David, who immediately reacted by lifting Jonathan, sliding onto the chair, and pulling him onto his lap.

"Shhh. What's wrong, baby?"

David rubbed circles on Jonathan's back and tried to calm him. Jonathan buried his face in David's neck and a final shudder made its way through his body.

"Nothing's wrong. That just felt so good." Jonathan's voice was soft and full of wonder. "I didn't know it'd feel like that. Never imagined it'd be so good. Thank you." He kissed David's neck. "Thank you." He made his way to David's mouth and gave him another gentle kiss. "Thank you."

David was stunned and didn't know how to respond. He'd heard Jonathan's earlier comment in the bar bathroom about never having done this before when they were kissing, but he'd written it off when the man asked to be fucked over the sink—not exactly a virginal request. Plus, the blow job Jonathan had delivered in the entryway couldn't have been his first. Fact was, David had had sex with several men over the years, some with a vast amount of experience, and not one of them had been able to take his entire length into his mouth, not even close. Yet Jonathan had done it right away, without so much as flinching and certainly without gagging. David continued to stroke Jonathan's back as he thought about how to best express his confusion.

"Was that the first time anyone's gone down on you, baby?"

Jonathan blushed and nodded. He wiggled against David, as if trying to dig himself even deeper into David's embrace.

"But you've done it before?"

Another blush and, if possible, Jonathan's scarlet color deepened. David didn't want to embarrass him, but he needed to understand the dichotomy in his experience, so he plunged ahead with another question.

"And you've, umm, had sex before? Been, ehm, penetrated?"

A little nod was Jonathan's only response. Okay, so he hadn't ever been kissed, never had his dick sucked, but some guy had taken his pleasure with both Jonathan's ass and his mouth. Given his delicate features and narrow frame, David figured it was probably one of those assholes who claimed he wasn't truly gay if all he did was fuck a guy or get sucked off but never gave anything in return. Or maybe it was one of those "gay until graduation" college kids.

Selfish motherfucker! A wave of anger more powerful than any he'd ever experienced shot through David. He opened his mouth to talk with Jonathan about his ex, let him know that whoever that guy was, Jonathan deserved better and he'd get it from now on, but then Jonathan raised his head and looked at David with a tortured expression.

"Can we please not talk about this? Please?" Jonathan pleaded.

His voice was so weak, and the look in his eyes so imploring, that David's heart broke. Well, he wanted to make Jonathan feel good, and if that meant leaving talk of his ex out of their conversations, that was fine. He'd show the charming beauty how he felt with his actions, so there could be no doubt things would be different with him than they'd been with whatever guy came before. David took a deep breath and smiled at Jonathan.

"Should we eat here or in the kitchen? The dining room is an option, too, but I've been in the house for about two years and I've never used it. It feels too big or stuffy or something, and I don't have people over much, or ever, really, so…"

Jonathan's smile lit up the room, and David noticed his dimples for the first time. His breath caught in his chest. Damn, but Jonathan was appealing. Dark hair that seemed to go this way and that, an angular face and chiseled jaw that was masculine yet pretty, a frame that was very lean but still had a seriously hot bubble butt, a wide mouth, and silver eyes. Not blue, not gray, but silver. The man was mesmerizing, a combination of sexy as hell and adorable at the same time. David found him irresistible. He stroked his thumb across Jonathan's lips.

"Is that smile for the food? I thought you said you weren't very hungry."

"Well, I was distracted before, but, ehm, I am hungry. The smile isn't for the food, though. You just make me feel good, is all. Being with you makes me happy."

Jonathan blushed when his brain caught up with his mouth and he realized what he'd said. So not cool. He was going to scare David off if he didn't stop sounding like such a heartsick little kid.

"That's the nicest thing anyone's ever said to me, Jonathan. I want to make you happy."

David wasn't sure what was stranger—the fact that everything that came out of his mouth around Jonathan was sappy as all hell, or the fact that he meant every word. He shrugged, not letting himself think too hard about it. He made this sweet, delicate, trusting guy happy. That was all that mattered.

"Kitchen's fine. I'm kind of a klutz and I'd hate to mess up your couch."

Jonathan flushed at his admission, but better to be truthful than ruin the expensive furniture. David stood and took Jonathan with him. He put his hand on the small of Jonathan's back, led them into the entryway, where he picked up the food bags in one hand, then walked them through the dining room to the arched doorway.

"The couch has stain guard or something. I eat dinner on it most nights while I watch TV, so it's had its share of spills. Caleb, my friend who decorated this place, promised there'd be no way to mess it up. But the kitchen's probably better anyway, because that way we'll be close to the drinks. Frankly, the fridge and the microwave are the only uses I have for that room."

CHAPTER SEVEN

WHEN THEY got to the kitchen, Jonathan understood why David didn't use it. The space was incredibly dark with peeling veneer paneling on the walls, laminate oak cabinets, and avocado green appliances.

"Yeah, I know. Tragic seventies remodel. I bet the original stuff was great, but one of the previous owners tore it out during what I can only assume was an unfortunate acid-induced do-it-yourself weekend. This room is the last thing on my to-do list. Well, that and the bedrooms, because they're essentially empty. Oh, and the yard. But that's it—kitchen, bedrooms, and yard."

David laughed and combed his fingers through his shiny black hair. Jonathan's fingers itched to do the same.

"Have a seat and tell me what you want to drink. I'm a disaster in the kitchen, so the fridge is a receptacle for beverages and the occasional takeout container. Beer? Wine? Soda? Water?" David pointed to the two mismatched chairs pulled up to the part of the counter that dropped down to table height. One of the chairs had a woven back with several tears and the other had a padded seat with a hole showing some of the stuffing. "The previous owners left those chairs when they moved out. I figured I'd wait to replace them until I remodel this whole room. But who knows when I'll get around to that."

Jonathan didn't know much about housing prices in Emile City, but he knew which neighborhoods were more blue collar, like the one where he grew up and his folks still lived, and which were higher end, like the one he was in at that moment. There was no question that David's house was in an expensive part of town. And based on the large lot and the incredible condition of the house, kitchen aside, he knew David had to have a good bit of money. Yet, his attitude indicated a person who didn't fixate on the material things surrounding him, which gave Jonathan comfort. After all, he'd never be able to match David in the income category, seeing as how he was just a glorified cook and dishwasher. Okay, not even glorified.

"I'll get the drinks."

Jonathan walked to the refrigerator and opened the door. It took quite a tug. David laughed and shrugged.

"I don't know if it's rusted shut, if the hinges are bad, or if that's some sort of diet plan—lose ten pounds in a week by making your fridge so hard to open that you'll never get to the food."

Jonathan smiled and propped the heavy door open with his entire body weight while he searched the fridge. He pulled out a bottle of water for himself, then looked up at David questioningly.

"Water's good for me too. Thanks, Jonathan."

Two bottles of water later, Jonathan was sitting at the counter, watching David dig through drawers. He couldn't believe he was sitting in his dream guy's kitchen, about to share what smelled like a fabulous meal. And that the man was just so damn *nice*. And hot. Monumentally hot. Can't forget that. Nice and hot. Jonathan reached his right hand to his left elbow and pinched hard enough to make himself jump and whimper.

When he looked around and still found himself in David's kitchen, rather than alone in his own bed, waking from the best dream of all time, Jonathan shot his eyes toward David, hoping he hadn't seen that little move. The amused grin on David's perfect face made Jonathan realize the pinch hadn't gone unnoticed, which set off a full-body blush.

David had been getting paper plates from the cabinet (he didn't own real plates, so he stored the paper products in there) when he saw Jonathan's head dip and the red take over his body once again. He walked over to the counter, set the plates down, and rubbed Jonathan's arms. He could tell Jonathan was embarrassed and it wasn't the first time that night. But the thing was, David found Jonathan's exuberance and honesty refreshing and endearing.

"You're beautiful and adorable and sexy. I can't believe you're sitting in my kitchen. Maybe you should pinch *me*, because I think I'm probably the one who's dreaming."

Jonathan's posture straightened, and he gave David a grateful smile. David kissed his cheek then spooned the food from the takeout containers onto the plates.

"I don't know if I can eat all of this."

David looked at the overflowing plate he'd served Jonathan, then at the slender man, and considered the portion size. He shrugged and grinned.

"Hmm. Well, whatever. Eat what you can, and we'll put the rest in the fridge for later. Microwave works, so you can always reheat it if you wake up hungry for a midnight snack."

Those silver eyes sparkled as Jonathan dug into his food.

"Thanks."

"You're very welcome."

It wasn't until David was swallowing the second bite of his own dinner that he realized what he'd said. Wake up hungry for a midnight snack...which implied Jonathan would be spending the night. Of course, that had been David's intent from the moment he'd invited the intriguing man over to his house, he just hadn't thought about it.

David hadn't ever been into the bar pickup scene or the online sites where guys met to hook up. Instead, he preferred to have sex within the confines of a relationship. Yet, despite having had several long-term boyfriends over the years, David could count the number of times he'd shared a bed until morning on one hand, and without using all of his fingers. And not one of those occasions was intentionally planned. They'd resulted from drinking too much to drive or being without his car.

Plus, he'd never allowed another guy to spend the night at his place. In fact, David had never invited his past boyfriends back to his house (or dorm room or apartment) specifically so he could avoid the awkward "early meeting tomorrow morning" after-sex conversations. If he went to their places, he could have sex, do the obligatory post-coital cuddle for as short a period as he could finagle, and then go home and have time to himself, sleep without anyone stealing his covers, and wake up without having to share the bathroom.

So why, for the first time in his life, had David picked a guy up at a bar and taken him home? And why, all of a sudden, did David want nothing more than to go to sleep with his arms wrapped around the man sitting next to him and to wake up seeing that beautiful man in his bed? It didn't make any sense, but it felt good and right. And Jonathan seemed to be on the same page. A shy smile aimed at him snapped David out of his musings.

"You haven't eaten anything, and I managed to get halfway through this Bigfoot-size mound of food. Is everything okay?"

David shook his head and brought himself into the present.

"Sorry. I was lost in thought. So, tell me about yourself, Jonathan."

The silver eyes looked down, and Jonathan pushed the remaining food around his plate with his fork.

"What do you want to know?"

Jonathan's voice was quiet, almost a whisper. David swallowed the bite of lasagna he'd just taken.

"You know, the usual. Where were you born? What do you do for a living? Are your parents still married? Do you have any siblings? Are you religious? What's your deepest, darkest secret and most explicit sexual fantasy? Just the regular first-date info." Jonathan looked panicked until David winked at him.

Okay, he was joking. That was a joke. Not that Jonathan minded answering most of those questions, but the last couple would end the night on the spot. Really, how would David react if Jonathan answered truthfully? *"My darkest secret is that I used to get gang-banged for a living, and my most explicit sexual fantasy became a reality earlier tonight because it was to kiss you."* Yeah, like that wouldn't simultaneously disgust and scare David off.

"Umm. Let's see. I was born here in Emile City. I've lived in EC West all my life. My parents are still married. They met in high school at Kennedy High. I have a brother, Brennan, who's six years older than me, and a sister, Shannon, who's eight years older. I was raised Catholic, but I'm not practicing. And as far as my job, I'm just working for my brother at my family's restaurant for now."

"What restaurant? I've probably tried it. Have I mentioned my ineptitude for all things kitchen-related? Restaurants and I are like this." David crossed his fingers and chuckled.

"The Dubliner. It's an Irish restaurant and pub. Not quite in EC West but not in Central, either. More like on the border."

David nodded and swallowed his latest bite of food.

"Sure. I've been there a few times. Good food, great atmosphere."

"That's the one. So, your turn."

Two more bites of food, a drink of water, and then David wiped his mouth with a paper towel, stretched his legs, and leaned back in his chair with his muscular arms crossed over his massive chest.

"Okay. I was born in California, but we moved around a lot. My dad was climbing up the corporate ladder, so we had to move for the next opportunity all the time. We ended up here in Emile City for high school, and I liked it, so I stayed, even when my dad moved to New York when I was nineteen. I'm not any religion, wasn't raised in any church to speak of, and never felt the desire to find one as an adult. I'm a Realtor, which is how I got this house. I'm lucky enough to hear about some things before they're on the market, and this was one of them. Same thing with Where Cowboys Dream— bank foreclosure, excellent price, so I snapped it up. I have a manager who runs it, so I don't have to do much—except, as you know, fill in occasionally and purchase a coffee maker." David winked.

Jonathan smiled. He was focused completely on David and the information he was sharing. He wanted to know whatever he could about the man who'd occupied all his fantasies for over three years. And so far, he liked everything he heard.

"That's great. I really like that bar. It's a good thing you bought it before some big company turned it into a chain coffee store or something."

David laughed.

"Yeah. I'm a big believer in spending local—restaurants, stores. EC West is a great place for that, actually. We don't have any of the big chains or box stores here. They're mostly in North and a good bit in East, but this area has a lot more character."

Jonathan nodded. It was true. He loved that about his hometown. Folks who lived there worked there, owned the businesses, and had an investment in the community.

"So tell me about your family. Your father works in New York?"

David took another drink of his water and tried to decide what to say next. He never talked about his family. Not ever. He missed them too much. But he'd brought this on himself by asking Jonathan those same questions. Not that he couldn't get out of answering. He was an expert at avoiding conversations about things that were too personal—meaning anything having to do with his family, his childhood, or his feelings. Frankly, anything other than work, movies, or current events had always been pretty much off the table.

But for the first time in his life, David didn't want

to hold back. Not from the refreshingly honest man sitting next to him who seemed to share whatever thought popped into his head. Even if the sharing inevitably resulted in an embarrassed wince, lowered eyes, and a blush.

"My mom had a stroke when I was in high school. She didn't make it. After that, it was just my dad, my sister Ellie, and me." David tried to calm the shake in his voice before continuing. "Ellie had always wanted to be a mom. That's it. So she married a great guy out of college, got pregnant a few years after that. About six months into it, they realized she had preeclampsia. They couldn't control it, and the baby was too little to induce, so they had her on bed rest, tried everything. But it wasn't enough to save Ellie. She managed to hang on long enough to have a healthy baby boy, though. Greg, her husband, called me when she went into labor. I took the first flight out and made it to New York in time to say goodbye. Don't know if she heard me."

David wiped a stray tear from his eye with the back of his hand, and Jonathan did what he'd wanted to do in that hospital years earlier. He got up from his chair, went over to David, and sat on his lap. Then he wrapped his arms around that strong body, rested his cheek against the crook of David's neck, and rubbed his head with one hand and his back with the other. He didn't offer any words. After all, what was there to say? He just held on tight, nuzzled David's neck, and hoped it was enough to express his support.

David was endlessly thankful for that compassionate

reaction. He clutched Jonathan, pressed his nose into his thick hair, inhaled his fresh, earthy scent, and knew without a doubt that he was completely and totally lost in Jonathan. And he'd never been more grateful for anything in his life.

"You still hungry, Jonathan, or are you ready to go to bed?"

That comment caused an immediate swelling in Jonathan's nether regions, and he shifted in David's lap. Jonathan swallowed and cleared his throat.

"Bed. Definitely bed."

David combed his fingers through Jonathan's hair, propped their foreheads together, and spoke quietly.

"You feel right in my arms."

And how fucking cheesy was that? True, but still, *cheesy*.

The joy that spread over Jonathan's face in response to David's comment made the normally reserved man forget all about cheesy. If it put that smile on Jonathan's face, David was willing to go all sap, all day. Totally worth it.

"David, can I use your phone? I need to call my parents to let them know I won't be coming home tonight." Jonathan chewed on his lower lip and dipped his head. "I mean, that is unless you want me to go home. I just…I mean, you said…"

David kissed Jonathan to stop the flow of those hesitant words. It seemed like almost every word or action he uttered tugged at David's chest.

"Will you please stay with me tonight, Jonathan? I

meant it when I said I don't want to let you go."

Really, it was a wonder David didn't ask the man to stay with him forever, because that was how he felt. And where in the hell had that feeling come from?

CHAPTER EIGHT

JONATHAN BEAMED when David confirmed his desire to have him stay the night. Seeing the magical smile take over that beautiful visage made David feel more accomplished than when he'd closed his highest dollar sale. *I made him happy.* David leaned down and brushed his lips over Jonathan's, enjoying the resulting whimper and glassy-eyed gaze that met him. He stroked Jonathan's cheek with his thumb.

"I don't have a landline because I'm almost never home, so you'll have to use my cell phone to call your parents. It's in my jacket pocket, and I think I left that in the car. Be right back."

"I'll get it. I don't mind."

Jonathan gave David's hard body a final squeeze, then crawled off David's lap and swiped the keys David had dropped on the counter earlier. David grasped Jonathan's hand as he walked by and pulled him against his chest. He caressed Jonathan's cheek and gave him a soft kiss. Damn, he couldn't get enough of him.

David had a feeling Jonathan wanted some privacy. Maybe he was embarrassed about still living with his parents, or maybe he didn't want David to hear whatever excuse he was going to use to explain where he was rather than telling his folks he'd be spending the night with a man he'd just met. Whatever the reason, David didn't want Jonathan to stand outside in the cold in order to be able to talk without David listening in. So he wanted to make it clear that he'd stay in the back, leaving the front of the house empty and available for Jonathan's use.

"I'm going to put these leftovers in the fridge, so I'll be in here for a bit."

Jonathan nodded and walked out of the room, after nuzzling David's neck and giving him a final, chaste kiss. David put away the food, dug through the drawers for a book of matches he'd need later, then walked into the empty room adjacent to the kitchen. It was supposed to be a family room, or television room, or something. But the yellowing linoleum tiles and the psychedelic wallpaper made it feel more like a step back in time. He planned to redo that room along with the kitchen, since they were connected. David would avoid the space altogether if it didn't have french doors leading to an enclosed back porch, which he loved.

The porch ran along the entire length of the house; it had ceiling fans for use in the summer and heaters installed along the baseboards for the winter. And it had a view of David's huge backyard. He didn't have much furniture there, just two white Adirondack chairs he'd picked up at a garden store. Of course, only one of those chairs ever got used. Maybe it was finally time to change that.

David stood on his porch and thought about his life. Things were good. He had wonderful friends, a successful career, and a beautiful house. So why all of a sudden did he feel like that wasn't enough?

"David?" Jonathan's voice floated through the door, and David's chest automatically constricted in response.

"I'm out here."

David walked over to the french doors and opened them to see Jonathan looking around the kitchen, the cell phone clutched in his hand. When he saw David, the handsome man bounded over and flung himself into David's arms.

"Okay, we ate dinner, I talked to my parents, now we can go to bed, right?"

David laughed and gave Jonathan a squeeze.

"Your excitement is going to give me a swelled head, Jonathan."

It was true. David had never felt so desired. And while that might've scared him off with other men, he absolutely adored the sentiment coming from Jonathan.

"Feels like it's already swelled."

Jonathan leered at David and ran his palm over David's crotch. David groaned out a laugh and pulled Jonathan down the length of the porch to another pair of french doors on the other side.

"Come on. I need to get you naked in bed so you're too distracted to make bad puns."

They walked through the doors and into a spacious

bedroom. David reached down and flipped the switch on a small lamp, casting a soft glow around them. Jonathan noticed the ceiling had the same diamond pattern as the other rooms in the house. There was an archway at one end of the room, a door—which he assumed led back to the main part of the house—on another wall, and those beautiful diamond windows on the remaining wall. The only furniture in the bedroom was an old bed with a milk crate next to it, holding a lamp.

"I've never looked at this room through someone else's eyes, so I'm just now realizing how pathetic this seems. I promise the mattress is comfortable, and I'm going to get new furniture soon. Really."

David stood behind him, the length of his broad, hard body pressed against his back. One big hand was splayed against his stomach, the other was caressing his neck, and David's mouth was right next to his ear. Jonathan didn't care about furniture. The smell of his dream man, the feel of his breath against Jonathan's neck, and the sound of that low, sultry voice rolling over him were the only things he registered.

He turned in David's arms and raised himself up on his toes. David met him halfway, and they fell into more of those gratifying kisses. Jonathan nipped and licked David's lips, making small, needy noises. When a big hand cupped Jonathan's ass and pulled him tight against David's groin, Jonathan opened his mouth in a gasp, and David took the opportunity to push his tongue inside and taste him.

"Need skin," David grumbled as he grazed his teeth against the side of Jonathan's neck. But when Jonathan immediately reacted by reaching for the button on his own pants, David stopped him. "Let me."

Feeling like he was unwrapping the best present of all time, David lifted the threadbare sweater and shirt over Jonathan's head and got his first look at the sinewy muscles on that lean chest. He lowered Jonathan to the bed, then knelt at his feet and removed his shoes and socks. The sound of Jonathan's heaving breath filled the air, and his entire body trembled. And if those signs weren't enough to let David know how into the encounter Jonathan was, the erection trying to poke its way out of his pants would have done the trick.

One button, one zipper, and one gentle pull, and David had the most beautiful man he'd ever met lying naked in his bed, looking for all the world like that was exactly where he belonged. At least, that was how he looked to David. A tightness made its way into David's chest, and he knew that the only way he could breathe would be to touch Jonathan right fucking now.

He caressed Jonathan's hair and ran his palm down the length of his body—ear, neck, collarbone, chest, stomach, and hip. Jonathan raised his hips and uttered another of those little whimper-moans, which were quickly becoming an aphrodisiac for David. David let a single finger glide on Jonathan's hard cock and enjoyed the shudder he saw take over that slender body.

"Like that, baby?"

Jonathan nodded. He liked all of it. The touching, the kissing, the endearment. All of it. But most of all, he liked David.

"Mmm hmm."

"Want me to do it with my tongue?"

Jonathan's eyes widened, his hands fisted the sheets on either side of him, and his mouth went completely dry. He couldn't speak, couldn't think. A need like nothing he'd ever felt consumed him, and he knew he'd just die if it didn't get met. When David's soft tongue lapped at his dick and balls, he swallowed and somehow managed to speak in a shaky voice.

"Need you. Please, David. Need you now."

David looked up at Jonathan's beautiful, adoring face, and his heart stuttered. How had he gone thirty-two years without this man in his life? He stood and quickly stripped off his own clothes. Then he fumbled in the side of the milk crate for the lube and rejoined Jonathan on the bed, blanketing him with his own body.

"Ungh. Feels good. Your skin on mine. So good."

The caveman talk might have made David laugh if it weren't such a turn-on that he could reduce Jonathan to incomplete sentences so easily. Frankly, the feeling was mutual.

David kissed Jonathan's neck, sucked on the skin, but refrained from leaving a mark, even though that was exactly what he wanted to do. The urge to somehow stake his claim on Jonathan was almost overwhelming. But David's thoughts shifted in another direction when Jonathan wrapped his legs around David's waist, rested his heels above David's ass, and thrust his hips up against David's belly.

"Please, David. Please."

"Oh, Jesus. I love hearing you beg."

He did too. David had never gotten off on needy, smothering men. He'd always wanted his space, both literally and emotionally. But all of that went out the window with Jonathan. He wanted this man to need him, wanted to hear that pleading voice asking David for something Jonathan thought only he could give. And, more than anything else, David wanted to meet each and every one of those requests, leaving Jonathan in a constant state of satisfaction and bliss.

David raised himself off Jonathan's narrow body and kneeled between his legs. He watched Jonathan's rapturous face as he caressed his testicles and the area beneath them. Jonathan made another of his happy noises, propped his thighs and ass on David's thighs, planted his feet on the bed, and let his knees fall to the sides, leaving himself completely exposed. That trust and vulnerability took David's breath away.

"You're beautiful."

David took a slick finger and breached Jonathan for the first time. So hot and soft. Had other men felt that good inside? When he had two fingers in Jonathan, David leaned down and kissed him. Jonathan was thrusting up and down, riding his fingers and moaning.

"More. Please more. Want you."

David removed his fingers, lined himself up with Jonathan, and braced himself with one hand planted next to Jonathan's head on the pillow and the other holding Jonathan's hip. He was about to push home when he realized he wasn't wearing a condom. Holy Christ! That was a mistake he'd never even come close to making.

He didn't keep any rubbers in his bedroom, since he never brought men home, but he probably had a couple in his wallet. They were old, but hopefully not expired. It took a concerted effort for David to pull away from the eager body beneath him and reach for his discarded jeans. He quickly found a condom and rolled it down his long, thick length. Then he dripped a good amount of lube onto his glans and rubbed it up and down his cock. With that preparation complete, David immediately returned to Jonathan's entrance.

David wanted to go slow, let Jonathan adjust, but the combination of his own attraction to the man and Jonathan's eager thrusts didn't let that happen. Before he knew it, David was buried balls deep in the tight channel and Jonathan was crying out in pleasure.

"Oh fuck, that's so good. You feel incredible wrapped around my cock."

David growled out the words through gritted teeth as his body moved fluidly over Jonathan's. His movements were graceful, his voice rough, and his expression raw and powerful. He reminded Jonathan of wild animals he'd seen stalking their prey in nature shows.

Jonathan moaned and his eyes rolled back in his head. David was kneeling between his legs, supporting Jonathan's thighs on top of his own, and gripping his hips as the strong man moved in and out of his chute. David's cock was so long and thick that he filled Jonathan's body in the best possible way and rubbed against his gland on every slide. Nothing had ever felt so good, and Jonathan knew that if he hadn't already come twice that evening, he'd have blown his load already.

As it was, the feeling of that hard cock inside him and David's rippling stomach muscles rubbing over his dick were putting him over the edge. Jonathan hadn't realized he was saying anything until David's husky voice washed over him.

"Those noises you make are so fucking hot, so needy."

David draped Jonathan's legs over his arms, folded his body in half, leaned down, and looked into Jonathan's eyes, never stopping the in-and-out motion. The pure pleasure showing on Jonathan's face turned David on beyond belief. He'd never been with a man who so obviously enjoyed this act.

"You really like this, don't you? Like having my cock in your ass?"

The roughness in David's voice, the dirty talk, and the heated look David gave him, combined with the feeling of the strong, handsome man plowing into him, were too good for Jonathan to be able to hold back. His eyes widened at the realization that his orgasm was coming, and he cried out as ropes of cum left his cock and coated his stomach and chest.

David gasped in shock at the sight of that hard cock spasming beneath him. He'd been holding himself up above Jonathan's folded body, so he hadn't been stroking Jonathan off. While David knew his previous sexual partners had enjoyed their prostate being stimulated and the friction of his stomach rubbing across their cocks while he fucked them in that position, he'd never been with someone who'd spontaneously released with such minimal stimulation.

David fervently wanted to shoot his seed deep inside that willing body clenching around his rock-hard cock. But he forced himself to hold back, wanting to see the look of ecstasy take over the beautiful face beneath him once again. He scooped Jonathan's ejaculate off his chest and stomach and rubbed his dick with his own seed, not letting it soften.

"I'm not done with you, Jonathan. Gonna make you feel so good that you'll come again."

The speed of David's pushes into Jonathan's channel increased continuously until he was on his knees, one hand on the bed and the other flying on Jonathan's dick while he slammed into him. David was grunting, panting, and making harsh sounds, again reminding Jonathan of a wild animal, which served to excite him further. His cock ached from filling again so quickly.

"Ungh! David! David! David!"

Jonathan locked his ankles around David's waist, arched his back, canted his hips, and clawed at David's arms and shoulders. Though he was normally restrained at all times, including in bed, something in David snapped and he growled, "I'm gonna fuck you so hard you won't stop feeling me for days, Jonathan. That's what you want, isn't it? You enjoy being filled? Want to feel me in your ass all the time?"

"Y-y-yes! Yes, please. Fill me! Oh God, fill me."

Jonathan bucked against David and wailed as hot liquid spilled over the big hand tugging mercilessly on his cock. The smell of the silver-eyed beauty's seed and the feel of that lean, hard body trembling beneath him tore David's orgasm from him, and he gave a final push as deep as he could into Jonathan's ass and sprayed his release into the latex.

When he finally stopped shooting, David collapsed, half his body on the mattress and the other half on Jonathan. He nuzzled Jonathan's neck, kissing and licking, while he stroked the soft skin on his inner arm and rubbed his leg up and down Jonathan's thigh. Holy damn, that had been amazing.

CHAPTER NINE

AFTER A few minutes of showering Jonathan with tender caresses, David's body calmed enough to reflect on the coupling they'd just shared. His immediate reaction was horror at the crude things he'd said and the roughness of his actions. He'd never lost control that way, never felt so completely wild and unrestrained during sex. And to act that way with such a sweet, gentle soul was terrible. He leapt away, scrambled to a sitting position, and hoped that he could redeem himself by groveling.

"Oh, Jonathan, I'm so sorry. I didn't mean it. I don't know what came over me, but I won't do it again. I promise. I'm sorry, baby."

Jonathan's eyes grew wide with fear, and his response, in a soft, shy voice, was completely unexpected.

"Why not? Didn't it feel good to you? I can do better. Really, I can."

Relief pulsed through David's body. He climbed over Jonathan, propped himself up on his elbows and knees above the slender body, and gazed into those silver eyes.

"You're amazing, Jonathan. I am so attracted to you, it's scary. And I don't know how you think you can improve on what we just did, but I'm pretty sure better would kill me. I was just worried that I was too rough. That I hurt your feelings with the things I said."

Jonathan reached his head up, kissed the base of David's neck, and licked his way over to David's ear. He closed his eyes, as if he could hide himself with that action. David had to strain to hear his whispered voice, even though he was speaking directly into David's ear.

"I liked it. A lot. Am I too weird?"

David's heart ached at those unsure words, at Jonathan's insecurity. Didn't he realize how sexy he was? How incredibly irresistible David found that mix of innocence and sensuality?

"Jonathan, will you please open your eyes and look at me?"

The long lashes fluttered, and silver eyes met his.

"You're not weird. You are a kind, gorgeous, passionate man, and I feel incredibly lucky that you're here with me. But you have to know, there's something about you that makes me lose all sense of reason. So you need to tell me if I do anything that makes you uncomfortable. I know you don't have much experience, and I don't want to take advantage of you." A haunted look passed over Jonathan's face, and he squeezed his eyes shut again.

He hadn't lied to David. Hadn't said anything that wasn't true. But he wasn't correcting him, either.

Did it count as a lie if he didn't speak up and explain that he had more experience than most men gained in a lifetime? That he truly couldn't remember the number of guys who'd fucked him during the two months he'd spent essentially naked and cum-soaked in New York? He owed David the truth and knew it was a bad idea to start a relationship with lies. Of course, if he told David about his past, there'd be no chance of a relationship, anyway. And that wasn't a risk Jonathan could take. He looked into his dream man's captivating eyes and shared the only truth he could.

"You're not taking advantage of me. The things you said, the feeling of your body on me, in me, stretching me hard and fast and deep... I liked it. I want to be with you like that again."

He wanted to add more. *I've wanted to be with you for three-and-a-half years. You're actually the only person I've ever wanted to be with. The others were just warm bodies to pay the bills and help with loneliness, but I think it actually made things worse. I never wanted them, didn't know them and never cared to, because you were all I could think about since the moment I laid eyes on you.*

Of course he didn't say those things. He couldn't risk scaring David away.

David groaned and shifted his body, amazed when, despite his very recent orgasm, his cock started filling in reaction to Jonathan's professed enjoyment of hard, fast, and deep. If he leaned down and kissed that soft mouth, sucked on that delicious tongue, and felt that warm skin against his, he'd recharge completely and push his way back inside the tight heat of Jonathan's ass.

No, no, no. The man had to be sore. Plus David had something else he needed to do before midnight, and Jonathan would probably appreciate a chance to wash off the sweat and semen covering his gorgeous body first.

"Hey, you want to share a shower with me? I remodeled all the bathrooms in this house, so it's a good-size stall. We can both fit."

Jonathan smiled and nodded. "Sure thing, tiger."

David leaned over Jonathan and grinned. "Tiger?"

Jonathan flinched and blushed down to his toes. Had he said that out loud? "Oh, ah, ehm, I just... You, um, you were growling earlier and you had this, um, wild look in your eyes. And you were moving on me, in me, with so much power and grace. It made me think of a tiger and..."

"So that's a good thing, right? That I reminded you of a tiger, I mean?"

Jonathan nodded. "It was hot."

"Cool. I've never had a nickname."

David hopped out of bed and reached his hands down to Jonathan, pulling him to his feet and leading him through the archway at the end of the room. He flipped on the lights and Jonathan walked into the clean, modern space. There were tiny, white, octagon-shaped tiles on the floor, with black tiles in the same shape thrown into the mix in an apparently random pattern. The cabinets were white with silver handles, covered by white Carrara marble countertops. White subway tiles lined the walls from the floor to shoulder height, topped by a row of small, square black tiles. Despite the lack of color, the space didn't seem cold, just clean and fresh.

"Green would look nice."

"What's that?"

David was standing right behind Jonathan, his body heat warming Jonathan's naked torso, making it hard to concentrate. Jonathan pointed to the stretch of wall space between the where the subway tiles ended and the ceiling began.

"For this room, a green color would be nice. A light shade so it doesn't change the fresh feel of the space, but just adds a little oomph."

Did he just say "oomph?" And did he actually tell David how the man should paint his own bathroom walls? Honestly, his only chance of not sending David running in the opposite direction would be to keep his mouth good and shut, something that hadn't ever been difficult for Jonathan. The only upside to being shy was that he never said much, which kept the weird at bay, or at least kept it mostly contained. But for some reason he couldn't seem to hold anything back from the one person whom he really wanted to impress. Well, anything other than his porn career and his child. Jonathan groaned inwardly. *Wonderful, I can keep back the worst and best parts of myself—coincidentally the two parts any future partner would want to know—but I have untreatable diarrhea of the mouth about everyfuckingthing else.*

"Light green. That's a great idea." David rubbed his hands up and down the sides of Jonathan's arms. "I'm sick of all these white walls. I've been meaning to get a painter in here, just haven't gotten to it. What about the bedroom? I haven't painted or done anything with that room."

Jonathan's tense body sagged in relief. David liked his idea. And he wanted Jonathan to help choose a color for his bedroom too. That had to be a good sign, right?

"Green just a few shades darker than you paint the bathroom would be good for the bedroom."

He could feel David's head nodding behind him. "That's perfect. We can choose paint for the kitchen and the adjoining room once we figure out cabinets. Everything in there needs to be pulled out and replaced."

He kissed Jonathan's neck and gave him a squeeze. David couldn't seem to keep his hands off Jonathan. The feeling of his skin, the warmth of his body, his earthy scent. All of those things called to something deep within David and made him want to wrap himself around Jonathan and cuddle. Yes, as out of character as that was, he actually wanted to cuddle.

"I need to make a quick pit stop in the bathroom. Towels are in the cabinet under the left sink. Extra toothbrushes in the bottom drawer." David landed a quick kiss on Jonathan's shoulder, then forced himself to pull away.

He disappeared behind a door at the end of the

bathroom, so Jonathan figured that space housed the toilet. He heard David's stream hitting the water and shivered a little at the intimacy of the moment. He was naked in David's bathroom, sharing normal day-to-day stuff like a real couple. Was that what they were? Was that how David saw them, or was this just Jonathan's stupid, immature imagination running away with him?

He walked toward the cabinet and shook off those thoughts. David seemed to like him, from the things he said, and the way he looked at Jonathan. It wasn't a fantasy Jonathan was concocting. It was real.

The comfort from that internal pep talk lasted exactly the length of time it took Jonathan to open the bottom drawer to see a lifetime supply of toothbrushes. He stood perfectly still and tried to come up with any possible reason why a single guy would need all those extra toothbrushes other than a revolving lineup of men coming through that bathroom... and the bedroom next to it. He was so lost in thought that he didn't hear the toilet flush or the door open. David's arms snaked around Jonathan's bare chest, and he felt the broad body wrap around him, and the flaccid cock and balls press against his lower back.

"My dental hygienist has a crush on me, so *she* insists on giving me all this stuff every time I go in for my cleanings. I explained that I'm gay years ago, but strangely enough, it just seemed to enflame matters. I usually bag up all those extra toothbrushes and the travel-size toothpastes and floss beneath them and donate them to the youth shelter for their toiletry drive in January. So it's a good thing you're not here a month from now, because then you'd have to share my toothbrush. Not that I'd mind."

Jonathan's body relaxed and he sighed.

"Really?"

David chuckled.

"Of course. I've had your dick in my mouth and I swallowed. Do you really think I'd have trouble with you using my toothbrush?"

"Not what I meant," Jonathan whispered.

"I know," David whispered back and gave Jonathan a little squeeze. "You're the first guy I've ever had in my home, and in my bed."

When Jonathan turned and flashed that happy smile, it was all David could do not to finish his thought and say he wanted Jonathan to be the last. And wasn't that realization a kick in the pants?

JONATHAN WAS standing under a showerhead, his neck tilted back and eyes closed, rinsing suds from his thick black hair. The expression on his face was content and happy. David's heart raced in reaction to the sight of the beauty before him. He looked at the floor and gauged whether his torso was tall enough to allow him to sit on his ass while he blew the shorter man or whether kneeling would be better.

"So why do you have two showerheads when it's just you living here?"

At first, hearing that voice speaking rather than moaning, as it had been doing in the fantasy sequence playing in David's mind, took him off guard, but he turned off the dirty slideshow and tried to answer the question.

"I don't know, really. That's just what came to mind when I was deciding what I wanted for the remodel."

He'd also put in double sinks, closed the toilet off in its own little space, and insisted on a closet with two sides that were mirror images of each other—each containing its own built-in drawers, shoe racks, and hanging rods. Those touches spoke to a bathroom shared by two people, and building all of them had required enough space that he'd had to turn a four-bedroom house into a three-bedroom. David knew better than anyone the negative impact that had on property values, and it wasn't as if he'd ever considered inviting someone to come live with him. Hell, he hadn't ever considered inviting someone to spend the night. So why had he chosen permanent and expensive construction that created a space for two?

His unusual moment of self-reflection was waylaid by the feel of a wet, slick Jonathan falling into his arms and squeezing him in a tight hug. David could feel Jonathan's cock lengthening and hardening against his thigh. Once in the bar, again on the couch, twice in bed, and that hot body was ready to go again. It was like screwing the Energizer Bunny, but without the annoying drumming noise and unfortunate pink color. David covered Jonathan's smooth, hard dick with his large hand and stroked it a couple of times.

"This for me?"

"Mmm hmm. I like being here. With you. I like being here with you."

"Damn, you're good for my ego. Let me show you that I'm worth the sentiment."

David dropped to his knees, sat back on his haunches, and took Jonathan's cock into his mouth down to the root. The moans coming from above him let him know Jonathan didn't mind getting right to the good stuff. Long sucks up and down Jonathan's cock made him shiver, his legs unsteady. David cupped his ass and held him firm while he worked that dick in and out of his mouth, hollowing his cheeks when he pulled out and tickling with his tongue when he pressed back in.

When Jonathan's moans turned into cries, his fingers tangled in David's hair, and his body trembled, David fumbled for a bottle of shampoo on the floor, managed to open it so his hand was slick, then pressed a finger deep into Jonathan's ass.

"Oh, David!"

Hot, salty ejaculate drizzled into his mouth, though not as much as the first time—which wasn't a surprise, considering the fact that Jonathan was probably close to dehydration from the volume of fluid he'd been expelling.

David kept his position on the floor, moving his finger languidly in and out of that tight ass and licking the softening cock and balls. Eventually Jonathan's legs really did give out, and he collapsed onto David's lap, his head resting on David's chest and his fingers playing with the fine hair that grew there.

David kissed the top of Jonathan's head, wrapped one arm around his back to hold him tight, and never stopped finger-fucking that sweet ass. He hadn't ever enjoyed being in somebody like that. Never sought the connection in either a literal or figurative way. It felt good. The ass and the connection.

The glide of Jonathan's hands over his skin slowed, and his body went limp in David's lap.

"Bedtime, baby."

"Mmm. Can't move."

David chuckled, slid Jonathan off his lap, and propped him against the wall, then stood to turn off the water and scoop up the towels they'd hung on the two hooks he'd installed next to the shower enclosure. Two hooks. David shook his head at the recognition while he dried off his body and feet. When he was sure he was dry enough that he wouldn't slip and drop his precious cargo, he leaned down to Jonathan, covered his thin body in the large bath sheet, and carried him into the bedroom.

"You snuggle up under the blanket. I'll be right back."

Jonathan clung to his arm and held him in place.

"Where're you going?"

He kissed Jonathan's head and smoothed the thick, black hair.

"Kitchen. I'll just be a minute."

"'M 'kay."

Jonathan crawled under the covers and pressed his nose into the pillow, inhaling David's scent. *Please let this be for more than one night. Please let him be mine.*

CHAPTER TEN

"HAPPY BIRTHDAY, Jonathan."

Jonathan sat up in bed and looked toward the door to see a naked David walking into the dark room, carrying a plate that held a slice of cake topped with a single candle. His head swam with emotion.

"H-h-how, ehm, how did you know it's my birthday?"

David dropped onto the bed on his knees and raised his elbows, releasing two water bottles that had been pressed between his arms and the sides of his body.

"I looked at your license when you passed out at Where Cowboys Dream, remember? I noticed that today's your birthday, so I included a piece of cake in our dinner order from Magiano's. Hope you like chocolate."

Tears glistened in Jonathan's eyes. Other than his parents and siblings, nobody had ever remembered, let alone acknowledged his birthday.

"I like you so much."

His cheeks still heated, but Jonathan didn't avert or shut his eyes during this confession. He gazed at David's face and enjoyed how his blue eyes sparkled in the candlelight.

"I like you too, Jonathan. Blow out the candle and

make a wish."

Jonathan closed his eyes, pursed his lips, leaned down, and gave a soft blow.

"I hope it comes true," he whispered with his eyes still closed. David's warm palm stroked his cheek.

"Me too."

They shared the cake, drained the water bottles, and collapsed. Jonathan pressed himself right up against David's side, used David's chest as his pillow, flung one arm over David's waist and a leg over David's hip, and fell straight into sleep. And David, who'd never enjoyed touching unless it was leading up to an orgasm, wrapped both arms around the slender man and tried to pull him even closer.

DAVID WOKE before the sun and let his fingers wander over Jonathan's soft skin. It was Thursday, close to end of the workweek for most people. But David wasn't most people. He worked seven days a week. Always had. When he was in school, it was working on his papers and studying for exams so he could graduate with a perfect grade point average. Then, when he'd started his career, he'd put that same dedication into building his client base by finding people the perfect house or office space. He loved his job and he was good at it. So good in fact, he'd had the highest dollar volume sales of any Realtor in Emile City for the past four years running.

But for the first time in his life, David didn't want to preview houses so he could find just the right spot for his clients to live their lives. Instead, he wanted to live his own life, which meant being at his own house with Jonathan. He wanted to try out the wood-burning fireplace in the living room and see the flames reflected in Jonathan's silver eyes. He wanted to paint the bedroom green and buy furniture to fill the empty space, so he and Jonathan could enjoy spending time there. He wanted to cuddle up together and watch old movies on cable.

He rubbed the heel of his right hand over his eyes and groaned in frustration at the realization that he'd already made appointments with clients for that weekend, promised to show them spaces, decide on list prices or offer prices, and everything else that usually filled his days. Jonathan shifted in his sleep, causing David's left hand to slide over that firm ass, and Jonathan's dick, hard again, to rub against David's thigh. David kissed the top of Jonathan's head and, though his eyes remained closed and his lids still, his lips turned up in a smile and he mumbled David's name.

David felt a responding tug in his chest and, in that instant, decided to hire the agent he contracted with when things were really busy or when he needed to leave town. She'd been asking to come work for him as an associate Realtor on a full-time basis for years, and he'd put her off because he wanted to give clients that personal touch. But Alice was actually a good agent, clients liked her, and the bottom line was this: David would rather have some free time so he could use his personal touch on Jonathan.

He'd call Alice that morning and offer her a job. If he was really lucky, and if Alice was as anxious to join his firm as she'd seemed, he might even be able to move things around and unload some of that weekend's work onto her plate, so he'd be able to spend a lot of time with Jonathan. His body relaxed with this decision. Well, most of his body relaxed. His dick had woken up and asked for attention as soon as it became aware of Jonathan's presence.

"Mmm."

Jonathan moaned, kissed David's neck, and moved the arm that was draped around David's waist so that his hand was caressing David's erection. David hissed and thrust his hips up toward that gentle touch.

"'S nice," that sleepy voice mumbled into David's chest while Jonathan's hand stroked him and his hips pumped against David's leg. David caressed that firm ass and tickled the cleft.

"You sore?"

Jonathan wiggled and clenched his ass.

"In a good way."

He scooted off David and onto the mattress on his stomach, then tucked his knees up and continued the wiggle. This time it looked a lot like an invitation, one that David couldn't refuse. He leaned over the side of the bed and fumbled for the discarded bottle of lube and the extra condom he'd gotten out of his wallet the previous night.

Note to self, David thought as he dropped a kiss on Jonathan's lower back, *move the box of condoms from the bathroom to the nightstand. Addendum to the note: buy a nightstand.*

After finding the supplies, David rolled a condom onto his cock and positioned his body behind Jonathan's inviting ass. He caressed Jonathan's back while he admired the lean muscles leading to the round globes. For a crazy moment, David thought about tasting those globes and the area between them. Never having been interested in rimming, the sharp desire surprised him. He shook it off and satisfied himself with light kisses on Jonathan's back while his lubed fingers made their way into that tight ass.

Jonathan sighed and dropped his arms so his shoulders and forehead were flat on the bed and his ass was still raised in the air. David draped himself over Jonathan's back, lined his cock up to that inviting opening, and whispered to Jonathan while he pressed in.

"You're so sexy, Jonathan."

He buried his nose in the soft, black hair, covered Jonathan's hands with his own, twined their fingers together, and found a slow rhythm. Jonathan made those whimper-moan noises David found so enticing and moved back and forth with David.

"God, you feel good inside me. So good."

"Like being inside you, baby. Wanna make you feel

good."

Still in that state between asleep and awake, Jonathan's face was soft, his skin warm, and his voice a little hoarse. David thought he was adorable. Part of him wanted to see if he could make Jonathan come just from fucking him; the man had been so damn responsive to the feeling of his prostate being massaged the night before that David thought it might actually be possible. But he knew that experiment would require a harder fuck than the sleepy, early-morning Jonathan moaning beneath him would enjoy. So David stuck with dropping tender kisses on Jonathan's shoulders, kept his slender body warm by covering it with his own bigger body, and eventually removed one of his hands from Jonathan's grip and jacked his cock slowly.

"Ready to come for me, baby?"

David's hand moved up and down Jonathan's hard cock, the thumb gliding over the tip every few strokes. His grip was loose, matching the slow, gentle rhythm of his thrusts in and out of Jonathan's body. It was completely different from the rough, frantic coupling of the night before, but Jonathan enjoyed it just as much. He was thrilled that the same man could bring him to ecstasy in such different ways.

Jonathan's soft, barely audible moans filled the air before a shiver went through his body and wet heat poured over David's hand. David looked down at the profile of the handsome face below him, eyes closed, mouth open in pleasure, pillow-lines still slightly visible on the skin, and felt his own orgasm overtake him. He moaned and shivered in delight with his release, landed a few more kisses on Jonathan's neck, then pulled out of that welcoming body. Jonathan curled onto his side, eyes still closed.

"What time is it?"

David reached for his cell phone and checked the time.

"Just a little after six. Still early enough for you to get more sleep. I'll get a washcloth to clean you up."

David stumbled into the bathroom, disposed of the condom, and wiped off his dick. He got a fresh washcloth and ran the water until it was warm before wetting the cloth and returning to the bedroom. He was surprised to see Jonathan sitting at the edge of the bed, pulling his sweater over his head. What was even more surprising, however, was the profound disappointment that racked David's body.

"Why are you getting dressed? It's early." David heard the whine in his voice but he couldn't control it.

Jonathan pulled on his pants and ran his fingers through his messy hair. "I have to go home before…" He sighed deeply, rubbed his eyes with the base of his hands, and chewed on his bottom lip. "I just have to go home."

David went over every word, every touch from the moment they'd woken up. What had he done to drive Jonathan away? He couldn't think of an answer, and refusing to take the man back to his car and tying him to the bed instead wasn't a viable option, no matter how much David wished otherwise—partially because David's bed didn't have any slats that could hold a rope. In fact, it was the realization that he had such a wish that motivated David to turn around and walk back through the bathroom and into the closet.

He got dressed with shaky hands and gave himself a mental flogging. *He wants to go home, so you're going to take him to his car and apologize for whatever you did to fuck things up. Then you're going to ask him out again.*

With that plan in order, David straightened his clothes, cleared his throat, and walked back into the bathroom feeling more composed. He found Jonathan at the sink, brushing his teeth. David halted. He stared at the vision before him and wondered if he'd ever seen anything more perfect. *He belongs here with me.* The thought came into his head unbidden, but he didn't even try to dispute its accuracy.

Jonathan rinsed his mouth, then wiped loose drops of water off his face with the back of his hand. Just then his eyes met David's in the mirror. He smiled, not the wide joyous smile from the day before, but a more hesitant, questioning version. Never having had an issue with confidence, David decided now was not the time to start. He strode over to Jonathan, removed the toothbrush from his hand, and dropped it into the wall-mounted holder where he kept his own toothbrush.

It wasn't a declaration of undying love, a marriage proposal, or a tattoo over the heart, but it was the only way David could show his intentions. Jonathan turned, wrapped his arms around David's chest, and gave him a tight hug. David stroked his hair, kissed the top of his head, and sighed.

"Let's go," David said reluctantly.

They drove back to Jonathan's car in silence. He kept trying to think of what he could say to explain himself, but other than the truth—I have a son waiting for me at home and I want to be there when he wakes up—nothing came to mind.

"I want to see you again."

Oh, thank God. He was getting a reprieve, despite his weird behavior. Jonathan's relief was palpable. "Me too," he replied.

David pulled up at Where Cowboys Dream, put the car in park, and looked over at the man sitting next to him. He ran a finger along Jonathan's strong jawline and thought about not being too pushy, about waiting some predetermined period of time before asking him out, about all the things he'd heard his friends say when they were interested in pursuing a guy. But David had never paid close attention to those conversations. He'd never had an issue meeting men, or getting dates, and, until that moment, he'd never cared one way or another whether any particular guy decided to turn him down. Not that any guy ever had.

"How about Friday night? We can go to dinner and you can stay the weekend with me."

David would figure out what to do with his clients if Alice couldn't jump in on such short notice. Hell, even if he lost the clients, it'd be worth it. Jonathan was pulling away, and David had to put a stop to it. He couldn't do that if they weren't together.

Jonathan's eyes widened. He blinked a few times and cleared his throat. "I can't." Suddenly, he was grappling with the door handle and scrambling out of the car. "I'll call you."

David was too surprised by that hasty exit to point out that they hadn't exchanged numbers. By the time he got his wits about him, Jonathan had jogged around the corner and disappeared.

"Shit!" David slammed his hand onto the steering wheel in frustration. He didn't have Jonathan's number, didn't know where the man lived, and he had no idea what had scared off the one person who had ever managed to burrow his way into his heart.

CHAPTER ELEVEN

DAVID DROVE home, feeling frustrated and deeply disappointed. Too keyed up to go back to sleep, he yanked on his workout clothes, downed a canned protein drink, and drove to the gym. Two hours later, his muscles ached but his head was clear. Jonathan had probably turned down the date because he had to work Friday night. No big deal. He'd go to The Dubliner, see Jonathan, and figure out a time when they could get together. Problem solved.

He went home, showered, then called Alice and offered her a job. She was positively giddy and agreed to start that morning. Perfect—one task down. David drove to his office, walked Alice through the client meetings he had planned for the weekend, then left to go have lunch at The Dubliner. Well, he was going to find Jonathan, but it was lunchtime and he hadn't eaten, so technically, he was going there to have lunch.

As soon as he pulled up in front of the darkened building, David remembered that the restaurant didn't open for lunch. He'd known that, but in his determination to find Jonathan, David had forgotten. He dropped his head down against his steering wheel and groaned.

Okay, fine. I just need to revise the plan. I'll go into work and start calling The Dubliner at about three. They're bound to have people there before opening hours, just to prep, and Jonathan said he worked in back. Maybe I'll catch him.

Feeling slightly deflated but still hopeful, David returned to his office. At least Alice had agreed to work that weekend, so he'd be free to spend it with Jonathan. That was, if he could talk to Jonathan. David swallowed his groan. *I'll find him.*

A few hours later, David picked up his phone and called The Dubliner for the fourth time that day.

"Dubliner. What can I do for ya?"

It took David a couple of seconds to process that someone had actually answered the phone. He was so used to the endless ringing that'd met him all day.

"Oh, yeah, hi. I'm, uh, actually looking for someone. Jonathan Doyle. Is he working right now?"

There was a long pause, and then the voice answered, sounding confused, "No, Jonathan's not here."

David's shoulders sagged. He couldn't keep the disappointment from his voice. "Okay. Thanks." He'd almost ended the call when he heard the voice come back.

"Do ya want me to give 'im a message for ya?"

"Yes, that'd be great. Can you please tell him David Miller called? My number—"

"David? Yeah, got it. Will do."

The line went dead and David slammed his hand on his desk.

"Shit!"

TRYING TO figure out how to find Jonathan played center stage in David's head the rest of the day. He managed to stay busy with work, introducing Alice to existing clients, getting through paperwork, even signing a few new clients. But thoughts of Jonathan never left David's mind. Unfortunately, the woman who answered the phone at The Dubliner when David called yet again said he wasn't in, and all David could do was leave another message because he had no other way of getting hold of his lover.

His lover. They'd met at a bar and spent one night together. Since when did that make a guy anything other than a one-off? David fervently shook off that thought. Yeah, they'd met at a bar, and, fine, it'd been only one night, but those things didn't matter. Jonathan was more than some hookup. David just had to find him and convince him of that undeniable fact. But it wouldn't happen that night, because Jonathan wasn't working and David didn't know where he lived.

David locked up his office and made another trip to the gym. Punishing his body did nothing to ease his mind. David left feeling sore and just as frustrated as when he'd entered the building. *I need to get good and drunk.* That wasn't a long-term solution to his heartache, but he had to find a way to take his mind off the man who'd been consuming it all day.

So David called his neighbors, hoping they'd want to go out and that one of them would act as the designated driver. Thirty minutes later, he was showered, dressed, and waiting for José and Adam to come pick him up. He snagged his jacket from the coatrack and ran out the door as soon as he heard their car pull up.

"Thanks for driving, José." David slid into the back of the car and bent over the driver's seat to give his friend's shoulder a light squeeze before settling back and leaning against the headrest.

"No problem. We were getting ready to go out anyway. Meeting Eli and Seth at Two of a Kind. That okay with you?"

David closed his eyes and tried to unwind. His shoulders ached from the tension he'd been holding since he'd walked into his bedroom and seen Jonathan getting ready to leave at six in the morning.

"Sounds good. So what have you two been up to today?"

José groaned. "We worked all day, then spent three hours at Walmart. Three hours. We're doing that holiday adopt-a-family thing and we had a list of toys and clothes, plus housewares and stuff. The case manager said we should go there to get everything. Have you ever been to that store, David?"

David shook his head. "Uh-uh."

"Yeah, me neither. We had to go all the way to EC

North, and then we had to navigate our way through three thousand aisles. I've never seen anything like it. There were whole families shopping together, like multiple generations. And I think we witnessed some life-cycle celebrations. You know, baptism on aisle three, quinceañera on aisle ten, wedding on aisle thirteen. I'm just glad we missed the birth on aisle twenty."

Adam and David laughed through José's story. David was still wiping tears from his eyes when they walked into the bar and saw Seth and Eli sitting at a table. Both men got up to say their hellos and exchange hugs and kisses with their friends.

"So you look about as tired as I feel, David. What's up?" Seth looked at David with concern.

The last thing David wanted to do was talk about Jonathan. He was at that bar to avoid those depressing thoughts. He waved his hand to signal there was nothing going on and sank into a chair.

"Not much—just woke up too early. How about you, Seth? Why so tired?"

Seth was David's age, with curly brown hair and kind brown eyes. Eli was younger, but not nearly as young as he looked. Both men were around five foot ten inches tall. Same height as Jonathan. Damn it! Did David's mind have only one channel?

"Eli moved in this week, so we've been busy packing, lugging, and unpacking. Every muscle aches and I'm exhausted, but at least we got it all done before Shabbat."

David was genuinely happy for his friends. Eli had been after Seth forever before he finally agreed to date him. Moving in with Seth surely thrilled Eli to no end.

"How about you, Eli, you feeling tired and, ehm, sore too?" David grinned.

Seth blushed deeply and suddenly became fascinated with his drink. Eli smirked and waggled his eyebrows.

"Oh, I'm sore all right, but it's not any trouble. In fact, I'm pretty blissful about it. I feel no pain. The sky is full of vivid colors. I see mushrooms growing. Oh, is that a unicorn walking by?"

David laughed and felt happy that he'd decided to go out with his friends. This was exactly what he needed—some lighthearted conversation to take his mind off silver eyes, unfocused with pleasure. And just like that his mind was right back to its regularly scheduled programming. Time for another distraction. David got up.

"Anyone need a drink?"

Eli raised his empty glass and nodded. "Vodka, straight." He looked around the table. "Save the pathetic joke attempts, ladies. Just because it has the word 'straight' in it, doesn't make it funny."

David shook his head and grinned as he walked toward the bar. A friendly face greeted him.

"Hey, sweetheart, how's it going?"

"I'm good, Joel, how're you?"

"Can't complain. Henry and I are taking off on Saturday for a couple of weeks to visit his family. Should be fun."

"Tell him I said hello. I haven't seen him in too long." David thought back to when he'd last seen his ex. "I think it was when we were working the polls a few weeks back."

A couple of guys standing close enough to overhear turned toward David, suddenly interested in their conversation. He rolled his eyes.

"During the election. We were volunteering at the polls during the election. You know, civic duty. Give it a shot sometime," David stated with emphasis, then looked back at Joel. "Anyway, we should get together when you guys get back in town."

Joel nodded. "Sounds good. What can I get for you?"

David placed his order and waited for his friend to get the drinks.

"I remember you." The slurred words hit him along with the beer-drenched breath. He turned to his right and saw the man who'd been harassing Jonathan at Where Cowboys Dream the previous evening.

"Yeah? I remember you too. It's not a good memory." He moved away from the drunk man before he decided to take his frustration over not being able to find Jonathan out on that only partially deserving target. Unfortunately, Nick didn't seem able to take a hint and he was teetering over on scrawny legs, another character flaw that made David dislike the inebriated half-wit even more.

"So are you done with him now? 'Cause I wanna take my turn. That boy can sure move his body."

David growled at the presumptuous jerk who was once again standing too close for olfactory comfort.

"Back off, man. He's my boyfriend, not some toy. And you met him for five minutes so you have no idea how he moves."

Okay, maybe boyfriend was overstating it, seeing as how David didn't even have Jonathan's number. And it didn't escape David's notice that he hadn't spent all that much time with Jonathan either. How much could he really know about a guy after one night? *Enough. You know enough. And it'll be more than one night once you find him and beg.*

David stormed away from Nick and back to his friends before he could say or do something he'd regret. Eli was leaning on Seth's shoulder, looking immeasurably happy.

"You look like you're about to break out into song, Eli."

"I just might," Eli said with a laugh. "Things are that good. I'm done with school and back in the gayborhood, where I belong. I have a dream job at the congregation where I grew up. Oh, and the cherry on top of the sundae that is now my glorious life is that I finally managed to get my boss into bed."

"I'm not your boss, Eli!" Seth snapped defensively. "We both work for your father and the other members of the congregation."

Gazing lovingly at Seth, Eli laughed.

"How long's it gonna take for you to realize I just say these things to rile you up, old man?"

"Umm, everything okay, David? You forgot these."

David looked up to see Joel standing by their table, holding the drinks David had ordered, then promptly forgotten when faced with the jerk talking about Jonathan.

"Sorry, Joel."

"No problem. Was that guy giving you a hard time? I can kick him out."

David got money out of his wallet and paid Joel for the drinks.

"Nah, don't worry about it. You know how I hate it when guys focus all their time on their upper bodies and completely neglect their legs. Makes 'em look ridiculous."

Joel laughed. "Yeah, okay. But I'm cutting him off. He's drunk as hell and he won't stop going on about some guy named Will to anyone who'll listen. If he starts driving customers away, he's out of here."

DESPITE COMING home exhausted after catching up with his friends, David tossed and turned all night, waking every couple of hours with a distinct feeling that something was off, something was missing. Then his consciousness would seep in just enough to fill in the pieces and make his chest ache. By the time the sun rose on Friday morning, David was dressed and ready to go out for a long and exhausting run. He didn't stop until he felt like he was ready to drop. Then he showered, dressed, and went into work.

He organized his office, finished every bit of paperwork, and signed a new client. None of those things kept David from noticing that Jonathan hadn't returned his calls, thereby making him feel progressively more dejected. What had he done to push Jonathan away? And how could he find the captivating man and apologize?

After eating a couple of protein bars for dinner, David hit the gym. The frustration he'd been trying to keep at bay finally found an outlet, and David worked the machines with a vengeance until one of his friends walked up and told him to call it a day or risk a muscle tear. He'd pushed his body too far, he knew that, but at least he was finally tired enough to get some sleep.

David dragged himself home, crawled into bed, and fell asleep smelling Jonathan on the sheets. Unfortunately, a couple of hours' reprieve was all he got before Jonathan entered his dreams, and David woke to find himself humping his mattress like a pathetic teenager. The first couple of times he beat off before falling back asleep, hoping that'd give his body the satisfaction it was craving so he could sleep through the night. But his hand couldn't compare to Jonathan, and his subconscious wouldn't let him forget that fact, so eventually he gave up and just lay in bed and stared at the ceiling. *I need to find him.*

CHAPTER TWELVE

DAVID WOKE at the break of dawn on Saturday after another mostly sleepless night. How he could feel so tense when he should be feeling nothing but exhaustion was a wonder, but short of finding Jonathan, the only way David knew to release his tension was to exercise. He drove by The Dubliner on the way home from another hard workout at the gym—not that the restaurant was actually on his way, of course. The building was dark, as he knew it would be until dinnertime.

He was too preoccupied with Jonathan and too tired from yet another nearly sleepless night to concentrate on work. Besides, he'd gotten through all of his paperwork and Alice was already slated to take his meetings that day. Not having that as an available distraction and not wanting to sit still for fear of the feelings of loss he knew would overtake him, David took a quick shower, picked up some coffee, and went to his friends' place.

He'd known Clark and Noah for years, and he'd just sold them their first house, a major dump on a great street not too far from David's place. Clark was excited about doing renovations, and Noah was excited about Clark. Perfect match. David rang the bell at the apartment they were living in until they finished remodeling and shifted from foot to foot impatiently.

"Just a sec!"

He heard Clark's voice through the door a few seconds before it swung open. His friend stood in front of him, blinking sleep out of his blue eyes and pushing his messy strawberry-blond hair off his face. He was wearing pajama pants that he'd obviously just put on in his hurry to open the door. At least that was David's guess, based on the fact that the pants were on inside out and backward.

"Morning, Clark. You'd better go put a shirt on before Noah kicks my ass. I'm too sleep-deprived to defend myself right now."

Not that David thought he'd actually be able to defend himself even after a restful night's sleep if Noah truly wanted to take him down. Besides being a trained kickboxer, Noah had a defiant personality and an almost uncontrollable temper. Clark seemed to have the magic touch that kept him in check, but there was no reason to test fate. After all, David knew full well that nothing provoked Noah's anger more than his possessiveness of Clark. So much so that, even after years of friendship, David knew better than to risk any possibility of standing too close to Clark. And as much as he admired the view of the handsome man's sinewy chest, it wasn't worth the reaction Noah would have if he walked in. Incredibly, Clark didn't seem to mind his jealous streak, even though to the outside world it sometimes seemed as if it bordered on controlling.

"Yeah, sorry. Was sleeping, didn't think. Be right back."

Clark stumbled down the hallway, and David set the beverages on the coffee table and sank back into the couch. He threw his arm over his eyes and thought back to Thursday morning for the hundredth time. What had he done to make Jonathan want to leave so suddenly?

"Did we have plans this morning, David? We had a late night and I guess we forgot. I'm sorry." Clark sat down in the fugliest armchair of all time and reached for a coffee, taking a sip and smiling. "Thanks for the caffeine."

"Nah, we didn't have plans. I just stopped by to give you a few extra keys to your new place." David pulled a set of keys out of his pocket and slid them across the coffee table to Clark. "The seller's agent dropped these off yesterday. I think they go to that scary-ass shed in back of the property, and maybe to one of the side doors. I'd rekey the whole house if I were you, but I thought I'd bring these just in case you wanted them."

Clark nodded and looked at David intently, as if he could see that something else was going on. The gaze and possibility of a conversation about his feelings fueled David to get it together and exude happiness, even if he didn't feel it. He straightened his posture and put on a smile that wouldn't fool anyone who knew him, but hey, it was the best he could do.

"So, you had a late night? Did you guys go out with

Frank and Tim?"

"No, we stayed home and made our own fun. It's the best kind." Noah's deep voice made both men turn toward the hallway.

Though his harsh features prevented Noah from being a man most would describe as traditionally handsome, he was certainly striking. Hazel eyes with depths of intelligence and immeasurable strength were his most intriguing feature. And with a tall, broad body that was all muscle, he certainly wasn't a man you'd throw out of bed. Not that anyone would ever have the chance, because Noah and Clark had been a matched set since college, and one glimpse of the way they looked at each other made it clear to any observer that their status wasn't going to change and there wasn't room for anyone else in their bed.

"What's up, David? You look like a dog pissed in your Fruity Pebbles," Noah grunted as he picked up a coffee and sat down in the space Clark had made for him between his spread legs. He lifted the drink toward David in a silent toast of thanks and took a sip. Clark wrapped his arms around Noah's chest and rested his chin on Noah's shoulder. Noah's free hand immediately covered Clark's and their fingers reflexively twined together.

David tried to think of whether he'd ever seen them sit apart, and he couldn't come up with a single example. Those two were always tangled up together. Why had he chosen to go visit the perfect couple on today of all days? He couldn't do this, couldn't watch them touching each other and see the love vibrating between them, when he couldn't be with the one person who'd ever made him feel that same emotion. David got up and took his coffee with him as he walked to the door.

"I'd better take off. I have to, umm... I just came by to drop off your keys. Sorry if I woke you. See you guys later."

David had one hand on the door handle when he heard Clark's voice behind him.

"Call us if you need to talk, David. Even if it isn't about keys."

David nodded and walked out of the apartment.

After another worthless drive by The Dubliner, David went home, showered, and flipped mindlessly through the television stations before throwing the remote down in disgust.

What am I going to do? He sighed. *I'm going to find him, that's what. I haven't waited my entire life to feel this way about another person only to give up so easily. I'm going to find him and show him that we're right together.* David remembered what Jonathan had said about green walls. *Oh, thank goodness, a task.*

He squared his shoulders and stalked over to his phone. Maybe his friend Caleb was free. The man was a little overly enthusiastic sometimes, but he was a great designer. He'd furnished David's living and dining rooms without making David give any input, and he'd also helped David with the bathroom remodels. David was suddenly desperate to have the bedroom and bathroom done in the colors Jonathan had mentioned as soon as possible and Caleb was the fastest and best way to make that happen.

NOT BEING a guy who liked to think about or—God forbid—talk about his feelings, David knew he had it bad when he slid into the booth opposite his two oldest friends that evening, ready to ask for help. He slipped off his brown suede jacket, rolled the sleeves of his starched white button-down shirt up to his elbows, and leaned on the table.

"So, I need you to tell me the truth. The absolute truth. No holds barred, no keeping anything back to spare my feelings. I want you to—"

"Enough! Truth. Got it. What in the hell do you want to know, Miller?" Frank cackled as he waved the waitress over and raised his glass. "Can we please get a couple more, Denise?"

The brunette nodded and looked at Tim. "Nice shirt, Tim."

Tim groaned. "Ugh, it's my fat shirt."

She put her hand on her hip and looked at him more closely. "What are you talking about, Tim? I wish my boyfriend looked like you. You're skinny!"

He smoothed down his slim-fitting red plaid shirt. "I

may be straight skinny, Denise, but I'm gay fat. All this talk is making me rethink my next drink. I'll just have a diet soda."

Denise humphed and walked away. Frank leaned over Tim's body and turned his head in a painful-looking angle so he could see an area next to the bar where Eric was bent over, cleaning something up off the floor.

"You're going to get a neck cramp, dear," Tim said sarcastically.

"It'd be worth it. That man has a great ass."

"He's straight, Frank." David laughed at his friend.

"Yeah? So is spaghetti until you heat it up." Frank waggled his eyebrows. "Oops. Did I say that out loud? The filter malfunctioned. Again."

"Charming." Tim took a sip from his drink and pouted.

Frank threw his arms around Tim and gave him a squeeze. "Oh, come on now, boo. I may browse the store but you know I'll never go to the cash register."

Tim rolled his eyes and crossed his arms, pretending to be upset.

"Whatever. Now, what is it you want to talk about, David?"

David chewed on his bottom lip and raked his fingers through his hair, feeling uncharacteristically anxious.

"Why haven't any of my relationships ever worked out?"

Frank laughed and took a sip of his beer while Tim rolled his eyes and threw a couple of pretzels from the bowl into his mouth.

"Because you keep dumping their asses, that's why," Tim said.

David had the decency to blush.

"I only break up with them because they're not happy with me. It just never seems to work."

Frank reached for Tim's hand and smiled at David, his eyes twinkling and the laugh lines at the corners of his mouth becoming more pronounced.

"Miller, nobody's happier than me about your poor track record—it gave me this guy." Frank motioned to Tim with his eyebrows. "But I've got to tell you, I'm surprised by this line of questioning. Want to tell us what brought on your sudden—and may I say exceptionally out of character— desire for self-reflection?"

David sighed and muttered, "Forget it, guys. Never mind. How's work?"

Tim dropped Frank's hand and clutched David's as he reached for his glass.

"Oh no, honey. You're not getting out of this so easily. Spill."

Why not? He'd started this line of conversation for a reason. He may as well see it through.

"I met someone."

His voice was low and his words murmured, but Tim and Frank heard David clearly enough. Frank leaned back in the booth, crossed his arms over his broad chest, and looked at David appraisingly. Tim made the sign of the cross over his body.

"Jesus, Mary, and Joseph. I never thought I'd live to see the day. David Miller wants to have a real relationship."

David knew his friends were teasing, but he didn't appreciate the joke. It simply wasn't fair.

"Hey. I've always wanted a real relationship. I'm not one of those guys who has a string of one-night stands."

Frank laughed. "No, not one night, true enough. You have a string of multiple-month stands. But they're as meaningless as bar hookups. Just because you're a serial monogamist doesn't mean you've ever wanted a real relationship, Miller."

David's face must have shown his reaction to that comment because Frank's expression softened.

"You said you wanted the truth, the whole truth, and nothing but that truth."

Tim chuckled. "So help us God!"

David nodded wearily. "Fine. What's your brilliant insight?"

Tim scooted forward on the booth and rubbed his hands together in excitement. "We're going to see if we can teach you to fish."

CHAPTER THIRTEEN

DAVID HAD a flash feeling of being trapped and exposed. He could change the topic or leave or set something on fire. Anything to avoid what was sure to be a maddeningly annoying conversation about his feelings. But he didn't do any of those things. He couldn't risk the increased premium on his fire insurance policy. Instead, he steeled himself and concentrated on whatever information his friends could share that would be useful in telling him what he'd done to drive Jonathan away, and how he could keep him once he got his stunning body back in his grasp.

"Tell us about the last guy you dated. The lawyer. What happened there?"

It'd been over a year since that relationship had ended, and David hadn't given it a single minute of thought. They were still friends, of course, but David had never focused on why things hadn't worked out. He'd never really cared.

David gulped the rest of his wine. Fine, he'd asked for honesty and they were willing to give it to him. He was thirty-two years old, he'd never had a decent relationship, and every part of his body knew he had to find out why. Because if he didn't, then there was no way he could be with the single most beautiful man he'd ever met. Just the thought that he couldn't have Jonathan made something in David's chest ache. No, not something—his heart. His heart actually hurt from the loss of the silver-eyed beauty. There was no point in pretending otherwise, and if talking about his feelings with his friends and answering their probing questions would help him fix things with Jonathan, then that was what he'd do.

"Umm. I couldn't satisfy him in bed, I guess."

Tim spit out the soda he'd just sipped and started coughing. David wiped drops off his forehead with the back of his hand and looked at his friends' gaping mouths.

"Seriously, Tim? Do I actually have to revert back twenty years and tell you to say it not spray it?"

Tim composed himself.

"David, honey, you've got the face of a model, the body of a professional athlete, and the cock of a horse. On top of that, I know from personal experience that you have the stamina of a long-distance runner. I know it's been years since you've been in my...bed, but I distinctly remember having trouble sitting after those nights. So tell me exactly what what's-his-name said that led you to believe that the beast you have between your legs isn't enough, because there's no fucking way he had a problem with your technique. *Trust me.*"

David's blush took over his neck and face. He wasn't sure how to respond to his friend after that outburst. He'd never been shy about sex, and yes, they'd been lovers, but that was ancient history, and Tim was talking about David's equipment in front of his own partner, which might be making Frank unhappy.

As if reading his mind, Frank moved his hand in a "go on" gesture. "Don't hold yourself back on my account, Miller. I've seen your dick too. It's been longer than ten years, but I still remember. That's not something a man can forget. Hell, I credit my ability to suck cock on the fact that I learned on your behemoth."

David and Frank had grown up together. When the two of them had figured out they liked watching their teammates in the high school locker room more than the cheerleaders on the field, they'd spent some fun nights practicing on each other. Their feelings had never blossomed beyond friendship, but by the time they finished high school, they both knew their way around a dick. Frank wasn't kidding about his skills, either, David remembered fondly. He was no Jonathan, but the man could suck a baseball through a straw.

Tim laughed and blew an air kiss to David.

"Thanks for that, by the way. I'm the lucky recipient of all that practice."

David rolled his eyes and groaned, wondering what had possessed him to talk to his friends about this. They were his oldest friends, that was what. In fact, he'd set them up. David had met Tim during his sophomore year of college at a gay-straight alliance gathering. They'd spent an entire semester getting coffee together after the monthly meetings before Tim finally gathered the courage to ask David whether he was on the gay or the straight side of the alliance. After that, they'd dated for two years, until graduation. When Tim finished graduate school two years later and came back to Emile City, David introduced the only two lovers he'd ever had to each other, knowing they'd fit together in a way neither had ever fit with him. He was right.

"What do you want me to say, Timmy? The man told me, ehm, he said I wasn't into it. When we were in bed together. That's not exactly a satisfied customer, so I cut him loose."

Tim and Frank exchanged a tender gaze and then looked at David with something that could only be described as pity.

"And before him? The doctor with the hot accent and the even hotter ass. What happened with him?"

Raul. David had dated Raul for two years, while he was in his residency. David had thought things were going well. Well enough, anyway. David shrugged.

"He said I wasn't present. But we both worked a lot. You know how my hours are. I never thought it bothered him because he had all those long shifts at the hospital. I actually thought it worked out with our schedules, that he'd understand because he was so busy too. But when he said I wasn't present, I figured it was time to move on."

Tim sighed and looked at David expectantly. When David didn't react, he tried again.

"And the one before him? The architect with the surfer

hair?"

Henry. David had met Henry through work. David had been a new Realtor, just learning the ropes. Henry was the low man on the totem pole with a local builder whose houses David sold. They'd hit it off and dated for about a year and a half, then stayed friends when it ended. David always remained friends with his exes. He'd never understood people who fought and hated each other when things didn't work out. A breakup was really no big deal. Why get all emotional about it? Of course it was easy to think that way when he hadn't cared all that much about those boyfriends. It wasn't so easy now, when he couldn't find Jonathan. And that was after only one night together.

"Henry and I broke up because..."

David furrowed his brow in thought. He honestly couldn't remember why he and Henry had broken up. It'd been too many years and, like with his other relationships, he'd never given it any thought.

"Damn it, Tim. I can't take it anymore. The man isn't going to figure out how to fish. Hell, I'm not sure he'll eat the trout if we catch it, fillet it, grill it, and spoon-feed it to him." Frank turned to David, his dark eyes flashing. "Do you want me to tell you why things didn't work out with Henry?"

David nodded dumbly.

"Because you fucking forgot you had a boyfriend, you dumb shit."

David would've been insulted if anyone else had

spoken to him that way, but he and Frank went back a long way and he knew the big man didn't mean anything by it.

"Okay, I'll bite. What do you mean?"

"It was an experiment. He thought if he stayed away, you'd realize that you missed him and then beg him to come back. Tim tried to tell him it was a stupid idea and that it wouldn't work, but he was sure it was a brilliant way to get you to pay attention to him."

David thought back to the time when he'd dated Henry, and then when they'd gone their separate ways.

"Bullshit. He was dating that guy with the really red hair, remember? Brought him to Clark and Noah's party."

Frank rolled his eyes.

"He didn't call you for four weeks and you didn't notice, so he took that guy to the party, hoping to make you jealous."

Tim started laughing at that point, so much so that tears welled in his eyes. "And you..." More laughter. "Ehm, you..." Coughing and laughter. "You patted his shoulder, told him it was great to see him, and that they made a cute couple."

David took a drink of his soda and felt his stomach rumble. He'd run that morning, then worked out that afternoon. Even more exhausting was all the time he'd spent shopping with Caleb. He'd tried to cut the designer off at paint colors, but that hadn't worked, so David had had to endure shopping for kitchen cabinets, appliances, and bedroom furniture until he finally threw in the white flag and admitted defeat. Oh well, at least he had paint samples in light green and a darker green picked out and an appointment with a painter for the middle of the week.

After the torture of shopping with Caleb, David had gone to the gym, then had just enough time to shower and dress before going to meet Tim and Frank at Where Cowboys Dream. And he'd been late anyway, because he went by The Dubliner first, hoping to find Jonathan...only to be told he wasn't working that night. When he felt the empty hole where his stomach used to reside, David realized that, other than a protein shake when he'd first woken up and a protein bar for lunch, he hadn't eaten anything all day.

"Maybe we should start serving food here. Nothing too heavy, but like appetizers or something."

Tim looked incredulous.

"That's it? You're changing the topic? Your need for revelations is over?"

"Fine, Timmy, I confess to being an oblivious asshole with Henry. But that was years ago. I'm pretty sure I haven't inadvertently broken up with anyone since then, so this isn't particularly helpful information. And I'd apologize to Henry, but seeing as how he's been shacked up with Joel for the last five years, I think his heart's all healed."

"Don't you understand that you did the same thing with every other boyfriend?" Tim's voice was suddenly high and squeaky.

"You're saying they all stopped calling and I didn't

notice?"

"No, I'm saying having a guy tell you that you're not into it when you're having sex or that you're not present all basically means the same thing that led Henry to try his goofy experiment. When you're with a guy, you're not really *with* him."

David was hungry, the conversation with his friends was going nowhere, and his head hurt. He hadn't been able to sleep for two nights because his bed was suddenly missing something critical and he knew exactly what—or, more accurately, *who*—that was. He needed to think about how he could find Jonathan and either force the man to see him again or get down on his knees and plead. Deciding to call it a night, he downed the rest of his drink and started to get up. "That's deep, man, really. You should call the fortune cookie people or something. Confucius says you're not there when you're there." David downed the rest of his drink and started to get up.

"Don't be such a dick, David. Tim's trying to help you. We've always stayed out of your love life, even though we've known about this issue for a long time. Tim was the first in that line of boyfriends, remember?"

Something about the anger in Frank's eyes and the way he suddenly squeezed Tim's hand in support let David know he'd gone too far. He lowered himself back onto the bench seat and looked at his friend.

"Timmy? Did I do something wrong when we were

together? You got into grad school out of state and moved away. That's not exactly me breaking up with you. We stayed friends and everything, so I thought things were fine between us."

Tim raised his glass to his mouth and took a drink. When he set the glass down, he looked straight into David's eyes, but David could tell it wasn't done with ease.

"I went to school out of state to get away from you."

David was shocked. His mouth dropped open. What had he ever done to make Tim feel like he had to flee?

"Jesus, not like that, David." Tim started playing with his cocktail napkin and looked at Frank for support. "I know you never meant to hurt me. I know we were friends. That's what makes the whole thing with you so…insidious."

Tim's words trailed off, and David could see the frustration in his eyes. He suddenly wanted to understand what his friends were trying to tell him. "Frank? What's he trying to say? And do I owe you an apology too?"

Frank snorted out a laugh. "Hell no, dreamboat, there was nothing between us but blow jobs and football. I never thought of you as a boyfriend. That's what made it work. Well, that and the fact that we were horny teenagers."

All right, at least David had an accurate read on his relationship with Frank. They were two tops before they were old enough to understand what that meant. It wasn't like things between them could've ever gone anywhere. He was glad Frank saw it the same way. David focused his attention on Tim and waited for his friend to continue speaking.

"You're a smart, successful, wealthy guy, David. You don't cheat. You don't yell or fight. You're generous in and out of bed. Even without getting into the whole pinup-model thing you've got going on, it's enough to make guys fall for you. Hard." Tim rubbed an unsteady hand through his white-blond hair. "But you're not really available, so they end up feeling frustrated. It's like you're almost theirs, but not. And if they try to point that out to get you to change and, I don't know, fucking attach or something, you bolt. I'm not trying to hurt your feelings, but you asked. You said you wanted to know why your relationships don't work out, so I'm telling you. They don't work because you don't really want them to."

David still didn't understand what Tim was saying, but he was ready to sit patiently if his friend had anything else to add, pretend to be grateful for the confusing advice, apologize for whatever he'd done wrong, and then go home and hope he could still smell Jonathan on the sheets. But then he felt a tentative tap on his shoulder. David turned his head and saw scared silver eyes looking at him.

CHAPTER FOURTEEN

"S-S-SORRY TO interrupt. I, umm, I just thought…"

Jonathan couldn't finish his sentence because he was pulled onto David's lap and kissed to within an inch of his life. When David finally removed his tongue from Jonathan's mouth, he slumped against David's chest and panted for air. David wrapped his left arm possessively around Jonathan's waist and caressed Jonathan's hair with his right hand, almost making him forgot they weren't alone.

"I'm so glad you're here. I was just trying to figure out the best way to avoid getting arrested while camping out in front The Dubliner so I could see you next time you're working."

Jonathan smiled and looked up at the navy-blue eyes that had haunted him for years.

"So it's okay that I just showed up here? My parents told me you called the restaurant, but they didn't hold on to your number. I figured I'd come by and see if I could get the bartender to give it to me or call you for me, but then I saw you sitting here. If I'm interrupting, though, I can go and…"

David kissed him, a closed-mouth, soft peck this time, and dropped his hand from Jonathan's hair to his cheek, continuing the gentle caress.

"You're not interrupting anything. And you can show up anytime. But I'd like your number, so I can call you, okay? I was starting to think stalking charges were a real possibility, given the number of times I've called The Dubliner. And driven by." David squeezed Jonathan tightly, feeling immeasurably grateful that he was back in his arms and seemed happy to be in that position. "I missed you, baby."

Jonathan's body relaxed and he sighed in relief. David still wanted him.

"I don't have a cell phone. I'll give you the number to my parents' house, but they're not so good with the messages."

Jonathan whispered the admission into David's ear. David could feel that face heating. Would it be weird to buy him a phone? Really, it was for selfish reasons, so it wasn't even like a present or anything.

"Ehm."

The sound of Tim clearing his throat disturbed David's thoughts. He looked up at his friends' amused faces, then down at the adorable, sexy man in his lap.

"Jonathan Doyle, these are my friends Tim Burgess and Frank Dupree."

Jonathan slid off David's lap and reached a shaky hand across the table. "Nice to meet you both."

Tim and Frank each shook his hand but kept their

eyes focused on their friend. David had wrapped his arm around Jonathan's shoulder and pinned him to his side. He was rubbing Jonathan's upper arm. When Jonathan was done shaking hands with Tim and Frank, he dropped his palm to the table, and David immediately twined their fingers, and stroked the top of Jonathan's hand with his thumb.

"You thirsty, baby? Want me to get you a drink? We don't have any food here, something I'm thinking of remedying, but I was just going to go get dinner. We can leave now if you're hungry."

Jonathan looked nervously at David's friends and chewed on his bottom lip. He'd spent the past three days thinking about David and trying to come up with a way to tell his dream man about his son without driving David away. Ultimately, he hadn't come up with a genius solution— probably because he wasn't a genius—so he'd decided to just take the chance and tell the truth. It wasn't as if he had another choice.

Having his heart broken was going to be difficult enough; Jonathan didn't need an audience, which made him want to take David up on his offer to leave the bar together. But his parents had plans that night, so they were only able to watch Samuel for an hour. The clock was ticking and there was no way he could fit dinner and a trip back to David's house into the schedule.

"It's nice to meet you, Jonathan, but we're late to, ehm, something, so we need to go. Come on, Frank."

Tim slid out of the booth and held his hand out to Frank.

"Very subtle, Tim. David, we'll call you later. Oh, and forget about what we just said. Seems like you've worked through it."

And then they were gone and Jonathan was left alone with David. Okay, no guts no glory. You can't win if you don't play; no pain no gain. In for a penny, in for a pound; nothing ventured, nothing gained. *Ugh, stop thinking of ridiculous proverbs and* speak.

"I can't go to dinner with you tonight. I actually can't stay long." Jonathan swallowed down the lump in his throat and forced himself to continue. "I just came here because I need to tell you something. Well, more like I need to tell you about someone. He's the most important person in my life and I should have mentioned him the other night, but I was worried you wouldn't want me if you knew and..."

David was looking at Jonathan like he was a runaway truck headed straight for him and he couldn't move out of the way in time to save himself. The arm that was wrapped around Jonathan's shoulders stiffened, the hands stilled, even David's breathing seemed shallow.

Jonathan took a steadying breath and plunged ahead.

"I have a son. His name's Samuel."

"Oh, thank God!"

Huh. That wasn't the reaction Jonathan had expected. He'd prepared for anger, disappointment, and, in an optimistic second, even reluctant acceptance. But not...was that relief?

"I don't...I don't understand. You're not mad? It's okay?"

"Jesus, Jonathan. Why would I be mad that you have a son? Unless...you're not, like, married or something, are you?"

The idea that Jonathan could be with a woman hadn't crossed David's mind until that moment. The man was just so clearly gay. When Jonathan had first started his explanation, David had been sure he was going to tell him about a boyfriend. Now, that thought was horrifying in and of itself, because given Jonathan's self-professed lack of experience with all things sexual except, it seemed, taking it up the ass good and hard, that boyfriend would've been a selfish prick and David would've had to step in and put a stop to it. Protecting Jonathan would've been the only reason for that, of course. David wouldn't have done it to clear the way for Jonathan to be with *him*. No, nothing so self-serving and sinister.

"No! Of course not. I was with his mother once, in high school. It was just a stupid mistake, and she had a boyfriend so she couldn't take the baby, and I wanted him, so I kept him. And he's beautiful and sweet and funny and just all-around wonderful."

Jonathan babbled nervously and twisted his ratty shirt in his hand. David kissed him, hoping to calm him down.

"He sounds just like his father. When do I get to meet him?"

That beautiful face lit right up. "Really? You want to meet him? So does that mean we can still...still..."

Oh, crap. How was he going to finish that sentence? We can still meet in bars and screw like bunnies? No, that wasn't what Jonathan wanted. We can still ride off into the sunset together and live happily ever after? Umm, no, too much too soon. Plus, there was the whole lack of horses thing.

"Jonathan, I really like you and I want to keep seeing you. I'm trying not to be insulted that you thought I'd be scared off by your son. Admittedly, I don't know much about kids, but it's not like I think they're diseased or something."

When David said it that way, the whole thing really did sound sort of silly. Jonathan laughed a little too hard, letting out the anxiety that had been building in his chest for the past few days.

And David sat at a booth in his bar and considered the fact that he'd never put himself in a position to meet any of his exes' parents because things hadn't ever seemed all that serious, and now, after just one night with a guy, he was asking to meet his child, something that seemed a hell of a lot more important and harder to unravel. Oh, well. David didn't want things with Jonathan to unravel. He wanted them to get all knotted up and twisted together so there'd be no way to keep them apart.

"So did you say no to dinner tonight because you already have plans or was it because you thought I was wearing my child-repellent jacket? Because I left that at home and I'd love to take both you and Samuel out. There's a great pizza place not too far from here. Kids like pizza, right?"

Jonathan nodded dumbly. He was completely flabbergasted by David's reaction, his openness to meeting Samuel. It was so much better than he had allowed himself to expect.

"Sam loves pizza. Pasta too. And broccoli. He's actually a really good eater."

David gave him one of those loving smiles he remembered from the night at David's house. Thinking of that time immediately made Jonathan's cock fill, and he had to shift in his seat, hoping that'd move his pants around in a way that'd make the hard-on he was suddenly sporting more comfortable.

"I missed you."

David's husky voice washed over him, and a big hand made its way into his lap and palmed his erection, causing a full-body shudder to go through Jonathan's small frame.

"Missed this too. I've probably beaten off a half-dozen times thinking about the other night. You've got me in a perpetual state of horniness, baby." David's voice was low and sultry, his breath hot against Jonathan's neck and ear.

"Only a half-dozen? I've barely had my hand out of my pants long enough to pick up a fork for meals."

Jonathan groaned and thrust his hips up toward that big hand, seeking more friction on his cock. David gave it to him, pressing down and rubbing his hand back and forth across Jonathan's dick. Just when Jonathan thought he'd explode, David stopped and pulled him out of the booth.

"What...where're we going?"

"Bathroom," David grunted out the one-word answer and hurried their pace.

Once they made it into the bathroom, David quickly kicked each stall door. When they all swung open, confirming that the two men didn't have company, he pulled Jonathan into the last stall, closed them in, and dropped to his knees.

Jonathan's worn khakis were unbuttoned and down to his ankles in the blink of any eye. David nudged his balls with his nose, made an appreciative murmur, then sucked them into his mouth. The sound of a zipper being lowered and a corresponding moan let Jonathan know that David had taken himself in hand. Confirmation in the way of the unmistakable sound of skin slapping against skin followed.

"Ungh."

Jonathan whimpered at the realization that David's cock was so close. He wanted to see it, feel it, taste it, but he couldn't move because David's free hand was on his dick, leading him into a warm, wet cavern. It didn't take more than a few hard sucks in David's mouth before Jonathan was crying out and pouring himself into David's throat.

David kept Jonathan's dick in his mouth and looked

at up at that stunning face while he gave a few more furious strokes to his own impossibly hard dick and shot all over the floor.

He rested his head on Jonathan's thigh and panted, waiting for his heart to slow down and his breath to return to normal. Jonathan's knees gave out and he collapsed, his chest on David's shoulder and his head facing down. David caressed Jonathan's naked ass, letting his fingers wander into the cleft, while his mouth covered every bit of naked skin he could reach with kisses and licks.

That deep voice spoke into the soft crease where Jonathan's inner thigh met his groin. "I've always made fun of my friends for hooking up in bar bathrooms. Can't believe we just did that."

Jonathan edged down so that he was kneeling in front of David, his legs spread to avoid the cum that streaked the floor. David reached his clean hand under the faded black sweater and stroked Jonathan's back.

"It felt so good. Thank you."

Oh, that hesitant voice, those shy eyes and flushed cheeks. Jonathan was heartbreaking.

"Yeah, baby, it felt good for me too. Really good. Let's get you dressed."

Jonathan stood on wobbly legs, turned, and bent down to lift his pants. That put his naked ass directly in front of David's face, and he had to use all his self-restraint not to bury his mouth and tongue into that enticing cavity.

Jonathan was making David want things he'd never even considered—sleepovers, family meet-and-greets, and his tongue in that ass, that irresistible ass.

David snaked his tongue out to take a lick, but just then a pair of white briefs, followed by Jonathan's pants, took his target out of view. He groaned in frustration and forced his all-too-quickly recharging dick back into his briefs and pants. A few quick wipes on the floor with toilet paper to clean up his ejaculate and they were ready to leave the bathroom.

"I'll go home and get Sam and then we'll meet you for dinner. Where are we going?"

"Have you been to Donatello's on Third Street?"

Jonathan colored slightly, but kept himself from telling David that he rarely ate out at restaurants. His family hadn't had much money growing up because The Dubliner hadn't been all that profitable, even when the kids were old enough to help out. Things were better now. His brother, Brennan, was a good businessman, and he'd managed to make the once-struggling business very successful. His latest idea was to open the place for lunch during the week and brunch on weekends. Hopefully that would bring in enough income to finally allow his father to retire and leave Brennan at the helm completely.

"I know where it is. We can be there in about twenty minutes. Is that okay?"

David nodded and pulled Jonathan in for a kiss. Soft

lips met his, and Jonathan melted against him, so warm and pliable, so perfect. When he pulled away from Jonathan's mouth, David kissed his still-closed eyelids. They fluttered open and silver eyes were revealed, wearing an expression that couldn't be mistaken for anything other than adoring.

I need to make sure I keep this. The thought slammed into David's head, almost knocking him off balance with its strength.

"Twenty minutes is great. I'll get us a table."

CHAPTER FIFTEEN

FIFTEEN MINUTES later, David was sitting in a booth at Donatello's Pizza, drinking a glass of wine and willing himself to calm down. He felt like he'd been connected to an electric current from the moment Jonathan had given him that dreamy look and shy little smile at Where Cowboys Dream. There was no question about the force of the attraction between them; it was like nothing David had ever experienced. And it wasn't just a physical reaction. Jonathan was beautiful, no doubt about it. But David had dated other good-looking men and they'd never come close to heating him up *inside*. But a mere look from Jonathan's silver eyes lit a fire somewhere deep within David's chest and belly that threatened to burn out of control. No, it wasn't just his appearance.

There was an almost naïve sweetness to Jonathan that drew David in. And he was so refreshingly honest. Most men David knew were constantly playing games. Don't seem too interested, call after some predetermined period of time, show up where you think he's going to be and pretend it was inadvertent. The games were so varied and numerous that David couldn't keep track of them. He'd been on the receiving end of enough attempts to reel him in that he felt like a damn fish.

It was different with Jonathan. There was no deception, no ruse. Jonathan just let it all spill out—his desire, his attraction, even his insecurities. Everything showed in those silver eyes, that slender body's language, and those softly spoken words. Jonathan was like an open book, a vulnerable, good-natured open book, trusting David not to hurt him. It killed David to know that Jonathan had been concerned that he'd be rejected because of his son. Sure, there might be guys who wouldn't be interested in taking up with a man who had a kid. And, okay, fine, David could admit to himself that he very well could have been one of those guys. But not with Jonathan. David would take that man any way he could get him.

"Papa, can I have ice cream for dinner?"

David looked up from his menu to see the source of that little voice—a tiny boy with hair as black as Jonathan's, but not as thick, iridescent skin, and wide blue eyes so big they seemed to take over his entire face. And holding his hand was Jonathan, a wide smile on his relaxed face as he looked at his son. A sense of rightness came over David when he watched the pair approaching him, much like the feeling he'd had when he saw Jonathan brushing his teeth in his bathroom. *Mine.* David's body shook with the strength of that sentiment racing through him.

Rising to his feet, David wondered how he was supposed to greet his date in this situation. Jonathan solved the problem by pressing up against him and rising on tiptoe to kiss his cheek. He gave David a brilliant smile and bent down to lift the little boy up.

"Samuel, this is David."

Those huge blue eyes took him in.

"Hi. Can I have ice cream for dinner?"

David felt a tug at his chest in response to that earnest voice and hopeful look.

"Of course you can."

Oh, damn. He probably didn't have the right to answer that question, but how on earth was he supposed to resist that little voice and those big eyes?

Jonathan laughed. "Well, I guess he found the weak link. Ice cream it is. Chocolate or strawberry, Sam?"

The boy turned to David and gave his best smile. "Can I have bofe?"

Now it was David's turn to laugh. "I think I just got worked by someone who's barely tall enough to reach my knees."

Jonathan sat down and settled Samuel on his lap.

"He's a born negotiator. My sister says he's better than some of the people in her law firm."

David reached for his water glass and smiled at the sight of his handsome lover across the table. He looked so happy and in his element holding that little boy. And he was right there. Across the table. Close enough to touch. *Finally!*

"Shannon, right?"

Those silver eyes sparkled with joy.

"You remembered."

And that right there was one of the things that drew David to Jonathan. He didn't hide the fact that something so small made him happy, didn't act nonchalant about his feelings. Nope, he was into David and he didn't pretend otherwise.

"I remember everything you told me, Jonathan. I know we've only known each other a few days, but I meant what I said—I really like you. A lot."

Jonathan reached a hand across the table, and David took it in his bigger one, stroking soft, smooth skin.

"Shannon's a paralegal. She works for a big law firm in downtown Central. She's the smart one in the family. Well, Brennan's smart, too, but he's more practical, like with the business and stuff, and Shannon's the book-smart one."

David noticed Jonathan hadn't included himself in the positive descriptions of the Doyle siblings. He didn't seem upset or resentful about his impression that his brother and sister were brighter than himself. He was just describing them with a tone that he could have used to talk about differing hair color. David didn't know how to react, so he decided to change the topic.

"Okay, ice cream for Sam. How about you, Jonathan? What do you like on your pizza?"

David passed the menu, but Jonathan didn't pick it up.

"We can get whatever you want. I'm not picky. Oh,

except for anchovies." He scrunched up that cute nose. "Yuck."

David wanted to lean across the table to kiss Jonathan. He was just so damn adorable.

"Mushrooms and black olives?"

Jonathan nodded, and David felt a socked foot slip under his pant leg. He raised an eyebrow in surprise.

Shrugging, Jonathan laughed and said, "Hey, it's the best I can do, considering the circumstances."

Why would a foot on his ankle be causing David's body to tingle? It's a *foot* and an *ankle*. The internal reminder didn't seem to make a bit of difference. David shuddered. Any touch from Jonathan aroused him, no matter how innocuous.

"Circumstances?" David's voice sounded rough, so he cleared his throat.

That big bright smile met him from across the table again. "I can tell you want a kiss, but I'm trapped under this heavy person, so I can't get up to give it to you. My foot's about the only thing I can move."

David chuckled. "Oh, *those* circumstances. I just don't know what's okay and what's not in front of..."

David looked at Sam pointedly. Jonathan set the boy down on the empty seat next to him.

"You sit here and play with your trains, dumpling. I'm going to see if they have crayons here like at Grandma and Grandpa's place, so you can color too, 'kay?"

The little head nodded and Jonathan got up. He stopped next to David's chair, leaned down, and gave him a chaste kiss on the side of his lips.

"Be right back."

David's heart fluttered. *Fluttered. What am I, a twelve-year-old kid or something now?* But he wasn't upset about that thought. It actually felt good to be excited about someone, to be so interested and engaged.

"So you like trains, huh?"

Sam had a blue wooden train and a red metal train in his hands, and he was rolling them around the table, making "vroom" noises.

"Uh-huh. You wanna play?"

David smiled and nodded.

"You can have the red one. Blue's my favorite color."

David took the train and rolled it along behind Sam's for about thirty seconds before Sam stopped playing and started banging the toy against the wall.

"I'm bored."

David bit his lip and held back a laugh. "Wanna learn how to make an airplane?"

"Can I drive it?"

The expression on that little face was so serious that David struggled to hold back his laughter. "Well, you can't fly it like a pilot. But after dinner we can go outside and you can fly it in the grass. Here, I'll show you."

He picked up the paper placemats and started folding while huge blue eyes stared at him, completely enraptured. By the time Jonathan came back to the table with crayons,

David had finished one of the four paper planes he'd make that evening. Samuel started decorating them.

An hour later, everyone was done eating, and David felt like he'd fallen even harder for the man in front of him. He was so incredibly easy to be with, so even-keeled and good-natured. Nothing seemed to upset him.

Not the glass of water that Sam spilled all over Jonathan's pizza and lap when he was throwing a temper tantrum for no reason. "Terrible twos," Jonathan had said with a smile and an eye roll.

Not the ice cream that smeared Jonathan's shirt in little handprint shapes. "Let's go clean you up, Sam," was the only reaction as Jonathan picked up the sticky boy and walked into the bathroom.

And not the phone call David had taken in the middle of their meal to calm a panicked Alice, who couldn't remember the code to a client's lockbox. Any of David's exes would have probably pouted for a good twenty minutes if he'd taken a call during dinner. They'd always expected to be the center of his attention, and gotten angry if he worked while they were out.

Jonathan had just smiled and said, "I think that's your phone."

David hadn't even noticed the ringing because he was so focused on a story Jonathan was telling him about his family. He fished the phone from his jacket and frowned when he looked at the screen. "It's work."

"Go ahead. I understand," Jonathan told him with

complete sincerity. Then he picked up the crayons and colored with Sam while David spoke with Alice.

The complete lack of drama, the fact that Jonathan wasn't obsessed about looking just-so, and the ever-present smiles and laughter from the other side of the table were contagious. David never wanted to eat another meal without them.

After dinner, they took a walk around the block and made their way to a grassy area where Sam could fly the paper airplanes. The merchant's association had put in winter grass, planted red gardenias, and hung strands of white lights in the trees. The setting was pretty and romantic. David and Jonathan sat on a bench, held hands, and watched Sam run around and giggle as the planes came crashing down at his feet.

"So, Samuel, I forgot to ask how old you are. You look like you're, hmm, like maybe thirteen or fourteen?"

The little boy giggled furiously. "I'm two." Two little fingers went up in the air. "But I'm going to be free soon."

Two more fingers joined the first two. Jonathan rolled one finger down gently and pointed to the three remaining digits in turn.

"One. Two. Three." He looked at David. "He'll be three on February twenty-eighth."

"Hey, the twenty-eighth is a great day to be born! You were born on February twenty-eighth. Your dad was born on November twenty-eighth. And I was born on October twenty-eighth."

A little giggle and Sam started hopping up and down. "We match!"

Funny, David was just thinking the same thing. And it had nothing to do with birthdates.

Jonathan turned to David and squeezed his hand. "October twenty-eighth of what year?"

"Trying to figure out how old I am?"

Jonathan grinned and nodded. "Yup."

"Thirty-two. Does that bother you? Too much of an age difference?" David asked as he drew little patterns on the back of Jonathan's hand with his finger.

"Nope. Does it bother you?"

David shook his head and whispered in Jonathan's ear, "The only thing that bothers me about you, Jonathan, is that at this moment you're wearing way too many clothes."

Jonathan's eyes twinkled. "Oh yeah? How many is too many?"

David leaned down and continued talking directly into Jonathan's ear. "Any stitch of clothing on you is too much clothing."

"Hmm. So you want me naked in a public park in the middle of December? I think I might get frostbite in choice parts."

David frowned. "Hmmm. Good point. I like all your choice parts, wouldn't want them damaged. Plus, I don't like the idea of all these people seeing you naked. In fact, now that

I think about it, I might get you a burka for Christmas."

Jonathan laughed. "Umm, you do realize burkas are for women. For *Muslim* women. I'm thinking giving a man a burka for a Christian holiday might be, like, a cultural insult or something. Plus, I don't think it'd look good on my ass."

"My point exactly. There have been wars fought over things less precious than your ass. Covering it is worth some slight discord among the various religious groups."

Jonathan's voice suddenly got serious and husky. "You like my ass?"

David's cock immediately woke up and tried to say hello. He adjusted himself as unobtrusively as possible. Jonathan's eyes followed the movement of that big hand.

He leaned close to David's ear and whispered, his breath warming David's skin, "I'll take that as a yes. A really *big* yes. A thick, long, deeply satisfying yes."

David coughed out a strained laugh. "Jesus Christ! You are temptation incarnate. I'm about to come in my pants from the word 'yes.'"

A quick squeeze to David's upper arm and a peck on his cheek, and Jonathan bounced off the bench and joined Sam in the grass.

"Come on, dumpling. It's almost bedtime and you still need a bath."

"Aww. Not yet, Papa. It's early. Please. Please. Please."

David wondered whether the begging would work if he joined in, because he wasn't ready to say goodbye yet either. Something told him that he'd never be ready to say goodbye to Jonathan.

He held himself back from pleading with Jonathan not to leave him, like some sort of deranged woman in a B movie. Taking pride in the incredible inner strength he mustered to avoid that public humiliation, David walked Jonathan and Sam back to their car, keeping his arm around Jonathan the entire time. David hadn't understood Frank and Tim's advice while it was being given earlier that evening, but now, walking down the street with that beautiful, sensitive man and his son, David knew his friends were right.

He was a workaholic who wanted things his way and he had no problem breaking up with any man who pushed too hard or wanted too much. And none of those breakups had been difficult because every boyfriend David had ever had was really nothing more than a consistent, convenient location for his dick. He flinched in horror at that realization, but he couldn't deny its truth. His heart had never been remotely engaged, even with men he'd dated for close to two years.

Yet there he was, with his heart trying to beat its way out of his chest over a man he'd known for just a few days and with whom he'd spent just one night. And shouldn't the neediness that was clear with every look Jonathan gave him be driving David away rather than pulling him closer? But there was nothing about Jonathan that made David want to run, at least not in the opposite direction. No, David wanted to pull Jonathan in so tight that he wouldn't be able to feel, see, or smell anything else. The desire to capture and possess was completely unfamiliar, but painfully powerful. David ached from it.

CHAPTER SIXTEEN

"WHEN CAN I see you again?"

David knew his voice was shaking from the depth of the emotions shooting through him. He wasn't sure whether it was because of his confusion over the dramatic shift in his feelings or because of the restraint he knew he'd be forced to endure that night. No matter how much he wanted Jonathan, David would be going home alone to an empty bed. Again. He kissed the top of Jonathan's head.

"I'm sorry it won't work out tonight. I want it...want you too," Jonathan replied.

Surprised that Jonathan seemed to be reading his mind, David cleared his throat and raised one eyebrow. Jonathan reached his hand behind his back and trailed it over David's fingers.

"This kind of sign language is pretty easy to read."

David looked down and realized that his fingers were pressed firmly in Jonathan's crack. He'd started out with his hand on the small of Jonathan's back, but his grip must have moved lower subconsciously. If those pants hadn't been in the way, David surely would have been pressed inside the warm cavern of Jonathan's body. David quickly looked over at Sam, who was skipping ahead of them, giggling at various things he saw on the street, thankfully oblivious to the fact that his father was being molested.

"Jesus! I'm sorry, Jonathan. I promise you, I'm not usually like this. Really, I don't fondle people in public and I don't act like a horny teenager. You just press all my buttons and turn me on so damn much that my body seems to act without checking with my mind. I'll rein it in."

"I wish you wouldn't," Jonathan whispered back hurriedly. "I like feeling like you want me. That way I'm not alone in this thing."

David caressed Jonathan's cheek. "You're not alone, baby." Not alone in the feelings and not alone in life, not if David had any say in the matter.

They had made their way back to the front of the restaurant and were standing in front of Jonathan's car.

"David?"

"Yeah?"

Jonathan rose up until his mouth was no farther than a couple of inches from David's. "Tell me what you were thinking. You know, when your hand was on me. Tell me what you'd do to me if we could go back to your house for the night."

That voice was low and slightly husky, the cheeks were red, whether from the cold or from slight embarrassment over the subject matter, David didn't know. But David's focus was on Jonathan's eyes; the silver shimmered in the streetlight and the gaze was locked on him like he was the only person on earth. Never having been one for dirty talk, even when he was in bed, David shocked himself with his response.

"I'd take you as soon as we got inside. Bend you over the entry table and fuck your ass so hard those whimpers you make would turn into screams loud enough to bounce off the walls. Then I'd carry you into the bedroom and do you again. And again. I'd keep my dick in your tight ass all damn night if I could. Fill you up so much that you'd know you belong to me even when you're sleeping."

A shiver ran through Jonathan's narrow body. He licked his bottom lip, then stood on his tiptoes and spoke into David's ear.

"I already know that. When I'm asleep and when I'm awake. I've known that I belong to you for a long time."

He licked David's ear, gave a quick suck to his lobe, and stroked his hard cock through his pants. When David gasped, Jonathan smiled, walked over to the old sedan, and opened the back door.

"Say goodbye to David and hop in, dumpling."

Sam waved to David, climbed into his car seat, and rolled his trains over the armrests while Jonathan buckled him in. David's eyes were glued to Jonathan's as he got into his own seat and started the car. When Jonathan pulled out and drove away, David groaned with frustration over his denied need. He stepped into the alley behind the pizza place, pried his hard dick out of his pants, and gave himself two strokes before he sprayed the wall with his seed, barely taking the edge off his desire. He leaned on the rough brick with one hand, his other hand holding his only slightly wilting and painfully sensitive dick.

What the hell is the deal with this guy? And how can I get more time with him?

THE RELIEF over reconnecting with Jonathan calmed David enough to allow a full night's sleep. He woke Sunday morning still feeling empty without Jonathan's presence, but no longer anxious that he had driven the man away or wouldn't see him again. *Jonathan.* Silver eyes, thick black hair, smooth skin, firm ass. David's hand was in his pajama pants, stroking his hard dick, when his phone rang.

He reached for the phone on his makeshift nightstand with one hand and kept the other in his pants, slowing his strokes.

"'Lo?"

"Hi. I didn't wake you, did I? Oh, it's Jonathan."

David groaned.

"I recognize your voice, baby. And, yeah, you did wake me. But not with this call." David moaned and tightened his grip on his cock. "I woke up thinking about you. Dreamt about you last night too."

Jonathan's heart rate doubled, and his breath came out in sharp gasps.

"You, ehm..." Jonathan cleared his throat. "You dreamt about me?"

"Mmm hmm." David pulled his hand out of his pants, reached for the lube, coated his hand and cock, and increased the speed of his strokes. Jonathan was likely able to hear his heavy breaths over the phone. Good. The man needed to know what he did to David.

"What did you dream?" Jonathan's voice was hoarse.

"Dreamt of tasting you. All over." David moaned. He was so close. So damn close. The memory of Jonathan's skin, his cock, those were driving him wild. But that wasn't what he'd tasted in his dream. "Oh God, Jonathan!"

David's orgasm rocked his body and spilled over his hand. He raised his sticky fingers to his mouth and licked his seed, listening to Jonathan's whimpers over the telephone line.

"Everything okay, baby?"

"Uh-huh. I just need to change my pants."

David laughed. "Wish I was there to help you with that."

Jonathan sounded breathless when he answered. "That's why I was calling, actually. I wanted to invite you to come to the zoo with us. Me and Samuel, that is."

There was nothing David would rather do then spend the day with Jonathan and Sam. A smile spread across his face, and he jumped out of bed, feeling energized at the prospect.

"Sure! I can be there in about thirty minutes to pick you up."

Jonathan laughed.

"The zoo won't open for another couple of hours."

David pushed his pajama pants down to the floor, lifted them with one foot, then reached down with his free hand to pick them up off his toe. He swaggered into the bathroom, feeling somewhat sated and very excited about the day ahead.

"That's perfect. We'll have time to go out to breakfast."

"Do you eat out for every meal?"

David paused. What was the alternative? "Well, no, not for every meal. Sometimes I just have a protein drink."

Jonathan's laughter made David grin, even though he had no idea what he'd said to cause that reaction.

"Look, Sam's all dressed. And I'm ready to go too— except for the sudden wetness in my pants, that is. Anyway, I'll change, we'll put breakfast together, and then we'll come over to your place and eat. How does that sound?"

David turned on the shower so the water would heat up. He shook his head reflexively, even though Jonathan couldn't see that motion over the phone.

"You don't have to do that. There are plenty of places nearby that serve breakfast."

"Yes, there are. But taking a two-year-old out to eat

two meals in a row is tempting fate. Besides, I don't mind cooking. We'll see you soon."

David had just gotten dressed and sent a text to his friend saying he wouldn't be attending their weekly Sunday brunch when the doorbell rang. He jogged over to the door and opened it to find the most beautiful man on earth on his doorstep. Yup, most beautiful man on earth. That was exactly who Jonathan was, inside and out, and David dared anyone to say otherwise. Okay, maybe he was a little hyped up, but the three days without Jonathan had all but destroyed him. The way David figured it, he was due a little happiness.

"Good morning, gentlemen!"

Jonathan took a couple of steps forward and fell into David's embrace, leaning up and kissing his neck.

"Mmm. You smell good."

David kissed the top of Jonathan's head and held him close. Damn, that felt right. After a few heartbeats, he released Jonathan, squatted down on his haunches, and reached his hand out to Samuel. "Good morning, sir."

Sam giggled and put his tiny hand in the big paw. "Hi, David!"

David lifted Sam up and rested him on his hip, the way he'd seen Jonathan hold him.

"Ready to come in?"

Sam's big eyes widened even farther. "You're high!"

Jonathan picked up the bag at his feet, followed David into the house, and closed the door with a nudge of his hip.

"Tall, dumpling. David's tall." He leaned forward and put his mouth right up against David's ear, so his voice wouldn't carry. "And strong. And thick in all the right places. Wanted you so bad last night, tiger. I had three fingers up my ass when I came and it still wasn't enough."

David almost tripped. Dear God! Jonathan was sex on legs. David's feet stopped working, so Jonathan was able to pass him by. Was that ass-shake intentional? David groaned. It was going to be an oh-my-goodness-I'm-so-damn-horny-I-can't-stand-it kind of day.

AFTER SPENDING three hours walking around the zoo with Sam sitting on David's or Jonathan's shoulders, eating soft pretzels, cotton candy, and caramel corn, and pushing Sam on the swings, it was time to head home. David was tired, but happier than he could ever remember being. He reached for Jonathan's hand across the car console.

"This was fun."

Jonathan beamed at him. "For me too. You're great with Sam, and he really likes you."

"I like him too. And his father. Even though he's an incorrigible tease."

Jonathan squeezed David's hand, then released it and reached for his thigh, trailing his fingers up toward the end of the V shape made by David's spread legs, and resting them on the hard warmth that greeted him.

"I'm not teasing. Just warming you up."

David groaned. "Come home with me?"

Jonathan let himself have a few heartbeats to pretend the invitation was for more than a few hours. That it was a request to share a home. That it was a recognition they could be each other's home.

"Sure. Sam's exhausted. He could use a nap. He'll probably fall asleep in his car seat, but we can move him inside."

When they arrived back at David's house, Jonathan lifted his sleeping son out of the car and followed David inside. He sat on the couch with Sam sleeping against his chest while David ran to the linen closet and came back with an armful of blankets, which he set up on the floor like a soft nest. Jonathan lowered Samuel onto the blankets, covered him with the edge of one, and then turned to find David standing right behind him. He raised himself up on his toes, pressed his chest to David's, held David's cheeks between his hands, and smiled up at him.

"Hi."

David leaned down and kissed Jonathan's forehead, the tip of his nose, and finally his mouth.

"Hi, yourself." David rubbed his nose against Jonathan's in an Eskimo kiss. "Wanna watch a movie?"

"'Kay."

Jonathan followed David to the couch. Both men

kicked off their shoes, then David sat in the corner of the sectional and reached his hands up to Jonathan, pulling him on top. They kissed and petted, enjoying each other's warmth and flavor, feeling happy to be together. And eventually fell asleep, tangled in each other's arms.

CHAPTER SEVENTEEN

MONDAY AFTER work, David stopped at The Dubliner for dinner. He hung his jacket on one of the coat-trees in the entryway and walked over to the hostess stand. A perky blonde approached him and smiled.

"You here for dinner or the bar?"

"Dinner, please. Is Jonathan Doyle available?"

The blonde seemed somewhat surprised. She smacked her gum, put one hand on her hip, and used the other to twirl her hair.

"Jonathan? You mean Brennan's brother? Sure, he's here. Come on, I'll seat you and tell him you asked for him."

David loosened his tie and followed the hostess to a table in the back. He noticed the restaurant was packed even though it was barely seven o'clock. It looked like he'd gotten the last empty table. He hadn't eaten at The Dubliner in a couple of years, and it hadn't been nearly as busy back then. Seemed like Jonathan's brother was doing well with the place.

He picked up the menu, started reading through it, and his stomach immediately rumbled. Everything sounded great and he'd skipped lunch.

"Hey!"

He heard Jonathan's happy voice just before a soft kiss landed on his cheek. Jonathan sat in the seat next to David and clutched his hand.

"This is great timing. I was just about to go home."

Even though it was the last thing he wanted to say, David forced himself to be an adult and managed to sound almost convincing when he said, "Oh, if Sam's waiting, you can go ahead. I don't mind."

Jonathan raised David's hand to his mouth and kissed it.

"I mind. I want to spend a little time with you. Well, I want to spend a lot of time with you, but the best I can do right now is just keep you company while you eat. My mother won't mind watching Sam for a little while longer."

A broad smile was Jonathan's reward.

"Great. So what's good here?"

"Everything's good. But I think my favorite is the bangers and mash or the shepherd's pie. You definitely won't go wrong with either of those."

The waitress approached and David ordered his meal. Then he turned his attention to Jonathan.

"How was your day?"

"Good. Really good, actually. My brother's gonna go ahead with his idea to open this place for lunch. A few servers said they'd actually prefer day shifts and one of the cooks wanted to switch, too, so Brennan has it all ready to go. His only hesitation was all the extra hours he'd have to work, managing the restaurant during the day and at night, so he asked me if I want to do the lunch shift."

Jonathan was happy and smiling, bouncing in his chair.

"I mean, I know it's just because I'm his brother and everything, but it's a really great deal for me. I'll be able to work more hours and make more money and I'll get home to Sam a little earlier. It's a total win-win!"

"That's great, baby. And I'm sure it's not just because you're his brother. I know a little something about hiring people, and believe me, it's hard to find someone you can trust to man the coffers. Especially in a bar, where it's so easy to lose alcohol or cash. You're honest and your brother's lucky to have you here."

Jonathan looked slightly uncomfortable in the wake of David's praise, but the food arrived before David could ask him about it. The smells wafting from the plate distracted David from their conversation, and he dug into this meal. After finishing every bit of food on his plate, David pulled a small phone out of his pocket and slid it over to Jonathan.

"I was, um, thinking maybe you'd want to use this phone. I got a group plan for my firm because Alice is working for me now, and it was no big deal to add another line, so I added you to it too."

Jonathan's eyes widened in surprise. "You got me a phone?"

David desperately tried to read Jonathan's features. Was he insulted? Had David overstepped? He didn't have to think for long to figure it out, because Jonathan hopped out of his seat, threw his arms around David's neck, and mumbled into his shoulder, "Thank you. This'll make it much easier for us to get ahold of each other."

David sighed in relief. Jonathan wasn't going to throw a fit about being able to afford his own phone or David being presumptuous or any of the other scenarios David imagined would have taken place with other men he'd dated. Damn, he enjoyed the lack of drama with Jonathan, that whole what-you-see-is-what-you-get personality was wonderful.

"I was thinking the same thing. I already added my number to the address book."

Jonathan sat back in his seat and played with the phone for a few seconds before looking up with a devilish grin.

"Cool. I'll call you tonight after Sam goes to bed. I'm sure we can find all sorts of fun things to talk about."

ON SATURDAY evening, David pulled up in front of a well-maintained 1950s ranch-style house. He was there to pick up Jonathan and Sam. They were going to go to dinner together, then they'd drop Sam off at Shannon's house until the next day. David was practically vibrating with excitement at the thought of being with Jonathan. Naked. In bed. Well, not the bed so much as being in a naked Jonathan.

They hadn't seen each other since dinner at The

Dubliner on Monday evening. That was pretty par for the course as far as David's past relationships. He'd always worked late during the week and he'd been busy showing people houses on Saturdays and Sundays. So that'd just left weekend evenings for dates. Spending two nights in a row with the same person had always seemed a bit much, so he stuck to either Friday or Saturday as date night and the other as time to hang out with his friends. Not being one to chitchat, he never called his boyfriends unless it was to make a date, but he always made an effort to return any calls within forty-eight hours.

Yes, he was that regimented—one date night, one friend night, forty-eight-hour callback rule. Hmm, it hadn't seemed weird or pathetic during the dozen or so years of his dating life, but thinking of it now, it was like Unabomber-level antisocial behavior. Anyway, it wasn't David's suddenly absurd-sounding habits that had kept him from seeing Jonathan. They both worked during the day, and Jonathan had Sam at night, so in-person get-togethers just hadn't been possible. Instead, they'd made do with nightly phone calls. Lengthy phone calls. Ball-drainingly steamy phone calls. There had been the whole get-to-know-you stuff, too, telling each other about work, family, and friends. But it wasn't the memory of those portions of the calls that made David's pants feel a little tight up front.

He managed to calm down enough on his walk up the steps so he didn't look like an overeager teenager or an old pervert. Then he knocked on the door and realized that he was actually picking his date up from his parents' house. The whole thing felt very Leave-it-to-Beaverish. Only without the Beaver. He snickered at his little joke then shook his head in self-disgust.

Christ, I really am like an adolescent. Beaver? Seriously?

"Hi. You must be David. Come on in, dear."

A blue-eyed woman a bit shorter than Jonathan with the same thick, black hair—except hers was streaked with gray—welcomed David into the house.

"I'm Colleen, Jonathan's mother. It's wonderful to meet you."

Now that he was standing in front of Jonathan's mother and no longer thinking of bad genital puns, David realized he was smack-dab in the middle of his first meet-the-parents moment. He would have been nervous, but Jonathan's smile greeted him from the open face of the woman in front of him and the only thing he could feel was happy.

"It's nice to meet you too, Colleen. Jonathan talks about you a lot. Your whole family, actually."

It was true. David had heard dozens of family stories over the past week. Like the time Jonathan's brother, Brennan, had played catch with his now brother-in-law, Keegan, in the middle of Thanksgiving dinner, using bread rolls, causing his mother to burst into tears and, as a result, turning his father from amused to red-in-the-face angry in the blink of an eye. And the time Jonathan's parents came home from work early and walked in on Keegan with his hand in Shannon's pants. Apparently, he'd tried to jerk his hand out, but the angle made it difficult and he'd ended up pulling her up off the couch with him, just increasing the visibility of what they'd been doing.

"Well, if we were talking about Brennan, I'd say you shouldn't believe a word he says. But with Jonathan, I'm sure they're all good stories. He's my sweet boy."

"Colleen, don't embarrass the boy or he'll never bring his young man round again."

A deep, gruff voice bellowed from around the corner. David looked over and was surprised to see a man who was around his height, but a good eighty pounds heavier, storming over. He had gray eyes and, despite the growl in his voice, a wide smile. The man's eyes raked over David's frame then squinted at his face.

"Huh. Ya're a big one, aren't ya? And not all that young neither."

Oh, shit.

A big paw clapped David on the shoulder and pushed him into the living room.

"Good. That boy needs someone to look out for him. I'm worried about him alone out there in the world. He's always g'ttin' 'imself in a bind. Too damn trustin' for 'is own good, that one. Nothin' like my other two, I'll tell ya that right now."

David was just starting to relax from the concern that Jonathan's father was going to disapprove of their age gap, or maybe it was their size gap, when the hand on his shoulder tightened into an almost painful squeeze and the voice got lower and more menacing.

"Ya are gonna look out for 'im, aren't ya, David?"

David reached back and pried the hand off his back, placed it in his own hand instead, and shook it.

"Yes, I will, Mr. Doyle. I'll take care of him from now on."

Yeah, it was kind of a big—and strange—thing to promise. On the fifth date. To a guy's father. But David meant every word.

A deep laugh rumbled out of his big belly. He patted David's arm with his free hand and vigorously returned the handshake.

"Good man. Good man. Ya call me Brady, ya hear? Can I getcha a beer? Colleen's probably gonna be fussin' over the baby's bag for a bit, makin' sure he has enough socks or whatnot. Jon-Jon did just fine with 'im on his own for almost three years there in New York, but that woman can't help but meddle."

"My mom was the same way." David smiled wistfully, remembering his mother always making sure he was dressed warm enough, had his hair combed, that kind of thing. He missed her.

"Was?"

David cleared his throat.

"She passed a while back."

"I'm sorry to hear that, son."

"David!"

A wet-haired Sam came peeling around the corner with Colleen hot on his trail, holding a towel.

"Samuel! I need to dry your hair. It's cold outside and you'll catch your death!"

Sam clung to David's knee. "Can I have ice cream again? No, cake! I want cake for dinner tonight. Chocolate cake. Can I? Pleeeeease?"

"Cake is not dinner, young man. Now get over here so I can dry your hair." Colleen stood in the doorway leading into the living room with one hand on her hip and the other holding the towel.

"Ah, leave the boy be, Colleen. Ya gotta quit coddling 'im."

"He's two years old, Brady. And I'm his grandmother. It's my job to coddle him."

David limped over to the doorway with a new appendage attached to his shin.

"Here you go, Colleen. Special delivery."

Colleen bent down, detached Samuel from David's leg, and restrained the twisting and turning little body with one hand while she towel-dried his hair with the other. David laughed at the sight. Just then, Jonathan walked into the room with a backpack and a small duffel slung over his shoulder.

His hair was disheveled, as always. He wore a gray sweatshirt, old, faded blue jeans with holes in the knees hanging loose on his thin body, and torn All Stars with laces that had snapped and been tied together. And he somehow managed to make that ensemble look sexy.

David instinctively reached over and pulled Jonathan into a tight hug and a quick kiss. They weren't groping, and it wasn't like there was any tongue involved, so David was surprised when Jonathan stiffened. He loosened his hold and noticed that Jonathan was bright red.

After shifting from foot to foot for a few seconds, Jonathan cleared his throat and looked at each of his parents in turn.

"Umm. Ma, Pop, I probably should've said something earlier, but, ehm, I'm gay."

No fucking way! David's head was swimming. Had he just outed Jonathan to his parents? Damn it, he wasn't usually one for public displays of affection. Hell, he rarely touched a guy unless it was leading to sex. But there was just something about Jonathan that drew in David's entire being—heart, mind, and body. This was horrible. Unforgivable.

David looked at Jonathan's parents in horror. He had no idea how they'd react to their son's sudden "I'm gay" announcement. There had been no build-up or preparation, just David kissing Jonathan and Jonathan blurting out something that David had thought was already common knowledge.

Colleen let go of Sam, stood up straight, and kissed Jonathan's cheek.

"Of course you're gay, dear."

Brady pried his big frame off the couch and hobbled over to his son, giving him a few pats on the shoulder.

"Ya boys have a nice night. We'll see ya tomorra. Nice to meet ya, David. I'm sure we'll be seein' a lot more of ya."

And with that, Brady left the room. Colleen followed a few seconds later, taking a protesting Samuel with her so she could brush his hair. David figured he had a brief reprieve. Jonathan had to be furious, but surely he wouldn't yell at him in that small house where his parents could overhear them.

"That sure went well," Jonathan said with a little laugh. He pressed himself up against David, got up on his tiptoes, then pulled David's head down for a soft, lingering kiss. "Hi, tiger. Missed you this week."

"Uh, Jonathan, what just happened here? I, um, I assumed your parents knew we were dating or I *never* would have done that. I'm so sorry."

Jonathan peppered David's neck with light kisses.

"Well, based on their reactions, I'm thinking they did know. And please don't apologize for kissing me. I love your kisses."

That was it? He'd just essentially pried the damn closet door open with a tire iron and pushed the man out to his parents and this was his reaction?

"Are you okay, Jonathan? Are you in shock or something?"

More laughter from Jonathan as he flung his arms

around David's waist and looked up into his eyes.

"I'm fine. Promise. I've been meaning to tell them for years, but I've always been too worried about disappointing them. It's not like I've hidden it or anything. It's just that there's never been cause to mention it. Well, until now, of course. So…thanks for helping with that."

Jonathan was actually thanking him for this? It could have gone a totally different way. Hell, his parents could have yelled, or cried, or thrown his belongings out on the street. And it wasn't like David had known enough about them to have worked out in advance that things would be fine. No, he simply hadn't been thinking. His body had just reacted to Jonathan's proximity in a way that felt natural.

Jonathan could see David's distress written across his handsome face. "David, it's okay. You saw how they were. It's clear they already knew. So, really, if anyone messed up here, it was me because I hadn't told them before. I'm sorry about that."

David stroked Jonathan's neck and ran his fingers through the hair on the back of his head.

"You're unreal, you know that?"

Jonathan's fingers clutched David's back, and he closed his eyes.

"Mmm. Feels good. Missed the feeling of you touching me." Those silver eyes opened and blinked a few times, then Jonathan pulled away. "Give me a minute to get some things from the kitchen and then we can go."

CHAPTER EIGHTEEN

AFTER JONATHAN left, David walked around the comfortable living room and looked at the various family photographs. The first thing he noticed was that Jonathan's brother took after their father in body type. He was just as tall and only slightly thinner. Shannon looked to be a bit taller than her mother and about as thin as Jonathan. Or at least that was how she looked in the high school graduation picture hanging on the wall. There were also pictures of a few children in addition to Samuel. David figured they were the niece and nephews Jonathan had mentioned during their nightly calls.

"Ready to go?"

David turned around to see Jonathan standing in the doorway, holding a large cooler in his hands and a backpack and duffel slung over his shoulder. David walked over to him and took the cooler.

"I've got this."

Jonathan beamed.

"Thanks. Let's get this stuff in your car and then I'll need to latch in Sam's car seat."

They put Jonathan's bags and the cooler in the trunk and latched the car seat into the back. Then Jonathan rescued

Sam from his doting grandmother, buckled him into the seat, and they were off.

"Do you have a preference on where to go for dinner?"

"Chocolate cake!"

The demand came from the backseat. Jonathan turned to look back at his son and laughed.

"You're going to eat some real food this time, dumpling."

"Where does your sister live? We can go to a restaurant close to her."

"She lives in EC West too. So does Brennan. We're a pretty tight family, so they didn't want to move far away."

David thought of a diner that served great burgers and fries and decided that'd be a good place to take Samuel. Plus, they made a fabulous chocolate cake.

"It's great that you're all so close. Sounds like you're the only one who ever left town. Why'd you move to New York?"

Jonathan didn't answer, so David turned to look at him. He could see only the back of Jonathan's head, because he was looking out the window.

"Jonathan?"

Jonathan turned back and there was an odd expression on his face. He chewed on his bottom lip thoughtfully.

"I was chasing my dream."

Yeah, him and thousands of other people who moved to New York every year. David wondered what Jonathan's dream had been and whether it was something he still hoped to achieve.

"Want to fill me in on the secret?"

Jonathan paled and his voice shook when he answered. "S-s-secret?"

David furrowed his brow, confused by that reaction. "You know, your dream. You said you were chasing your dream. I'm wondering if you ever caught it."

Jonathan coughed and gave David a relieved smile.

"Turned out everything I ever wanted was right here in Emile City all along."

That sounded typical. New York seemed to draw people with goals of making it big on Broadway, or in fashion, or art, but as far as David knew, most of them were chewed up and spit out pretty quickly. He was sorry Jonathan had gone through that. But, in a manner David had already realized was typical for him, he seemed to have picked himself up and brushed himself off just fine.

"So what do you think about burgers and fries at the Moonlight Diner?"

"Fries! Fries! Fries! I looove fries!"

David chuckled.

"Sounds like the backseat approves. How about you, Jonathan? You good with the Moonlight Diner?"

"Sounds great."

DAVID KNEW his hormones had officially been elected president of his body when he got hard at the sight of Jonathan sucking ketchup off his fries. Either that or his iced tea had been spiked with Viagra.

The second Jonathan sucked the final french fry between his enticing red lips, David cleared his throat and spoke with a voice that was hoarse with passion.

"Do you want anything else to eat or..."

Jonathan met David's heated gaze and his face flushed.

"Nothing they serve here, no."

David groaned, snatched his wallet out of his jacket and threw down way more money than a couple of burger specials, a kid's meal, and piece of chocolate cake could possibly cost.

"Let's go."

Jonathan gave one of his infectious smiles and scooped Sam up. Ten minutes later, they were pulling into the parking lot of Shannon's condo complex.

"I just need to get Sam's things from the trunk," Jonathan reminded David.

By that point, David needed all the reminders he could get because his blood had been pooled in his wrong head for way too long. He couldn't remember ever being anywhere near as easily and frequently aroused as he was with Jonathan. Then again, he couldn't remember what he'd eaten for breakfast either, because of the whole blood-loss-from-his-brain problem.

David popped the trunk and walked around to get the bags and cooler out while Jonathan unbuckled Sam.

"Oh, just the duffel. The backpack and cooler stay with us."

Jonathan swung Sam onto his narrow hip and cupped his arms under the little boy's body to hold him up. David thought about asking what Jonathan had stashed inside that cooler, but really, any extra words at that point would just further delay David's ability to stash his cock inside Jonathan, so he figured question time could wait until later. He snatched the duffel from the trunk, closed it, and followed Jonathan to Shannon's unit. Jonathan knocked on the door, then turned to David with wide eyes.

"Oh, I shoulda warned you. Be careful of the boys."

Careful? David thought back to what Jonathan had told him about his sister's family. Her husband, Keegan, was a firefighter, and they had three kids. All boys. The oldest was seven and the twins were six. What was he going to do, step on them?

"Okay, I'll be careful."

Jonathan shook his head way too fast, almost as if he was panicked. "No, you don't understand. The boys are like—"

"I can't take it anymore, Keegan!"

David heard the screeching through the door just before it swung open. A brown-haired, brown-eyed man a few inches shorter than himself stood with his hand on the knob, but he was looking back into the condo and not at them.

"Shannon, just calm down. I'll talk to them later, okay?"

The man turned to David and Jonathan and waved them into the combination entryway/family room, which was littered with toys. A man David recognized as Brennan from the pictures at the Doyle's house sat on the couch, which was pressed against the wall. There was a little girl with bright red hair who looked like she was about the same size as Sam sitting at his feet. Sam scrambled out of his father's arms, then ran up to the little girl and pulled her to the far corner of the room. The two kids laughed as they gathered toys off the floor and began stacking them into a tower.

Jonathan's sister, Shannon, stood in the middle of the room wearing nothing but a towel and dripping a puddle on the floor. Next to her was a tiny, red-haired, blue-eyed woman with a pregnant stomach sticking out so far it was a wonder she was able to remain upright. Her hand hovered right next to Shannon's back, seemingly trying to decide whether touching her would help calm her down or instigate things further.

"What'd they do this time?" Jonathan asked Keegan in a quiet, calm voice, as if walking into the middle of almost naked marital strife was an everyday occurrence.

"I'll tell you what they did! I was in the shower, washing up after cleaning this house all day. I picked up the bottle of shower gel, turned it over, and squeezed. And do you know what happened?"

The red-haired woman winced, presumably having heard the punch line already. Jonathan shook his head hesitantly.

"The lid popped right off and a bunch of cockroaches tumbled out onto my hand. *Cockroaches*! A couple fell to the ground and crawled up my leg. One jumped onto my arm and made it all the way to my neck before I could get it off. And another somehow landed on my hair! I'm telling you, Jon-Jon, I've never been more terrified. Do you think shaving my head and scrubbing off the top layer of skin is an overreaction? Because I'm seriously considering it. Maybe they've finally managed to give me full-on PTSD with this one."

"How did roaches get into the gel bottle?"

David leaned over Jonathan's shoulder and whispered the question into his ear, terrified by the scene playing out before him, but unable to neglect his curiosity. Jonathan shook his head and mouthed a "tell you later" to him. Keegan continued speaking to his wife from where he stood by the door, making no move to get any closer to her.

"I took care of it, Shannon. The roaches are all gone, and the boys are in time-out right now. Please, just go finish getting dressed."

"They're not in time-out! They're in protective custody. Well, it isn't going to work this time, Keegan. You either go in there and straighten those boys out or I will!"

Keegan turned to Jonathan and David, who were still standing in the doorway.

"Come on in all the way, guys. I need to close the door so the neighbors don't hear the screaming. Again."

As soon as they got inside, Keegan closed the door, then turned to David and reached out his hand.

"Sorry. Forgot my manners, man. I'm Keegan O'Brien."

David reached out his hand and smiled, instinct and upbringing taking over even in the midst of the completely insane situation.

"David Miller. Good to meet you, Keegan."

"Yeah, you too, David. We've heard a lot about you. Sorry about this..." Keegan waved his arm toward his still wet, almost-nude wife. "But you know how it is. There are two ways of arguing with a woman and neither one works."

He looked at Jonathan and back to David then shook his head. "Well, I guess you *don't* know. Lucky you, man. Taking it up the ass has to be less painful than this."

The red-haired woman gasped, the resulting movement bringing her perilously close to tipping forward, and Shannon growled at her husband, just barely catching her towel before it slipped to the ground.

"Damn it all to hell, Keegan! You know we're not supposed to say anything about that. We're supposed to let him come out to us on his own time!"

Keegan pinched the bridge of his nose with one hand

and waved in the general direction of David and Jonathan with the other.

"He's with his damn boyfriend, Shannon! What the hell am I supposed to do? Pretend the six-foot-four-inch linebacker standing in our house is a really big woman with five o'clock shadow?"

"Well, he could be a friend! Did you even think of that, Keegan? Maybe they're just friends!"

Keegan's patience snapped and he growled back. "Friends! Yeah, right. Because guys always spend the night with their buddies. We're watching Sam until tomorrow night, Shannon. What the hell do you think these two are going to do together until then? Wait, don't answer that. It's been so long that you've probably managed to forget!"

In response to those words, Shannon's eyes widened, she covered her mouth with her hand, burst into tears, and ran out of the room. Her husband uttered a few curses under his breath and chased after her. A few heartbeats later, Brennan got up from the couch with a sigh. He walked over to the kids playing in the corner, kissed the little girl on the head, tousled Sam's hair, then walked over to the front door.

"You got the little ones until Shan and Keeg work it out, right, Jon-Jon? Cuz we've got a movie to catch and it starts in twenty minutes. I don't want to miss the previews."

"Yeah, we've got them."

The red-haired woman remained rooted to the same spot on the floor, staring in panic at the hallway Shannon had run into. Brennan looked over at her, his expression softening. He walked back to where she stood, put his big arm around her narrow shoulders, and walked her toward the door.

"Come on, Gracie. You know they'll be fine. They just need a few minutes to sort things out."

The redhead let her husband lead her to the door. He opened it for her, but just as they were about to step out, he turned back to David and reached his hand out.

"Oh jeez, almost forgot. I'm Brennan Doyle, and this is my wife Grace." He pointed to the little girl playing with Sam on the floor. "That's our little one, Clare. Welcome to the family, man."

As soon as the words were out of his mouth, his eyes widened and he snapped his head toward Jonathan.

"Oh, shit. Sorry, Jon-Jon, didn't mean to, ah, assume or whatever. I just figured, with you bringing him around we can all stop pretending like we don't know you're into dudes. But I can go with the whole buddy thing if we're still doing that."

Jonathan smiled at his brother. "We're good, Brenn. Would've been nice if you'd told me that you've known all this time. Mighta saved me some anxiety."

Brennan shrugged.

"Yeah, well, sorry about that. See you later."

The door closed and the house was completely quiet except for the little voices coming from the corner. The toys Sam and Clare had stacked into a tower fell, and they laughed and started the project over again. David reached over to Jonathan and pulled him against his chest, wrapping him in his arms.

"You okay?"

Jonathan's body softened against him. He heard him inhale deeply, then felt Jonathan's hands slip into his back pockets.

"Yeah, I'm good. I'd make up an excuse for my family and say they all just picked the same week to quit sniffing glue or something. But the truth is, they're always like this. Don't get the wrong idea—Shannon and Keegan have been together as long as I can remember and they really love each other. The boys are just a major handful, and it gets to them sometimes."

David kissed Jonathan's forehead. "You know, um, no offense or anything, but are you sure we should leave Sam here? Maybe he should come with us."

Jonathan's heart pounded, and he had to hold back tears. David was thinking of his son first. He knew the man was just as excited as Jonathan about being alone together, yet he was willing to give that up because of his concern over Sam.

"He'll be fine. The boys like to torture adults, but they're actually pretty sweet with Clare and Sam. And this place is like an amusement park for kids. They have tons of toys and there's always someone to play with him—Sam loves coming here."

David heard the break in Jonathan's voice. He held the man who had become so precious to him close to his chest and found himself instinctively rocking back and forth. He was smack-dab in the midst of what was surely the strangest date of his life. Hell, it was the strangest date he'd ever heard of. There'd been a kid's meal, a meet-the-parents experience, an inadvertent coming out to said parents, a family feud involving an almost naked sister, a pregnant chick, a reference to getting fucked and not in the traditional I'm-making-an-offer kind of way...let's see, what else? Oh, right. Strangest of all, David was in love.

CHAPTER NINETEEN

"SO HAVE I managed to scare you off yet?" Jonathan asked David as soon as they were settled in David's car and pulling out of Shannon's complex. His tone was teasing, but the worried look in his eyes and the way he chewed on his thumbnail told David he was actually concerned.

"I like your family." Jonathan looked at him in disbelief, so David chuckled and continued. "Seriously, I do. They're funny and they seem to care about each other and I'll come up with more good things to say about them once I've spent more time with them." He gave Jonathan a big smile and squeezed his knee. "I mean it."

Jonathan relaxed back in his seat and covered David's hand with his own. "I guess you really do like me."

David laughed and took another quick look at his passenger. Jonathan shrugged.

"My family's nuts. If you truly like them or are even willing to pretend to like them, that means you like me."

Jonathan was smiling and joking around, those silver eyes were gleaming, and David wanted to correct him—not just like, *love*.

I love you. Don't know how it happened so fast, but

there's no doubt about it.

The words somehow got stuck on the way out and all David could do was nod and keep driving. He heard a click from Jonathan's seat belt and looked over to see Jonathan scooting over to the edge of his seat and bending over the console. Jonathan's hand was on David's zipper before he processed what was happening.

"What are you doing?"

Jonathan looked up with a wicked grin and fished David's quickly hardening dick out through the opening in his boxer briefs. He licked his lips and ducked his head.

"Sucking you."

The words came out as Jonathan lowered his mouth to the head of David's cock and began to suck.

"Oh, God!"

David grasped the steering wheel so tight that his knuckles were white. This was dangerous—probably illegal too. And it'd be embarrassing as hell if someone saw them. Oh, but it felt so damn good. Jonathan could suck cock like none other. He pushed his mouth down and took David into his throat, then pulled up with a tight suction all the way up to David's glans, only to drop back down again. Up and down he went, his tongue making little swipes along the way; slurping noises filled the car, and that ever-present suction drove David out of his mind.

Just when he thought he'd go off in the car and cause an accident, David realized his house was in sight. He'd been driving on mental autopilot, only partially paying attention to his surroundings. Thank goodness the drive from Shannon's condo wasn't very long and didn't involve terribly busy streets. He put the car in park and petted Jonathan's hair.

"We're here, baby. Let's take this inside."

Jonathan released David's dick with a popping sound and smiled up at him. He wiped the wetness from around his mouth with the back of his hand.

"I love how you taste and smell down there."

David groaned. Damn, that was hot and his dick was *so* hard. He forced it back into his pants and winced as he zipped up, not bothering with the button. Then he stepped out of the car and held his hand out for Jonathan.

"We need to get my backpack and cooler."

Right. Backpack and cooler. How was it that Jonathan seemed to be perfectly fine, remembering all these details, and David was about two seconds away from forgetting his own name? David walked over to the trunk, handed Jonathan his backpack, and looked at the large cooler. He'd need both hands to carry it so he turned back to Jonathan and held out his keys.

"You get the door, okay?"

Jonathan nodded and bounded ahead. David lifted the cooler out of the trunk, balanced it on one knee while he shut the trunk, then followed Jonathan inside. He flipped on the lights in his entryway and stared at Jonathan's ass encased in his tattered, loose Levi's. Those jeans were nothing like the cut-to-hug-every-muscle expensive designer brands his dates usually wore. No. On Jonathan, those old jeans were much sexier. Jonathan turned his head back toward David, his silver eyes heated, a pink tongue darting out of that enticing mouth and licking his lips.

David remembered where that tongue had just been, and he wasn't able to hold back his moan. He set the cooler down and pulled Jonathan up against him by the loops on his jeans, hoping the hard cock Jonathan was sure to feel would give the man a clue of what they needed to do right fucking now. He leaned down and sucked on Jonathan's neck, covering it with kisses and licks. Jonathan lowered his hands to David's ass and massaged the hard muscles. David moaned again and ground his dick against Jonathan.

"Should we take the cooler to the kitchen and unload it?"

David knew his voice was strained. It was taking every ounce of self-control he could muster to keep himself upright and off the tempting man in front of him. Jonathan whimpered and pulled David's pants down. It wasn't a difficult task, because he hadn't refastened the button after their little escapade in the car. Once the pants and briefs were down to David's knees, Jonathan gave David a gentle nudge toward the bench in the entryway.

David felt the edge of the fabric against the back of his legs and sat down. Jonathan leaned down and kissed him while he toed off his own shoes and his hands made quick work of unbuttoning his own jeans. The loose denim fell to the ground with ease, and Jonathan's white briefs followed. After that, a half-naked Jonathan climbed onto David's lap, wrapped his legs around him, and began rutting.

"Damn, yes." David moaned and grasped Jonathan's ass, squeezing and encouraging his movements.

Jonathan's hard dick rubbed against David's as he snapped his hips and sucked on David's neck.

"Gonna, tiger. Gonna, gonna."

His voice got higher, the sucks harder, the thrusts faster, and then Jonathan pushed hard against David's body and shouted out in pleasure as wetness covered their bellies. David buried his face against Jonathan's shoulder and cried out his own release. Their bodies relaxed against each other, but their breathing was still heavy, hearts still racing.

"Missed you," Jonathan whispered quietly.

David laughed softly.

"Missed you too. Come on, let's get cleaned up."

Jonathan unfolded himself from David's lap and swiped his hand through the drying cum on his stomach. He peeled off his shirt and wiped the wetness from his body. Then he snagged his briefs and jeans off the floor. David had gotten up and lifted his own briefs and pants back up. He was looking admiringly at Jonathan's naked body.

"So, in all seriousness, should we unload this cooler?"

Jonathan shook his head as he started walking toward the bedroom. "Nah, the icepacks will keep everything cold enough. Now I, on the other hand, am definitely the wrong temperature. It's freezing."

Jonathan curled his arms around himself and squeezed his clothes in a bundle between them. Then he rubbed his hands up and down on his upper arms as much as he could. David pressed his chest against Jonathan's back and wrapped his arms around the thinner man, engulfing him in muscle and strength. Jonathan sighed and leaned back.

"How does a bath sound? I haven't had a chance to test out those jets, but Caleb promised it'd be heavenly when it was being installed," David whispered into Jonathan's ear.

Jonathan nodded and walked with David into the bedroom.

"You painted." Jonathan sounded awed.

David smiled broadly, pleased that Jonathan had noticed.

"Yeah, green like you said. A few shades darker in here than in the bathroom."

Jonathan dropped the bundle of clothes, turned around, and absolutely melted against David. Nobody ever listened to him. Not that he usually offered his opinion on things, but that was mostly because he never felt like anyone really cared what he thought or had to say. He mostly stayed invisible in the background, trying not to get in the way. But David had listened and acted. Jonathan hadn't done more than mention the color in passing, and the room had been painted.

"I...I..." Jonathan wasn't sure what to say. He looked at David and blinked back tears. "Thank you."

David stroked that precious head and dropped a kiss on top.

"Why are you thanking me? I'm the one who's grateful. The color already helps make this room feel warmer. Now we just need to pick out furniture."

Jonathan sighed and squeezed David tightly. "You make me feel so good. It's like...it's like you *see* me."

David held Jonathan in his arms, rocked them from side to side, and mumbled into Jonathan's hair. "Of course I see you. I just wish I could see you more often."

After several minutes of silence, the two men padded into the bathroom. David went into the closet to take off his clothes and throw them in the hamper, and Jonathan fiddled with the knobs on the tub until he had the temperature just right.

"I don't have any bubble bath because I've never used that tub, but maybe shampoo will work."

David was standing behind Jonathan, gloriously naked and holding a bottle of salon shampoo. It looked like it cost ten times as much as the grocery store generic brand Jonathan used.

"You sure you want to waste that on bubbles?"

David leaned over the edge of the tub and squeezed a generous amount of the product under the running water.

"I want to be all slippy with you in there. That's not a

waste."

He kissed Jonathan's cheek, set the bottle on the counter, and climbed into the tub. He settled with his back against one end and his legs stretched out down the length of the tub and spread open. Raising his arm and reaching a hand out to Jonathan, David looked at the beautiful man standing above him and felt his breath catch in his chest. *I love you.* Why wasn't that coming out? He sure seemed to be thinking it hard enough.

Jonathan took David's hand and climbed into the tub. He settled in between David's legs, leaned back against that wide chest, and sighed happily when David drizzled warm water onto him.

"Tell me about your day. Anything exciting happen? Other than coming out to your entire family, I mean."

Jonathan laughed and started talking.

"That kooky old guy came into the restaurant again and insisted on sitting in Jessica's section. She threw an absolute fit and starting going off about how he stares at her boobs. She was so loud that I know he heard her, but he just sat there smiling, which made the situation way worse. Then Jessica..."

David closed his eyes, focused on the sound of Jonathan's voice and the feel of his body, and rejoiced in how right it felt. So much better than doing this daily catch-up over the phone. He caressed Jonathan's arms and chest. There had to be some way for them to spend more time together. He'd think about it and figure something out, but for now he'd enjoy having this wonderful man in his arms.

AFTER THEIR bath, the two men dried off and got into bed. They cuddled together under the comforter. Jonathan flipped onto his stomach, propped his arms on David's chest, and rested his chin on his hands.

"So tell me about when you came out to your family."

David brushed Jonathan's damp hair back off his forehead, then started rubbing circles on his back.

"Let's see. I was in college and my sister Ellie came to visit. Her flight was early, so she took a cab from the airport and sweet-talked the super into letting her into my apartment. She'd been up since the crack of dawn, so she was beat and wanted to get a nap in before I got home. I'd left a magazine next to the bed the night before."

He shrugged and raised his eyebrows. "When I got home, she was sitting at my table, eating a sandwich and flipping through the magazine. I didn't figure there was any other way to explain the pictures of naked guys in compromising positions, and she was getting ready to go off to college the next year, so it's not like she was clueless about the world."

He ran his hand through his silky hair and smiled as he remembered his little sister.

"SHE'D DOG-EARED a couple of pages and told me she'd been wondering about some things, but she couldn't ask our dad because his version of a sex talk had been to tell her to stay vertical and travel in herds. Our mom was long gone and Ellie figured her friends didn't know anything more than she did. Anyway, we sat and talked. She asked questions about guys and sex. I tried to answer honestly, even though it was hella uncomfortable to be having that conversation with my little sister. And that was that."

"What about your father? Does he know?"

David cleared his throat. "Yeah, sure. I called him when Ellie left. I didn't want her to be in a weird position if anything came up. My dad worked so much back then, even more than he does now, so the call was pretty short. I told him Ellie was on her way back, that we'd had a nice visit, and that I was gay. He said he'd have a driver waiting for her at the airport and to make sure I studied hard for finals."

David laughed. "I almost wondered whether he heard me, but then when he came into town for a business meeting a few months later, we met for dinner, and he told me I could bring a friend. I figured that was his way of being accepting."

Jonathan moved his body so he was completely covering David. He kissed his neck and nibbled on his ear.

"Do you get to see him a lot?"

David shook his head.

"No, usually only when he's in town for business. That almost never happens anymore. Plus, he's been living in London for the past few years, which makes the flight time longer. But we usually talk on the phone for birthdays and major holidays. We get along fine and everything. We're just both so busy with work that it's hard to find time to see each other."

Knowing how close Jonathan's family was, David realized that must sound pathetic. But Jonathan didn't say anything, and there was no judgment or pity in his expression. David found that he actually enjoyed opening up to Jonathan, telling him about his family, sharing anecdotes about what he'd done at work that day. He'd never met anyone who was so easy to talk to. The two men lay together in silence, sharing soft kisses and enjoying the feel of their naked skin touching. And David wondered what it would take to make those feelings a more regular part of his life.

CHAPTER TWENTY

DAVID'S THOUGHTS about seeing Jonathan more frequently were sidelined when Jonathan's licks and nibbles across his chest were joined by moans and Jonathan's hard dick humping David's thigh.

"What do you want?"

David's voice was low and husky with need. He caressed Jonathan's back and ass, let his fingers move into the crevice and massage the rosebud. Jonathan wiggled back and moaned.

"That works."

Jonathan reached down next to the bed where David had put a box of condoms and the lube. Then he scooted back and straddled David. He ripped the packet open, slid the condom down David's hard cock and covered him with lube. After that, Jonathan moved forward so he was just above his prize.

"Hold yourself steady for me."

David moaned and reached for his dick, holding it steady while Jonathan placed his opening on David's glans and pushed down, taking David's cock into his body. Leaning back and resting his hands on David's thighs, Jonathan slowly lowered himself until he'd consumed David's entire length within the tight heat of his body. David hissed and closed his eyes. It felt so fucking good.

Jonathan rolled his hips and shivered with pleasure. When David opened his eyes, the vision before him took his breath away. Jonathan was moving up and down, pure bliss shining on his beautiful face. David clutched his hips and bucked, meeting his motions and adding to their experience. The sounds of the bed squeaking and their skin meeting surrounded them.

Both men moaned and moved together for long minutes until David tightened his stomach muscles, raised his upper body, and flipped Jonathan onto his back with a thud, never severing their connection.

"So strong. 'S such a turn-on." Jonathan moaned, arched his back, and spread his legs, making as much room as he could for David to pummel into his channel. And David accepted the invitation with gusto. His eyes gleamed with a feral look as he raised one of Jonathan's legs up against his chest, changing the angle and allowing himself a deeper penetration.

"Oh, God!" Jonathan shouted as his body was pushed progressively farther up the bed from the force of David's thrusts.

The mattress shook and swayed. Jonathan reached his hands back and made contact with the headboard, pushing against it to counter the pounding from David's body. David's eyes locked with his, and he groaned.

"Almost there, baby. Come with me, please."

Jonathan reached one hand down to his cock and stroked himself in time with the motion in his ass.

"Oh, fuck, so close. So close, Jonathan. Gonna. Gonna. Now!" David shouted and released, giving a couple of final thrusts into Jonathan's welcoming body. Jonathan cried out and came all over his stomach and chest. Both men gasped for air, trying to refill their lungs, when suddenly they heard a loud squeak, felt the bed shake, and then heard a series of thuds as each leg collapsed in turn, until they were lying on a mattress resting on the floor and surrounded by snapped wood.

David looked at Jonathan with wide eyes, and both men started laughing uncontrollably.

"Holy crap! I guess we wore out the furniture."

"Hey, I said you were strong." Jonathan giggled. "Sorry about your bed."

"'S okay. We needed a new one anyway. Think we'll have time to go shopping in the morning? We can get nightstands too."

Jonathan nodded and reached up for a kiss just as he felt David's dick fall out of his ass.

"Be right back." David gave him a quick peck on the forehead and slid off the mattress. A couple of minutes later, he was back with a washcloth, wiping off Jonathan's body and holding him close as he fell asleep. He watched Jonathan's body relax and kissed his cheek.

"I love you." He whispered the admission and gave himself a mental smack for not having said it while Jonathan was awake. After rubbing Jonathan's back for a few minutes and enjoying the texture and warmth of his skin, David fell asleep.

JONATHAN UNTANGLED his legs from David's, slipped out of bed quietly so he wouldn't wake him, brushed his teeth, and then padded down the hallway, through the living room and into the entryway, where they'd dropped his backpack and cooler the night before. He dug through the backpack and pulled out a pair of sweats, a soft, long-sleeved T-shirt, his favorite sweatshirt, and thick socks. Not as warm as being nestled under the comforter with David, but it'd have to do.

He hoisted the cooler up and carried it into the kitchen. Well, hopefully the puke-green appliances worked. Damn, what had the person who picked these colors been thinking? He set the cooler next to the counter and unloaded the ingredients. He'd seen the contents of David's refrigerator the last time he'd stayed over and he knew it held nothing resembling food, unless you counted takeout containers. So Jonathan brought everything he'd need to make breakfast for them. The clock on the microwave told him it was just barely five in the morning. He knew David would be sleeping for hours yet, so starting breakfast right then wouldn't make sense. Oh well, he'd packed enough ingredients that he could cook up a couple of meals David could heat up later in the week if he worked too late to stop for his usual takeout.

Jonathan dug through the cabinets and confirmed his suspicion that there were no cooking utensils—no spatulas, no pots, not even a frying pan. He shook his head and chuckled quietly to himself. He'd packed a saucepan, a frying pan, and a couple of spoons just in case. He worked in waves, finishing a dish and then storing it in the refrigerator on paper plates covered with foil. Then he washed the pan and pot and started on the next meal.

While he cooked, Jonathan thought about how it'd feel to live in that house, to cook meals there every night, to have Sam sit at that counter and eat breakfast. He shook off those thoughts. It was too soon for that. Way too soon. Sure, he'd been fantasizing about David for years, but in David's mind, they'd just met. Plus, there was the issue with Sam. It was one thing for a man to want his boyfriend to move in. But inviting an almost-three-year-old into that perfectly appointed house seemed like too much for Jonathan to hope for.

He wouldn't allow himself to feel sad about that. He had found his dream man, he was lucky enough to talk to him every day, and to see him as often as they could manage. That was more than he'd ever had and it would have to be enough.

AFTER STUMBLING into the bathroom to take a leak and brush his teeth, David threw on a pair of sleep pants and T-shirt, then made his way through the house with a huge smile on his face. The previous night had been incredible. They'd literally broken the damn bed. The sweetest guy he'd ever met and the best sex of his life. How had he managed to find that combination in one person?

Once he got to the dining room, David could hear whistling coming from the kitchen. He stood at the doorway for a moment, watching a happy Jonathan bop around to a song playing in his head. There were smells of actual food being cooked coming from that room for the first time since David had moved in, and he was somewhat shocked that such things could originate from his appliances.

"Morning, handsome."

Startled, Jonathan jumped and held onto the counter with one hand, the other flying to his heart.

"Hey. You scared me." Jonathan cleared his throat then walked back to the stove. "Hungry?"

David came up behind the shorter man and looked over his shoulder.

"You made this? Like from scratch?"

Jonathan scoffed and turned in David's arms, pushing him back toward the seats at the counter.

"Pancakes, sausage, potatoes, and a Denver omelet. Yes, I made them *from scratch*, not really sure what the alternative is."

David stood next to the chair, looking adorably confused. "You can cook too?"

That earned him a belly laugh from Jonathan.

"You mean you thought the only thing I was good for was a hearty romp in bed?"

David's jaw dropped and he shook his head furiously. "No! That's not what I meant at all! I was just..."

Jonathan winked at him and laughed. "I'm teasing you. Yes, I can cook. I grew up in a restaurant, remember? I think I learned how to chop vegetables before I learned how to ride a bike. The Dubliner is a family place, so we all worked there. Besides, this is a simple meal. Even Sam knows how to beat eggs. And who exactly did you think made the breakfast I brought over before our zoo trip last Sunday?"

Still perplexed by the activities in his kitchen and horrified that he might have offended Jonathan, David hadn't moved, so Jonathan pushed him down onto the chair. With Jonathan standing and David sitting, they were eye to eye. Jonathan leaned over and kissed David's cheek and smiled at him. Okay, he wasn't mad. Of course not—Jonathan never got mad.

"I thought you bought breakfast on the way here. I didn't know you *made* the french toast."

Jonathan spooned food from the stove and the plates he had covered next to it onto a paper plate and placed it front of David. Then he brought his own plate to the counter and sat down.

David picked up his fork, scooped some eggs and potatoes onto it, and took a bite.

"Mmm. 'S good!"

"Glad you like it. Imagine what I could do with the right equipment."

David shoveled food into his mouth at a record pace.

"Mquip't?"

"Do I need to talk to you like I do to Sam? Chew and swallow before you speak."

David almost choked on his breakfast. He reached for the bottle of water Jonathan had set before him, and once his mouth was clear, he smiled sheepishly at Jonathan.

"Sorry. Nobody's cooked for me since my mom passed. I guess I'm a little overexcited."

Jonathan's heart broke, hearing David say no one had taken care of him in so long. Then again, Jonathan had been on his own since he'd turned eighteen. Maybe now they could be there for each other. He reached over and squeezed David's hand in support.

"Excited is good. Now eat. I have lots of activities planned for you this morning, and believe me when I tell you that you're going to need lots of energy."

Jonathan waggled his eyebrows and gave David his best leer.

David would've laughed, but his mouth was full of the most delicious pancakes he'd ever had.

"Mmm, 'kay," he mumbled.

Jonathan smiled, picked up his fork, and scooped up some eggs, feeling pleased down to his core that he'd made David so happy.

After finishing breakfast and sharing a long shower, the men shopped for bedroom furniture, then picked Sam up, spent a few hours at the park, and said their goodbyes. The next week followed the same routine as the previous one, with nightly telephone calls. One improvement was that The Dubliner was open for lunch, so David dropped by there almost every day, and Jonathan ate with him. Even though he spent considerably more time with Jonathan than he had with previous boyfriends, it didn't feel like nearly enough.

On Friday evening, David picked Jonathan and Sam up for dinner and then drove over to Brennan and Grace's townhouse. Jonathan carried Sam, and David held Sam's bag with one hand and rested the other on the small of Jonathan's back. The sound of a football game playing on TV greeted them well before they got to the door. David knocked, but there was no answer.

"They probably can't hear us over that racket."

Jonathan nodded and tried the handle. The door was unlocked, so they walked inside. Brennan and Keegan were sitting on the couch, drinking beer and watching the television with a single-minded focus. Clare had coloring books and crayons strewn all over the coffee table. As soon as she saw Sam come into the house, she jumped up and ran over to her cousin.

"Maybe you two should play in Clare's bedroom. I bet it's much quieter," Jonathan suggested.

The two kids ran off, and Jonathan and David turned to walk into the family room just as Brennan and Keegan leaped off the sofa in tandem and started yelling at the screen. Jonathan found the remote and turned down the volume when a beer commercial came on.

"Hey, guys."

Brennan looked over at Jonathan and David in surprise. "Oh, hey, Jon-Jon. Hi, David. Didn't hear you guys come in."

Jonathan laughed. "Yeah, I noticed. You might want to lock the door and turn the volume down to a respectable roar. Where's Gracie?"

"She's with Shannon, doing some last-minute Christmas shopping," Keegan responded.

David sat down on the couch and pulled Jonathan onto his lap. "What're you watching?"

"Yesterday's Broncos-Texans game. Recorded it. You like football, David?" Brennan answered as he got up from the couch.

"All-city, all-state," David responded.

Brennan and Keegan both looked impressed.

"Really? That's great. You guys are welcome to hang out." Keegan turned toward the two men and picked up a bowl of pretzel mix from the end table.

"I'm getting refills from the kitchen. Can I get you

guys anything? Beer?" Brennan asked as he walked out of the room.

"We're good, thanks, Brenn."

Jonathan hadn't gotten the sentence all the way out before they heard Brennan shouting, "Damn it, Keller! That's not funny." He stormed back into the family room and glared at Keegan as he shook the waist of his track pants and wiggled his legs. Ice cubes scattered on the floor. "That spawn of Satan you call a son just dumped a whole cup of ice down my pants."

"Keller, you're in time-out," Keegan responded reflexively while searching the bowl he was holding for his favorite kind of pretzel. He didn't bother looking up for even a moment.

"Keegan, that's not a time-out, that's you saying time-out." Brennan's voice was still angry. Keegan didn't seem to notice. He just kept digging through the bowl and throwing pretzels into his mouth. Brennan rolled his eyes. "Whatever, Keeg. But I'm not cleaning their shit. Get your fat ass up and wipe the floor."

Keegan stood, walked over to the area where the ice cubes had fallen from Brennan's shirt, and squatted down so he could pick them up. He moved one of Clare's dolls out of the way.

"I don't like these realistic baby dolls. They scare me."

"Yeah? Well, your children scare me. There's more to clean in the kitchen. Come on."

When they were alone in the family room, Jonathan

turned to David and kissed him gently.

"You want to stay here and watch this game or go home?"

Damn, David loved hearing Jonathan refer to his house as home. He was suddenly filled with emotion. He returned Jonathan's kiss, but with more passion and tongue.

"I watched the Broncos game last night. And whatever game your brother and Keegan are playing with each other just makes me nervous. Do you want to stick around?"

"Nope. I'd rather be alone with you."

"Okay, then let's go home."

CHAPTER TWENTY-ONE

JONATHAN HAD brought another packed cooler with him, and David carried it into the kitchen. He set it next to the fridge and leaned down to open it.

"Okay, this is silly. I'm sure there's a grocery store around here. I can buy this stuff so you don't have to keep lugging this cooler back and forth."

Jonathan pressed his body against David's.

"I haven't had your cock up my ass in a week. Maybe we can take care of that first, and then I'll deal with the cooler."

Those words were enough to snap David's mind. He stood up, scooped Jonathan into his arms—causing a small yelp—and marched into the bedroom, where he lowered Jonathan onto the new iron bed they'd picked together. He was breathless with the anticipation of being with Jonathan again, and a little bit from the exertion of carrying him across the house. While Jonathan was certainly shorter than David's six-foot-four-inch height and much more slight, at five foot ten inches, he was by no means petite. David stood back and looked at the gorgeous man in his bed and rubbed the base of his hand over his painfully hard dick.

Jonathan moaned, got himself naked in seconds,

then began working on David's clothes. He shoved his hand under David's sweater, and pushed it up and over his head. Trembling fingers worked on the buttons of the collared shirt while his tongue licked every area of exposed flesh.

"Want to feel your skin."

The licks turned into sucks as more of David's chest was exposed. When he finally managed to slip the shirt off David's body entirely, Jonathan caressed his broad chest and the corded muscles on his stomach, then rubbed his engorged cock through his pants. David growled, used the weight of his larger body to force Jonathan onto his back, and ripped his own pants open, shoving them down to his knees with one hand while his other hand braced him above Jonathan in a push-up position. He toed off his shoes, wiggled his way completely out of his pants and briefs, and blanketed Jonathan with his bigger frame.

Jonathan whimpered when David's muscles overpowered him. He moved his mouth toward David's, desperate for a kiss, and opened for David as soon as his tongue flitted over his lips. That tongue explored Jonathan's mouth while hands explored his body, peppering soft touches over his waist, hip, and thigh.

"You feel so good, baby."

A whimper and a frenzied increase in the passion of the kiss were Jonathan's replies to that endearment. David wanted to get off, but what he wanted even more was to make things good for Jonathan. So he held himself in check and concentrated on Jonathan.

"Tell me what you want, baby. What makes you feel good?"

That thin body rubbed up against him, bringing Jonathan's hard cock in contact with David's, and both men gasped. Jonathan gripped David's shoulders and panted into his mouth.

"Want you. Want this. Feels good."

David gyrated his hips, nibbled on Jonathan's chin, licked his neck, and reached into the nightstand drawer for the lube and condoms he'd stashed there. He quickened his actions when he heard another whimper-moan from the man underneath him as their heated cocks rubbed together more and more quickly. David raised himself onto his knees, flipped the cap open, and let a thin stream of lube trickle into the cleft of Jonathan's ass while caressing his chest with his free hand. Those legs spread open in invitation, the heartbeat he could feel under his hand quickened, and David realized he'd never felt more wanted, more welcome.

His thick fingers massaged Jonathan's pucker for a few seconds before he focused his attention on the condom, opening the wrapper and rolling it down his impossibly hard cock. Two thumbs pressed into the eager, willing tunnel, and Jonathan's entire body seemed to melt against the mattress in reaction to the breach of his opening, a sigh of relief escaping his lips. David leaned his head down so his eyes were scant inches away from Jonathan's.

"It's so hot how much you enjoy this. Your ass was meant to be filled, baby."

Jonathan's eyes rolled back in his head in response to the combination of David's words and the in-and-out motion of his thumbs.

"By you. Filled by you. Only you."

It didn't sound like a request or a demand. More like a statement of fact. And it called to every possessive bone in David's body. Surprising, really, because that wasn't one of David's personality traits. Competitive, yes, but not possessive, not jealous. Of course, that was before Jonathan. From the moment he'd seen Jonathan being harassed by that Muscle Mary in Where Cowboys Dream, he'd wanted to protect him, shield him from other guys, and keep him to himself.

David slowly withdrew his thumbs from Jonathan's chute and replaced them with his aching cock. He slid home slowly, enjoying the pleasure playing over Jonathan's face as his body was taken. He licked those full lips and held himself still, covering Jonathan inside and out.

"Only me?"

"Mmm hmm. Only you. Always."

That adoring look in Jonathan's eyes made David's chest constrict, almost taking his breath away. He burrowed into Jonathan, as deep as he could, then pulled out and pushed back in again. His mouth covered Jonathan's in an attempt to devour him.

"Mine," David growled into Jonathan's mouth as his hips snapped. He nipped at Jonathan's lips, his chin, his neck. "Mine."

Jonathan wrapped his legs around David's waist and his arms around David's neck. He rested his heels on the small of David's back and clung to the hard body above him, meeting each push, giving himself completely.

"Yours, David. I promise, just yours."

Oh, it was so good. So damn good. David pushed down with all his strength, and Jonathan joined him in every motion, thrusting his hips up and down to get David in as deep as possible even as he reached a hand in between their bodies to tug on his own cock. Both men grunted and moaned, harsh sounds of skin meeting skin filled the room, while David pummeled into Jonathan.

"So close, tiger! So close. Gonna, gonna..."

The smell and feel of Jonathan's seed joined his shouts of pleasure. David thrust a few more times into that warm cavern, then held himself deep inside Jonathan, digging his fingers into Jonathan's hips to keep him as close as possible while he released inside the condom, wishing there was no barrier separating them.

David collapsed onto Jonathan, moving his hips just enough to pull off the condom, tie it, and drop it on the floor. Sated, sticky bodies, curled together in the bed, petting and kissing, recovering from their joining.

"Missed you all week, baby. Wanted you here every

night when I came home." David kissed that precious head and closed his eyes, letting the feelings he had for the man in his bed overtake him. Damn, it felt so good to connect that way, to want that way, to love that way.

"Me too, tiger," Jonathan whispered.

David curled his arms around Jonathan, flipped onto his back, and took Jonathan with him. Jonathan nestled on top of David's body, traced his nipple with his tongue, and ran his fingers through the soft hair on David's chest.

"How was your day?"

David's hands made their way to Jonathan's head, petting his hair. "Good. I finally sold a house to Micah Trains."

Jonathan sucked David's nipple gently. "That's the guy you've been working with for months, right? The one who kept finding issues with every place?"

David chuckled. "Yeah, that's him. I finally realized the only way he'd ever be happy would be to build his own house, so I sold him this tear-down on a great lot. I had a friend who owns a construction company meet us and give him ideas of what he could build, and he was sold. Done and done."

David leaned down, kissed Jonathan's head, and gave his body a squeeze.

"How about you? Good day?"

"Yeah, it was good. One of the girls at work said there's going to be a vacancy in her building. The rent's a bit steep, but I think I can swing it, so I made an appointment to go see it on Monday."

David didn't like the thought of Jonathan moving into that apartment, and at first he wasn't sure why. He didn't even know where the place was yet. But after a few seconds, he recognized that his feelings had nothing to do with location. Or, more accurately, they had everything to do with location. Was it crazy that he wanted to ask Jonathan to move in with him? They'd known each other less than three weeks. That had to be too fast, right?

David was never impulsive. No, he was the type to think things through, analyze all the possibilities, lead with his head. Always. But this was different. He didn't need to take time, didn't need to weigh options. This thing with Jonathan was right, he knew it was right. And seeing the man only a couple of days a week, sharing a bed with him only when an overnight sitter could be arranged...it simply wasn't enough.

"Move in with me, baby."

After briefly stilling, Jonathan went back to caressing David's chest. "If I didn't have Samuel, I'd do it in a heartbeat."

David squeezed that gorgeous body and kissed Jonathan's forehead.

"I meant both of you. You're mine, Jonathan." The words rolled off his tongue naturally—so strange to say that to someone, but it didn't *feel* strange. "You're mine and he's your son. I get that it's a package deal and I want the package."

Jonathan pulled himself off David's chest and scooted off the bed. He held his hand out to the man he'd dreamt of, both in sleep and in consciousness, for years.

"Let me think about it. For now, how about a shower? I'm sticky."

That nose did the little crinkle thing David found so damn cute. He smiled and cupped Jonathan's cheek. Yeah, it was right. It was good and it was right, and though he'd never outwardly admitted it to himself, David had been waiting to feel that way, waiting for someone to share his life, for years. After all, wasn't that why he'd bought this big house and then made it a place meant for a couple to share? It wasn't like he could use two sinks, two towel hooks, and two closets all on his own.

Yup, he'd been preparing for this, even if it was on a less than conscious level. And now that he'd found Jonathan, David wasn't going to accept anything other than a complete joining. If Jonathan needed a little convincing, that was fine. David could be damn persuasive. All those houses didn't sell themselves, after all. Hell, it'd actually be fun to chase someone for once. Just as long as Jonathan let himself get caught. Fast. Because whoever said patience was a virtue clearly hadn't spent his nights in an empty bed while the man he loved was just out of reach.

JONATHAN TRIED to let the strong heartbeat under his ear lull him back to sleep. He was sated, washed, and cuddled in bed with his perfect guy. That should have been a recipe for sleep, but his mind was running a million miles a minute. David had actually asked him to move in. Not just for one night or a weekend. No, the man with the navy-blue eyes wanted to live with him and Samuel.

Jonathan had moved away from his family and across the country in pursuit of David. And not just one time. He'd done it when he'd finished high school and then again after Sam was born. Because something deep inside had told him he was meant to be with the blue-eyed man. Being with David was literally the only goal Jonathan had ever had for himself, the only one he'd ever pursued. That was, until he'd held Sam for the first time, and then he had one other goal—to be a good father. Jonathan had done that in every way he knew how, but he'd had to go it alone and with very few resources. So, to that point, Sam had spent his life living either in a tiny one-room apartment in New York or sharing Jonathan's childhood bedroom. And they couldn't continue living with Jonathan's parents forever; it was just a temporary arrangement until Jonathan got on his feet and...into another tiny apartment because, he had to face it, that was all he'd be able to afford.

So was there any doubt that he'd accept David's offer to move in? After all, moving himself and Samuel into that fairy-tale house, building a life with that kind, smart man, those were sure ways to accomplish everything he'd ever wanted for himself and his son. So, no, there wasn't a doubt that he'd accept the offer. The only question was how he was going to tell David about his past. He owed it to the wonderful man offering him the dream, he owed David the truth. And he'd give it to him.

But first, he'd give him breakfast. It was past seven, and he figured David would be waking up soon. He slipped out of bed, threw on some clothes, and walked over to the kitchen. Thirty minutes later, eggs were whisked with cream and shredded cheese in a measuring cup, bacon was spread on a plate, ready to be fried, soda bread was sliced, and potatoes were grated. It wouldn't take more than ten minutes to get everything cooked and onto plates. After covering the ingredients with foil and putting them in the fridge, Jonathan made his way back to the dark bedroom.

David was lying on his side, breathing heavily, with the comforter pulled over his body and up to his shoulders. A sharp need shot through Jonathan—the need to touch and be touched, the need to share and learn and dream, and the need to do all of those things with the man in that bed. *I'll just tell him about my past later.*

CHAPTER TWENTY-TWO

JONATHAN STRIPPED off his clothes, leaving them in a pile on the floor, and slid underneath the comforter. David reached for him in his sleep, muttering unintelligible words and pulling Jonathan's body up tight against him.

"Mmm, c'mere, baby." A leg draped over Jonathan's hip and an arm wrapped around his body, holding Jonathan against David's chest. "You feel so good. Never wanted to touch anybody like I wanna touch you."

That deep voice was rough with sleep, dark stubble covered David's cheeks and neck, and his hard dick pressed against Jonathan's thigh. Damn, was he ever sexy. Jonathan pushed David's hand down until it covered his hard cock.

"Rub me."

David groaned and moved his hand slowly up and down Jonathan's shaft while he nuzzled Jonathan's neck and humped his cock against his thigh. All the while, he chewed his way around Jonathan's jaw and mumbled with his husky voice.

"You're different from anyone I've ever known. The way you make me feel is different. So good. Never knew it'd feel so good. Hoped, always hoped, but never knew."

Jonathan wasn't sure what David meant; he wasn't even sure whether David was fully awake or whether his words were bits and pieces of dreams, his subconscious seeping out. It didn't matter. Even without understanding the exact meaning or the details, Jonathan grasped the sentiment: David wanted him. That was enough. No, it was more than enough; it was everything to Jonathan.

David moved his hand from Jonathan's hard dick and caressed Jonathan's back, making his way down to his tight ass with light touches. He rubbed and stroked the cheeks while nibbling on Jonathan's neck and ears. Soon those long, thick fingers made their way into Jonathan's cleft and rubbed over his entrance.

"I want in here so bad," David breathed into his ear.

Jonathan moaned and flipped onto his stomach, tucking his knees underneath his body and spreading them as much as possible to the sides, leaving himself as open as he could.

David gasped and raised himself to his knees behind Jonathan. He ran his hands over the smooth skin in front of him.

"You're beautiful. So incredibly hot. Oh, God, I...I need to taste you."

Such an uncharacteristic need, not something he'd ever wanted to do or even something he'd found to be a turn-on in stories from friends or porn. But he was salivating at the thought of it. He caressed Jonathan's ass again, then cupped each cheek in a hand, spread them apart, and leaned down, swiping his tongue up the length of the cleft.

Jonathan cried out in surprise and pleasure, and that reaction motivated David more. David pulled Jonathan up so his ass was higher, wrapped one arm around him to keep him steady and fisted Jonathan's cock. His free hand remained on that perfect ass, spreading it open while his tongue made quick work of circling that twitching hole and stabbing into it as deep as he could go.

"Oh God! David, what, oh my God!"

Jonathan's body was shaking, and his words sounded as if they were spoken through tears, as if he was becoming completely undone by David's actions. The blanket was pooled down by Jonathan's legs at the height of David's cock so when his hips began bucking reflexively, he brushed his cock against the cotton, providing just enough friction to make him moan. That moan was muffled against Jonathan's skin, because David had gone from quick darts with his tongue to full swipes outside and inside Jonathan's body.

"Please, please, tiger. Oh, please!"

He knew what Jonathan wanted—him. Jonathan wanted him. Needed him to find the release he craved. He'd reduced Jonathan to a shivering, whimpering, begging pile of need. And that made David feel like the most powerful, desirable man around. He took another deep swipe inside that ass and watched his saliva drip down the cleft and glisten on Jonathan's skin.

"Please what? Say it. I want to hear you say it."

"Uhh!" Jonathan moaned and moved his head from side to side, pressing his face against the pillow. "In me...fill me...help me. Ugh, please!"

Good enough. David kneeled behind that perfect, lean body, lined his cock up to the glistening hole, and pushed in hard with one sure stroke. Jonathan shouted out, screamed David's name, raised his head, arched his back, and fisted the sheets.

"Fuck yes! Yes, yes, yes."

David moved in and out of that body, feeling the friction of their mating, listening to Jonathan's cries of "Oh, God" and "Yeah, yeah, yeah." Sweat dripped from his forehead onto Jonathan's back, his grunts got louder and more animalistic, his fingers dug into Jonathan's hips, sure to leave bruises, and his pace became harder, faster, almost vicious.

"Gonna, gonna! David, David, David!"

That tight passage squeezed around him, Jonathan cried out his name, and David's hips jerked and snapped a couple more times before he felt his body turning inside out and he shot deep inside that willing body. It was only after his breathing had returned to normal and he pulled himself out of Jonathan's channel that he realized what he'd done. No lube and no condom.

Oh shit. His heart started racing, and not in the good way from earlier. He rubbed his eyes, willed himself to relax, and rolled Jonathan onto his side, tucking himself around that relaxed body.

"Baby?"

Jonathan shivered and pressed back against him. David flipped the blanket up with his foot, reached down to grasp the end of it, and pulled it over their bodies. He cradled Jonathan in his arms.

"Jonathan? Did I hurt you?"

"Thank you." Jonathan's voice was soft and dreamy. "You're amazing. So amazing. You make me feel so good, tiger."

David's already decimated heart melted.

"That's all I want. Listen, baby, I'm clean. I have a test in the filing cabinet in the other room from about six months ago, and I haven't been with anyone in over a year."

"'Kay."

"No, you don't understand. I sorta forgot to use a condom, so you really need to know. I'm sorry."

"'S okay. I'm clean too. Don't think I kept copies of my tests, but it's been about three years for me. I can go get tested today so you won't have to worry."

David was so relieved Jonathan wasn't angry. He hadn't been worried about his own safety; he'd been on the safer side of that transaction. Plus, he'd gathered Jonathan didn't have much experience, and that whatever he'd had likely took place long before. But he'd been concerned that Jonathan wouldn't take kindly to going bareback without his permission. Hell, most guys would throw a fit. Rightly so.

"We'll both get tested. We can go to the EC West HIV/ AIDS Center this morning. They're open Saturdays, and they have the ten-minute test."

Jonathan turned and buried his face in David's neck. He wrapped his arms around David and clung to the large, muscular body. Firm fingers cupped his chin and tilted it up to that gorgeous mouth. Damn, David could kiss him into a stupor; he was all tongue and teeth, gnawing and sucking on Jonathan until he was completely breathless.

"So no more condoms?"

David chuckled and stroked that thick, black hair.

"Guess we won't need them anymore, huh? It's just you and me now, right? No other guys."

"Thank goodness." Jonathan's voice was full of relief and joy.

DAVID DRIFTED off back to sleep, and when he woke again, the bed was empty. His first thought was that he'd dreamt the previous evening. He'd been thinking of Jonathan almost nonstop since the day they'd met, and that certainly included vivid nocturnal fantasies. But his sore cock and soiled sheets told him that he'd experienced the real Jonathan that night, so where was he?

He used the bathroom, brushed his teeth, and wandered into the kitchen, where he was greeted by delicious smells. After enjoying the food Jonathan had left in his fridge all week, David was excited to see what was waiting for him that morning.

Jonathan heard David come in and made his way over for a kiss. "Morning. You hungry?"

David nuzzled his neck and gave him a little bite. "Always. What'd you make?"

Jonathan pointed David to a seat at the counter and started putting food onto a paper plate. "Nothing special— eggs, bacon, hash browns. Want some orange juice?"

David was salivating in anticipation of his meal. "I don't think I have any juice."

Jonathan walked over to the fridge and wrenched it open with a grunt. "I brought OJ with me."

David was looking wistfully at his meal, but he hadn't touched his fork.

"You're not waiting for me, are you? Go ahead and eat."

That was all the encouragement David needed to dig in. Jonathan joined him a minute later. They sat side by side and ate in companionable silence, nudging each other's legs every so often and laughing. After they finished eating every last bite of food Jonathan had made for breakfast, David threw away their plates and plastic ware and turned to Jonathan with a triumphant smile.

"See how easy cleanup is when you don't have to wash?"

Jonathan got up and stepped into David's embrace.

"I broke two plastic knives trying to spread butter on my toast. Those plates leave moisture rings on the counter. And..."

Jonathan was distracted by the feeling of wetness between his cheeks. He shifted his stance and tightened his sphincter muscle.

"You okay?"

David was looking down at him, wondering why he'd stopped in mid-sentence.

Jonathan bit his lip, feeling embarrassed, but not knowing how to get out of answering the question.

"Yeah, I'm fine. Just, ehm, feel a little, um, my rear end feels a little..."

A concerned expression etched itself in David's face and he reached down to Jonathan's ass and softly moved his hand over his sweats.

"Are you sore? Did I hurt you? You don't have a fissure, do you?"

Jonathan shook his head and buried his face in David's chest. He shouldn't be ashamed of this. The man had had his tongue in Jonathan's bottom, for goodness' sake! This was no big deal.

"I can feel you leaking out of me," Jonathan confessed.

He was speaking quietly and mumbling against David's shirt, so the taller man couldn't hear him well. He gently raised Jonathan's chin, ready to ask him to repeat himself, when the words finally registered. His dick immediately hardened and he lost his breath.

"Did you say you could feel my cum leaking out of your ass?"

Jonathan nodded and David gasped.

"That is so fucking hot. Can I touch?"

He wasn't sure why David was turned on by his revelation, but the hard dick pressing against him immediately caused a similar reaction in Jonathan's groin. He nodded, and David slipped his hand in the back of Jonathan's pants, running two fingers in his crease and pressing one into his hole.

"Jesus! It's wet. I can feel it. Never done anyone bare— it's so hot." Another finger joined the first and David thrust them in and out of Jonathan's ass. "I need to take you again. Right now. Please, Jonathan, I...I..." He swallowed hard, groaned, and increased the pace of his fingers.

Jonathan grasped David's arm. "Stop." David tried to continue the finger-fucking. "David, stop."

Horrified that he might have taken unwanted liberties with Jonathan's body, David pulled his fingers out of that tight ass. Jonathan immediately pushed his pants down, turned around, and bent over the counter. He looked over his shoulder at David, his silver eyes hot with lust.

"Come on, take me. Feel yourself deep inside."

David's heart raced. In less than a second, he had his sleep pants down around his ankles and his cock pushing its way into Jonathan's chute, aided by his own cum from earlier that morning. He rested one hand on Jonathan's shoulder and another on his hip while he pumped in and out of that hot cavern. David gritted his teeth with the effort it took to prolong the pleasure. He grunted and moaned while he plowed that hungry hole.

"Ungh, ungh, ungh."

David's sounds were an aphrodisiac for Jonathan, who managed to squeeze his hand between his body and the counter so he could rub his cock. He let the pounding of David's body push him through his own fist. The pummeling he received was so hard Jonathan had to raise himself up on his tiptoes to take it. Within minutes, David's moans turned into loud yells, and he leaned down and growled into Jonathan's ear.

"Gonna fill you again. So deep, ungh, so fucking deep. Take it, baby. Oh, God! Take it."

One more deep push and David was spasming inside him, shooting into his body once again. Jonathan was pressed against the counter with such strength that he couldn't move his hand. Desperate for release, he whimpered, getting David's attention. Still catching his breath, David gently pulled out, slipped to his knees, turned Jonathan around, and went down on his hard prick.

Jonathan fisted David's hair and thrust into his mouth, crying out his release within moments. His body was trembling when David pulled his mouth off his dick, kissed the head, then stood back up and wrapped his arms around Jonathan, holding him tight.

"Shit, that was something." David's voice was husky. "Not sure how we went from talking about cleanup to that, but this definitely wins the award for best breakfast ever."

Jonathan nodded and leaned on David for support. They held each other, rubbing backs and exchanging soft kisses while their bodies calmed. Eventually, the two men headed for the bedroom. Jonathan picked his clothes from the previous night up off the floor and set them next to his backpack, then stripped off his sweats and shirt and added them to the pile.

"Tell me what equipment we need to buy for the kitchen, so you can cook whatever you want. We can go shopping this morning. We also need to check out the cabinets and appliances Caleb picked for the kitchen remodel."

"Caleb's your decorator friend?"

"Interior designer. If you call him a decorator, he'll bite your head off."

Jonathan laughed. "We should throw your sheets in the wash right now and then we'll be able to get them in the dryer before we have to leave to meet your friend."

David was standing behind Jonathan, leering at his naked body.

"Um, yeah, that's a good idea. Stripping the bed, I mean. We can just put the sheets in the hamper. I have a clean set in the hall closet."

Jonathan walked over to the bed and began removing pillows from the cases and the duvet from its coverlet. "We may as well throw these in the wash." He made a pile on the floor while he spoke. "Where's your laundry room?"

David tried to shake off the lustful thoughts evoked by a naked Jonathan bent over his mattress, pulling off sheets. At that angle, he could see Jonathan's entrance, glistening with his seed. Nothing had ever been more arousing.

"It's off the kitchen, but I don't do laundry. I take everything to Fluff and Fold."

Jonathan turned around with sheets bunched in his arms.

"Seriously? You don't cook *and* you don't wash your own clothes?"

Was that unusual? David nodded. Jonathan squatted down and scooped up the rest of the linens from where he'd dropped them on the floor. He walked over to David and pushed the pile of bedding into his arms.

"Well, with three of us living here, there's going to be a lot more laundry and there's absolutely no reason we can't do it ourselves. Since it's clear I'm going to be the one responsible for meals, what with your severe kitchen allergy and all, you're going to have to be in charge of laundry. May as well start now."

He gave David a firm look.

David cleared his throat and answered apologetically.

"I, um, I don't have any detergent." He bit his lip and

added quickly, "But we can get some today." Then the rest of Jonathan's words sunk in, and he dropped the sheets and lifted Jonathan up with a full-body hug. "You're moving in?"

Huh…Jonathan hadn't realized that he'd completely finalized his decision. The words had just slipped out. Oh well, he figured he'd ultimately come to that conclusion anyway. No way would he be able to stay away from David when his whole body had been screaming "He's the one!" from the moment he'd first seen him all those years ago. Why prolong the wait? Besides, who could resist the pure joy that spread over David's absurdly perfect face when he heard Jonathan agreeing to move in? "Yeah, we are. When do you want us?"

CHAPTER TWENTY-THREE

NINETY MINUTES later, the two men were standing in front of a kitchen design store, waiting for David's decorator—strike that, his *designer* friend. A black Hummer H-1 tore into the parking lot and squealed into two parking spaces. The door flew open and a thin man wearing low-slung tan pants, a lavender cashmere sweater, and a matching scarf jumped out. He reached into the vehicle, reemerged with a leather attaché case, and sashayed over to Jonathan and David.

"Sorry I'm late, David. I got stuck behind a lady who had stuffed reindeer antlers adhered to the doors on both sides of her sedan and a Guinness-Book-of-World-Records-sized stuffed animal collection squeezed into the back window. Snoopy, Tweety, Taz, Daffy, Daisy, Bugs, they were all there. Damn things were so crowded it looked like Odie was doing Garfield doggy style. And she was driving slow enough that we got lapped by an old lady in a wheelchair." Without taking any time to catch his breath, Caleb raised his sunglasses off his face and onto the top of his head, gave David an air kiss, and reached his hand out to Jonathan. "I'm Caleb Lakes, and you must be the fabulous man who finally mobilized David to do something about his kitchen. I've been nagging for years, but I've gotten nowhere. Maybe you can give me some tips later. Any man who can talk David into bed and into cabinets must be damn good at being convincing."

Jonathan flushed and dipped his head, clearly uncomfortable, so David took the attention off him.

"What's with the Hummer, Caleb? You plan on driving through a war zone after we're done here, or are you just set on doing way more than your part to speed up global warming?"

Caleb put his hand on David's arm and laughed brightly. "It belongs to a new guy I'm seeing. I stayed at his place last night and he drove, so I didn't have my Audi." He turned and looked back at the vehicle with a frown. "It's ridiculously huge, isn't it?"

David nodded and patted Caleb on the back. "Yeah, it is. Sorry about his ridiculously small penis."

Jonathan coughed out a shocked laugh and looked at Caleb with concern, but the man just sighed knowingly, walked over to the showroom door, and threw his hand up in the air.

"Yeah, it sucks, but so does he, and that's enough for me to stick it out for a while. Honestly, why a man with his, ehm, condition would want to advertise it by owning such an obvious compensation vehicle is beyond me. Anywho, you ready to look at cabinets?"

AFTER TWO hours in the store, they settled on cherry cabinets, soapstone countertops, and stainless steel appliances. Jonathan had been quiet the entire time, his shyness exacerbated by Caleb's extremely outgoing personality. When Caleb laid out pictures of all the final products in front of them, David took Jonathan into his arms, drew him close, and spoke softly to him.

"You good with all of this? It's what you want?"

Jonathan nodded and inhaled David's calming scent.

"You're the one in charge of meals, remember? So make sure this works, and I'll put all my focus on a new washer/dryer. Well, that is if we *need* a new washer/dryer. I guess I should check if the set that came with the house works first. Think you can teach me how to use it?"

That lightened the mood and gave Jonathan the laugh David had been hoping to evoke.

"The cabinets and countertops are beautiful. I like the appliances too, but I think the kitchen is big enough to hold a double oven and a six-burner cooktop."

"I have no idea what that means, but let's get those." David turned to Caleb. "Did you catch that, Caleb?"

Caleb was gaping at them. "I'm sorry, I don't know whether I heard that correctly or if I was overly distracted imagining the two of you naked. Did you just say he's in charge of meals? Is he moving in with you?"

David beamed and rubbed circles on Jonathan's back.

"Yeah, he is. Next weekend, so he'll be there for

Christmas."

"Holy, hell! Where'd I leave my hand basket?"

"ALL RIGHT, what's next on our agenda for today?" David asked as they were pulling out of the design store parking lot.

Jonathan reached for David's hand and twined their fingers together.

"Laundry detergent and STD tests. Wow, aren't we obsessed with cleanliness?"

David laughed. "The Center isn't far from here and they do walk-ins. Let's go there first and check that off the list. I want as much time as possible to focus on the laundry. I'm beyond excited about it."

"Ha ha."

When they walked into the EC West HIV/AIDS Center, they were greeted by a man who looked like nobody Jonathan had ever seen, even after having lived in New York for three years. His light blond hair was cut short to the scalp on both sides, with sideburns in the same length reaching all the way down to his jawline. The hair in the center of his head was several inches high and spiked in a bright blue Mohawk. His left eyelid had a bar pierced through it and his right ear had a spike through the lobe and studs all along the perimeter. A huge tattoo of two male symbols took up the entire bottom of his left forearm and his right forearm had the word "Pride"

tattooed on it. The ink peeked out from under a black shirt
he had pushed up to his elbows. On top of that long-sleeved
shirt, he was wearing a blue T-shirt with black block printing
reading, "Come out of your log cabins."

"Hey, David! Long time no see, guy."

The pierced man got up from behind the desk where
he was sitting and gave David a one-armed hug. Jonathan
noticed that he was as tall as David, but without the rippling,
broad build. He turned to Jonathan and licked his lips, showing
a metal ball in his tongue.

"Who's your friend, David? He looks delicious."

David immediately put his arm around Jonathan's
waist and pulled him tightly to his side. Jonathan almost
laughed at the possessive move, but it made him so hot that
his mouth went dry and he had to concentrate on swallowing.

"This is my partner, Jonathan Doyle. Jonathan, meet
Dr. Andrew Thompson."

The silver bar in the pierced eyebrow reached upward.

"Partner, huh? That's interesting. Hey, I got new metal.
Apadravya. You boys want to see it?"

Andrew's hands went to the buckle on the metal-
studded belt holding up his paint-splattered skinny jeans.
David winced and held his hand out in the universal sign for
stop.

"Just the knowledge that it's there is enough, Andrew.
We came in to get tested and we're in kind of a hurry."

Andrew clicked the stud in this tongue against his

teeth. "Sure thing. You can head back to room one, David. And, Jonathan, you can head back to room two, I'll come poke you in a sec." He waggled his eyebrows and chuckled.

David took Jonathan's hand and walked to the rooms, grumbling under his breath, "Was that supposed to be a joke? It's not that funny."

Jonathan bit his lip and held back his laughter. David was actually jealous. Jealous over him. There was absolutely no chance of Jonathan so much as looking at another guy now that he finally had David, so was it wrong to be a little giddy because his man seemed to be concerned? It was just so nice to be wanted. David's little growls and glares at Andrew made Jonathan feel noticed and important.

"I'll be right next door, 'kay?" David stroked Jonathan's cheek and gazed at him. "You're stunning."

Jonathan blushed and pushed himself against David's chest, throwing his arms around David's waist and holding on tight. David returned the hug and surrounded Jonathan with bulging biceps and hard pecs.

"You feel bigger."

David kissed Jonathan's head. "I've been working out a lot more than usual these past few weeks. Need a way to wear myself out so I'm too tired to be frustrated that you aren't with me at the end of the day." He cleared his throat and continued speaking in a lower voice. "Is it too much?"

Jonathan ground his hard dick against David and stroked his hard chest reverently. "I like it. Your body is amazing."

"All right, boys, let's get you into your rooms and get started."

David bent down and pressed his lips to Jonathan's. He nibbled on his lower lip and caressed his ass, not stopping until Jonathan practically melted against him. Only then did he pull back, look meaningfully at Andrew, and strut into room one. Andrew rolled his eyes, grasped Jonathan's arm, and pulled his limp body into an empty room.

"Let's go, cutie."

He led Jonathan to a chair, then closed the door. Jonathan's eyes were still hazy with lust, but the needle poking his finger snapped him out of it. Forty minutes later, he'd been given the all clear, along with a counseling session on safe sex.

"So are we done here?" He smiled at the most unconventional-looking doctor he'd ever seen and started rising to his feet. "Because David's waiting."

"Yeah, we're done. Well, the official part of our discussion is over."

Jonathan didn't know what that meant, but he focused on the "done" and the "over" and opened the door. Andrew put his hand on Jonathan's shoulder and cleared his throat. When Jonathan turned, Andrew dropped his hand and started talking.

"So, how serious are things with you and David?"

Jonathan blushed. How was he supposed to answer

that question without sounding like a love-struck thirteen-year-old girl?

"Serious."

Andrew clicked his tongue ring against his teeth a couple of times, sighed deeply, then continued talking.

"Look, it's not like it's my business or anything, and I swear I'm not trying to pick you up. But you should know that David's not really the commitment type." He groaned. "I'm not saying he's going to cheat on you or anything. He won't do that. It's just... Fuck, the way you look at him, I can tell you're a total goner. You seem like a nice kid, and if you're looking for something long-term and serious, you might want to reconsider. We run in the same circle, and I work with one of his exes, which means I know a bit about a few others, too, and they tend to walk away pretty broken-hearted."

"He's not going to break my heart."

Jonathan was surprised at how strong and sure he sounded—it was so unlike him. But he was absolutely certain things with David would work out. They had to. Because Jonathan just *knew* he was meant to be with the blue-eyed man. He'd known it from the first moment he'd laid eyes on David.

Dr. Thompson gave him a pitying look, as if he was a naïve child who had no idea what was coming, but he didn't say anything else. When Jonathan turned back around and stepped out of the room, he found David waiting right outside the open door.

"I won't, you know." David's voice was somber. Jonathan raised his eyebrows in question. "Break your heart. I won't break your heart."

Jonathan beamed at him, put his hands on David's shoulders, and raised himself onto his tiptoes for a kiss. David leaned down and brushed their lips together. He pushed Jonathan's hair off his forehead and smiled gently at the man who'd come to mean so much to him in such a short period of time. His heart hurt with the power of the feelings flowing through him, and he knew of only one way to relieve that pain.

"I love you, Jonathan."

"Love you too," Jonathan mumbled against his lips.

"Well, damn! I've always prided myself on being shock-proof, but you got me." Andrew's voice interrupted their kiss. The two men separated and looked at the green eyes watching them with amusement. "I'm guessing you heard what I said, David. So consider this me swallowing my words."

David laughed. Andrew got closer, put one arm around David's shoulder and used the other to give him a noogie.

"Are we good or do you want to hug it out?" He pulled back and held his open arms out to David. "Come on, let's hug it out, bitch."

David snickered. "We're good, asshole. But only because Tim and Frank pointed out that I may have been a bit of bastard in past relationships. Oh, and also because, despite your increasingly more ridiculous personal appearance, I know you're not the type to try to break people up, so I do believe you were just trying to look out for my guy."

"I look ridiculous? I don't know where you find shirts to fit around those tree trunks you have masquerading as arms. I'm surprised your veins haven't exploded yet, Popeye."

David smiled but it didn't reach his eyes. He held Jonathan's hand in one of his and put the other on Andrew's shoulder. "How are you, Andrew? Can't help but notice that you're working on a Saturday."

Andrew squeezed David's hand. "Hey, people appreciate the extended hours."

"You have staff, Andrew. And an MD isn't required to do testing," David answered dryly.

"Keith called in sick."

"And you were the only person available to fill in?"

The colorful man sighed and looked down at his hemp shoes.

"What do you want me to say, David? I work weekdays at the hospital and I'm not on call this weekend, so today my options are this place, home wallowing in self-pity, or chemical assistance. I'm choosing work." Andrew cleared his throat and looked back up, a determined glint in his eye. "I take the Goldberg depression test every day. If I see a real indication for concern, I'll handle it."

"You have friends, Andrew. You don't need to handle this by yourself. We're here."

Andrew nodded, but even Jonathan could tell he was just doing it to appease David. He practically pushed them the rest of the way to the clinic's door. David sighed in resignation.

"For a guy with a one-sixty IQ, you can be a real idiot, Andrew."

The doctor opened the door and held it open, making his intentions clear, but his smile took the heat away from his actions.

"It's one-sixty-five, David. And it was nice seeing you." He reached his free hand out to Jonathan. "And it was great meeting you, Jonathan. I'm sure I'll see you around."

Jonathan waited until they were in the car with the doors closed before indulging his curiosity.

"So what's the story with Dr. Thompson?"

David sounded sad when he answered.

"Andrew's a good guy. Wild, but good. He's some sort of a Doogie Howser. Graduated college before he turned eighteen, went to medical school, the whole bit. His boyfriend passed away a while back from complications related to AIDS, and he just hasn't gotten over it."

Neither man talked for several minutes. Each was lost in his own thoughts. Then David reached over and took Jonathan's hand in his.

"So you love me?"

Jonathan nodded. "Uh-huh. I love you."

"I love you too." David grinned. "Feels good to say it."

Jonathan laughed. "Feels good to hear it."

CHAPTER TWENTY-FOUR

"KAIDEN, I told you not to put your muddy shoes on the kitchen counter!"

Brennan swung his door open and waved Jonathan and David in. He stomped away, and they heard his voice from the next room.

"Kaiden! I mean it. This might fly at your house, but it sure as hell isn't acceptable here."

"But I took the shoes off the counter, Uncle Brennan."

"The table isn't an acceptable location either, Kaiden. Take them off now."

David started laughing.

"So Shannon's kids stayed the night too?"

Brennan stalked back into the family room and crossed his arms.

"Go ahead and laugh, man. It's your turn to take the kids next weekend."

David froze in mid-laugh and swung his head toward Jonathan. His face showed his panic.

Jonathan shrugged. "Well, it's a babysitting share. Shannon and Keegan were last weekend, Brennan and Grace had this weekend, and I'm on deck for next weekend."

"But you're moving in next weekend." David was too disappointed to worry about the whine in his voice.

Brennan laughed almost hysterically and slapped Jonathan on the shoulder. "Oh, this is just too perfect. Ma and Pop have been trying to get you a pardon from the share because you're living at their place, but now there's no excuse."

Jonathan slipped his arms around David's waist and looked up at him with a nervous expression on his face. "Are you going to change your mind?"

"No!" David's voice was louder and more forceful than he'd intended. He lowered his voice and relaxed his body. "I'm not going to change my mind and I'm fine with taking turns in this babysitting share." Then he added, in a tone that did nothing to convince anyone, "It'll be fun."

Brennan grunted. "Fun. Right! Having Shannon's boys around is like taking hallucinogenic drugs. The only thing missing is me sitting on the floor of my childhood bedroom, playing Pink Floyd backward."

Just then a boy ran by waving some clothes, chased by a similar-looking boy wearing nothing but underwear. Brennan shouted after them.

"Keian, Keller! Freeze!"

Two identical faces turned around.

"What, Uncle Brennan?"

"What did I say about getting dressed?"

"You told us to get dressed because Papa's coming to

get us."

"Is Keian dressed?"

The two boys shook their heads in unison.

"Okay, then. Get dressed. Your pop should be here any second."

Brennan turned around, and Keller shrieked as he ran down the hall with Keian fast on his trail.

"You can't catch me! You can't catch me!"

Brennan covered his face with his hands.

"You heard me tell them to get dressed, right?"

"Uh-huh," Jonathan answered.

"And you heard them admit that they heard me?"

"Uh-huh."

"And then they kept running without Keian putting any clothes on?"

"Uh-huh."

Brennan threw his shoulders back and glared down the hallway.

"Okay, good. Just needed to confirm that the whole thing wasn't in my head. I'm gonna go crack some skulls. Sam's in the kitchen with Clare and Gracie. His bag's all packed, and he was a perfect angel. I'll see you guys later."

"SO, SAMUEL, did you have fun at your cousin's house?" David looked at Sam in the rearview mirror as they pulled away from Brennan's townhouse.

"Uh-huh. 'Twas fun. We had candy and popped tarts and asghetti and chick nuts."

David bit his lip to keep himself from laughing. "That sounds like lots of eating. What else did you do?"

"Umm. We colored and played hidagoseek."

Jonathan smiled at David and clasped his hand. Then he turned toward the backseat and looked at his son.

"I'm glad you had a good time, dumpling."

"Are we going to David's house now, Papa? I wanna watch Diego on his big TV."

David positively beamed. The previous weekend, when Sam had woken from his nap in David's living room, he'd walked over to the couch and poked at David and Jonathan, waking both of them and asking to watch television. David had found one of Sam's favorite shows on his On-Demand television service, and Sam thought he was a hero.

"What do you say, tiger? You up to having us over for a couple of hours before we have to get home to go to bed?"

"Are you kidding? I'm up to having you over forever, starting right this second. Why even bother going back to your folks' house?"

Jonathan gave David a soft smile and answered quietly, "I need to talk to Sam, explain that we're moving, and make sure he has his things. He doesn't even have a bed at your place, David. He can't spend the whole night on a pile of blankets on the floor."

David's posture slumped and his face fell. "Yeah, okay. I understand. Soon, though. Okay? I need you to be with me, baby." They stopped at a light, and David turned to Jonathan and caressed his cheek. "I know it doesn't make sense because we haven't known each other that long, but I feel like I've been waiting for you forever. Don't want to wait anymore. I want you home, with me."

When Jonathan left David's house later that evening, David pressed a key into his hand.

"It's my spare key. I'll have another one made tomorrow. But I want to make sure you have this in case you end up wanting to move in early or something. This is home now, 'kay?"

"Okay. I want this too, tiger. More than anything. Thank you."

Jonathan reached up and kissed David's cheek. He couldn't believe he was actually reassuring his dream man about his feelings. Didn't David realize Jonathan was ass over teakettle in love with him? But he couldn't move in without telling David about his past.

He'd been telling the truth earlier that evening when he'd said he wanted to talk to Sam and make sure things with his son were in order before moving in. But that wasn't the only conversation he needed to have. He also had to talk to David. His parents didn't usually have plans on Sundays, so maybe they'd be able to watch Sam for a few hours the next day and he could go over to David's house to talk.

DAVID WOKE up the next morning, skated his hand over the cold sheet next to him and sighed. *A week from now, he'll be here with me. Just a week. That's no time.*

He stumbled into the bathroom, stripped off his sleep pants, and got into the shower. The warm water felt good splashing over his body. He reached for the soap and lathered up, enjoying the slippery glide on his skin, over his chest and stomach, on his cock. He gave himself a few strokes, feeling his member plump up from the attention. But he wasn't really into it. Not without Jonathan there. He slumped against the shower wall, resting his forehead on the tile. *One more week without him. That feels like forfuckingever.*

As David dried himself and dressed, he thought about what Jonathan had said. He needed to talk to Sam. Okay fine, what was that, like a five-minute conversation? David had spent enough time with Samuel to know he was unlikely to last even that long before becoming distracted with a meal, a show, or a game. So why couldn't Jonathan move in that evening? It wasn't like he had furniture or anything; he was staying at his folks' house. Furniture. He'd said Sam needed a bed. Always happy to have a plan and something within his control, David straightened and felt lighter.

I'll go buy a bed for Sam today. That way they can sleep over here. No reason to wait until next weekend.

He made the ten-minute drive to downtown EC West and parked outside the restaurant where he was meeting his friends for their weekly brunch. David had missed the previous couple of weeks because he'd been with Jonathan and Sam. Between work and time with Jonathan, David had been pretty out of pocket, so some of his friends didn't even know he was dating anyone. And he hadn't told anyone other than Caleb that the silver-eyed beauty was moving in.

Oh well, they'd meet Jonathan soon enough. His infectious sweetness would endear Jonathan to everyone, even though he did seem to be quite shy whenever someone other than David was around. He'd barely spoken to Caleb when they were shopping for the kitchen remodel the previous day. Then again, Caleb was so outgoing and bubbly that there really wasn't much room for other people to speak up.

"Hey there, gorgeous. We've been talking about you." Tim smiled at David and waved him over to the empty seat next to him. "Were your ears burning?"

David sat next to Tim and suppressed a smile when he saw the expectant eyes staring at him from around the table. Clark was stroking the tattoo on the back of Noah's neck, keeping him calm and happy. Eli was holding hands with Seth and practically bouncing, obviously thrilled that he'd finally settled down with the other man after years of courting (or begging, depending on your viewpoint). Frank was sitting next to Tim with his arms crossed over his wide chest and one eyebrow raised expectantly, waiting for David to talk.

Andrew sipped his water and stayed quiet. David knew the tattooed doctor well enough to guess that he hadn't said a thing about Jonathan to the group. Despite being brash and outspoken, Andrew was incredibly sensitive and he absolutely never gossiped. That fact was the primary reason David hadn't been angry when he'd overheard Andrew warning Jonathan about him. Andrew would never have done that for any reason other than genuine concern for Jonathan.

Caleb wasn't there yet, so unless he'd sent out a mass text (which wasn't out of the question), nobody knew that Jonathan was moving in with David. That meant their conversation had likely related to David's discussion with Tim and Frank and their brief introduction to Jonathan. David was trying to decide how to play the situation. Should he act confused, as though he had no idea why he was the topic of conversation? Should he pretend to be offended that they'd been talking about him behind his back? Should he pick up his menu and act nonchalant, brush the whole thing off as if he didn't care?

"I met someone. His name is Jonathan Doyle. He's sweet and funny, and I'm in love with him. He's moving in this week, so you'll all get to know him really well."

Huh, that little speech wasn't on his internal list of possible responses. Oh well, that was how he felt. He grinned at the shocked faces around the table. Eli started coughing uncontrollably, and Seth patted his back. When he got himself together, he dried the tears from his eyes and looked at David in shock.

"Moving in? How long have you known this guy, David?"

"Three weeks," David replied calmly, reaching for his water glass.

"Holy fuck. Who moves in with someone that quickly? Well, other than lesbians, that is."

The entire table rumbled with laughter. Seth turned to Eli and rested his hands behind Eli's neck. He raised his eyebrows in question and spoke in a teasing voice. "Really, Eli? You're saying it wasn't like that for us?"

Eli blushed, which was a rare occurrence for the confident man.

"I just moved in last month, and we've known each other for years."

Noah joined the conversation with a rumbling laugh and a slap to Eli's back.

"It took you so long to move in because Seth had his head up his ass. Don't try telling us you wouldn't have set up house in the man's shed the first time you met him if he'd have let you."

Seth raised his iced tea glass toward Noah in a toast. "Fuck you very much, Noah."

Tim laughed and clutched his heart dramatically. "Oh,

such nasty words coming from a member of the clergy. I'm appalled."

"Yeah, yeah," Seth replied with a straight face.

"You should see the nasty things he does when we're alone. It'd make your toes curl." Eli waggled his eyebrows, gave Seth a pointed leer, and dropped his hand under the table suspiciously.

Seth flushed and cleared his throat. "All right. All right. That's quite enough. This conversation has completely deteriorated. David, we're all happy for you and we can't wait to meet Jonathan."

"I've met him and I can guarantee you won't be disappointed." Caleb pranced over to the group, carefully arranged his jacket on the back of the empty chair next to Andrew, and sat down. "I had the pleasure of his company yesterday, and I can attest to the fact that Jonathan is a sweetheart."

"Yeah, right. A *sweetheart*." A voice David didn't recognize responded to Caleb's comment. The tone was sardonic, but the volume low. David probably wouldn't have heard him if the man hadn't been standing right behind David's chair.

He turned his head and saw Nick, the man who'd harassed Jonathan and then asked David if he was done with him. The guy was like a bad skin rash. He kept showing up unexpectedly and nothing could get rid of him. David was about to get up to tell the intruder to mind his own business, when Caleb pointed to an empty seat at the other end of the table without ever raising his eyes from the menu.

"You can sit there, Nick. Guys, this is Nick. Nick, these are my friends."

Well, if Caleb wasn't even bothering with names or making any effort to sit next to Nick, David guessed he wasn't really interested in the annoying man. He glared at Nick and willed him to go away. No luck. Damn that lack of paranormal powers. David turned to Caleb.

"Who's the Muscle Mary?"

Caleb rolled his eyes. "He's the Hummer. The vehicle, I mean, not the fun kind. Whatever, I'm over him. I tried to brush him off this morning, but he insisted on coming here for some reason. I'll tell him it isn't going to work out after we're done eating."

David enjoyed brunch with his friends, despite the annoying sneers Nick aimed his way from across the table. Eventually, he'd had enough and decided to excuse himself so he could go work out and then buy a bed for Samuel. He said his goodbyes and walked out of the restaurant.

"David, wait up. Hey, David!"

Why in the hell was Nick following him? David clenched his fists and turned around, willing himself to be patient. He plastered an obviously forced smile onto his face.

"What can I do for you, Nick?"

That maddening smirk made yet another appearance.

"Oh, it's not what you can do for me. It's what I can do

for you." Nick reached into his jacket and pulled out a disk, which he thrust at David. "Here."

David took the disk and looked at it. Plain silver with a handwritten note: *Will Dragon.*

"What is this?"

"It's a best-of compilation of that *sweet* boyfriend of yours. I knew you were friends with Caleb because I saw you in one of his pictures from that benefit last year, so I took a chance that you'd be at this brunch. That's why I came. I wanted to deliver this disk to you."

David looked at Nick with a blank expression on his face. He had absolutely no idea what the man was saying. The triumphant smile turned into frustration when Nick didn't get the response he'd clearly been seeking.

"It's porn. You said that I don't know how Will moves, but you're wrong. I've seen every movie he's been in. That's a disk of all his scenes. You'll note the dialogue is very minimal but the movements are plentiful."

Why was Nick giving him porn? And who was Will? Most of David's mind had already put the pieces together, but he had to ask.

"Who's Will?"

Realization dawned on Nick's face.

"Oh, right. *Jonathan.* That's what you call him right? But he's Will Dragon. I'd recognize him anywhere. A little older, maybe, but I know he's the same guy. When I get the chance to see him bare-assed and bent over, I'll be able to give you definitive confirmation."

Nick waited for David's reaction expectantly, but he didn't get it. David just turned on his heel and walked to his car without saying another word.

CHAPTER TWENTY-FIVE

JONATHAN LEFT Sam with his mother and drove over to David's house. He'd taken inventory of their belongings and knew he'd be able to pack everything in less than an hour. Pathetic, but true. And he had no doubt that Sam would be thrilled to move into David's house. His son talked about David all the time, and David was wonderful with him. Plus, there was the whole satellite television bonus, which to an almost-three-year-old was reason enough to choose a home. But Jonathan hadn't talked to Sam about moving in with David yet. He first needed to clear the air. David deserved the truth about Jonathan's past, even if it was late getting to him.

Jonathan rang David's doorbell and shifted from foot to foot nervously as he chewed on his nail. David's car was in the driveway, so Jonathan assumed he was home, but he wasn't answering the bell. After knocking and waiting another few minutes, Jonathan remembered he had a key to David's house. David's words as he had thrust the key into Jonathan's hand the previous morning rang in his head: *This is home now.* Jonathan fished his keys out of his pocket, unlocked the door, and let himself in.

"David?" Jonathan called out as he looked around.

There was no response. The house was quiet and none of the lights were on. Jonathan was starting to think that David was out, but then he heard the faint sound of water running. His head immediately filled with visions of David in the shower, water droplets running down his chest, every muscle gleaming with wetness. He groaned and walked toward the bedroom, unable to resist David's pull.

Jonathan noticed David's jacket thrown over the armchair in the living room as he was passing by, so he picked it up, thinking he'd hang it in the closet once he got to the bedroom. He flung the jacket over his shoulder, and something dropped out onto the floor. Jonathan squatted down, picked up the disk, and started putting it back in the jacket when he noticed the writing: "Will Dragon." Why did David have a disk with that name written on it? Jonathan's stomach dropped.

He knows. David knows. And Jonathan hadn't been the one to tell him, hadn't been able to explain. Oh, God. Had David *watched* the movies? Telling him about his old career was one thing. But actually seeing the things Jonathan had done, all those men. How could David forgive that?

Jonathan realized that David had dated other men before him, but he didn't let himself think about it. He wasn't naïve enough to expect to be the first person in his thirty-two-year-old boyfriend's life, but he didn't enjoy the fact. What would it be like to know that the number of men who came before was too high to count, and to have visual evidence of...well, those men coming on your boyfriend? How could Jonathan possibly expect David to accept this? What had he been thinking when he'd put off this conversation?

"Jonathan?"

Jonathan's head shot up, and he saw David standing in the doorway. At first he wasn't sure why David looked distorted, as if he was watching him through a fun-house mirror. But then he registered the wetness on his own face and realized he was looking at David through tears. Those blue eyes were as warm as ever, and David walked over to Jonathan, wrapped that strong arm protectively around his shoulder, and maneuvered them to the couch. David sat right next to Jonathan and cradled him in his arms. Then he looked at the disk Jonathan clutched in an iron grip.

"Want to tell me about it?" David's voice was soft and reassuring, and Jonathan could no longer hold anything back. Not his former career, not his tears, not anything.

"I was so stupid. It was just a couple of months. I wasn't thinking straight. I was lonely. Kathy had just told me she was pregnant with Sam, and I needed to decide whether I'd take him or we'd put him for adoption. And I couldn't find you, David. After that day in the hospital, I moved to New York to find you. But I looked and I looked, and I couldn't. I couldn't find you."

Jonathan knew he was babbling, but he didn't know how else to explain everything to David. Each sentence was broken up with tears and gasps until Jonathan's entire body shook and he clung to David.

"I didn't want you to see me like that. It's not who I am."

He looked up at David, tears streaking down his beautiful face and silver eyes pleading with him to understand. "I did those things, but it's not who I am. Do you know what I mean?"

David held Jonathan tightly and stroked his hair. "Shhh, baby. It's okay. I know who you are, Jonathan. I didn't play the disk and I won't unless you want me to. You can tell me what's on there or not. It's your choice and it won't change anything between us either way. I know who *you* are and I know how I feel about you. There's nothing on any disk anywhere that can change that."

David sounded so sincere and Jonathan desperately wanted to believe him. He almost did believe the man with the navy-blue eyes. But then he thought about David, about his kindness, his intelligence, his success in business, his large group of friends, his gorgeous house, his education. Jonathan thought about all of those things and wondered how a man like that could truly want a man like him.

He'd been cutting it close, anyway, but this latest development had to be too much. How could David tell him that playing bottom boy in two months' worth of gang-bang movies wouldn't make a difference? Unless, of course, David didn't truly know what was on the disk.

When Jonathan was able to stop crying, and when his

body was finally free of the hiccups and shudders that had racked him while his tears were falling, he braced himself to come forward with the truth. David deserved to hear it.

"David?"

"Yeah, baby."

"Do you, ehm, do you know who Will Dragon is?"

David held him even tighter and kissed his brow. "A pseudonym you used when you made movies."

Jonathan was surprised, but still certain that David didn't understand the nature of the movies.

"Do you...do you understand what I did in those movies?"

David rubbed circles on Jonathan's back. "It was porn so, yeah, I have a pretty good idea."

A cry escaped Jonathan's lips. He tried to be strong, put on a brave face.

"You don't have to stay with me, David. You didn't sign on for this. I know, ehm, I know you must be disgusted. That you don't want to be with someone who did those things."

David clasped Jonathan's shoulders and leaned back so he could look into his eyes. The pain and insecurity David saw in them nearly destroyed him.

"Oh, baby." David leaned down and kissed Jonathan gently. Then he rubbed his arms, petted his flank, and reached his hands under his sweatshirt and T-shirt. He caressed Jonathan's chest under that shirt, then lifted it over his head. Jonathan looked at him in confusion, but didn't say a word.

David reached down and covered Jonathan's lips with his own. He kissed him sweetly, taking Jonathan's lips between his own, nibbling on them, licking them, and eventually pushing his tongue between them. The taste of the kind, gentle man for whom he'd fallen so completely filled his mouth, and David moaned.

He devoured Jonathan's mouth, then pulled his tongue out and licked those bee-stung lips as he reached for Jonathan's loose jeans and yanked them off his waist. The silver eyes had gone from frightened to aroused, and David felt relieved that he'd taken the right approach. He dropped off the couch onto his knees, pulled Jonathan's shoes from his feet, then lowered his jeans the rest of the way down to his ankles and off his body.

Jonathan's trembling hands caressed David's hair, and the look of hope in those eyes called to David, made him want to prove to Jonathan once and for all how deeply he was loved and cherished. He placed each of Jonathan's legs on his shoulders, kissed Jonathan's inner thigh, and licked his way down to his testicles. The whimper-moans that David adored filled the air as he licked Jonathan's balls, and sucked them into his mouth.

"I know what you did in those movies, baby." David looked up at Jonathan and felt him tense, but then he continued. "And it doesn't change anything."

David took a second to make sure his words sank in. When he felt Jonathan's body relax, he clasped Jonathan's ass, pulled each of those hard globes apart, and buried his face in the cleft. He licked around the rosebud with quick darts, flattened his tongue and took long drags, covered it with his entire mouth and sucked, then pushed his tongue all the way in and fucked Jonathan with it. Jonathan grasped David's hair and screamed as his hips shot off the couch.

Like riding a bucking bronco, David stayed with that wiggling, thrusting body and kept his tongue steadily moving in and out of the dark cavern. After a few minutes of this treatment, David pushed a finger alongside his tongue into Jonathan's opening. He found the gland and massaged it as he swiped his tongue along the inner walls of Jonathan's chute.

"David! I...I... David, David, oh God! I'm gonna. Please, David."

Jonathan's incomprehensible sentence made David moan in satisfaction. He pushed his track pants down with one hand and yanked on his hard cock. His other hand moved away from Jonathan's ass and fisted his dick while his tongue continued to lick and fill Jonathan's ass. It didn't take long for Jonathan to shout as his dick pulsed and wet warmth covered David's hand. A few more tugs and David found his own release.

He wiped his hands on his pants and pulled them up. Then he crawled on the couch, pressed Jonathan onto his back, and covered his slender body with his larger frame. The tension had seeped out of Jonathan and he melted into David's embrace. David kept his touch constant, petting and gentling the man in his arms.

"Jonathan?"

"Uh-huh." Jonathan's voice was dazed and dreamy.

"What did you mean earlier when you said you moved to New York to find me?"

Jonathan sighed and looked up at David, meeting his gaze.

"That's exactly what I meant. I saw you there, David. That day in the hospital nursery, holding your nephew. I saw you. But then you were gone, so I couldn't talk to you. As soon as I graduated, I went back to find you. You're why I moved to New York. I was looking for you. All those years I searched in the wrong place. I moved away to find you, but you were here at home all along."

David's eyes widened in surprise. "Oh, baby, I'm so sorry." He held the precious man tightly.

Jonathan sniffed. "It's not your fault. You didn't do anything."

David knew that was true, but it didn't change his feelings. He'd give anything to go back and find that young Jonathan and take him home. Not because he had an issue with Jonathan's past, but because he could see that the actions from those days were now tearing the sensitive man up from the inside. And David wanted nothing more than to shield Jonathan from that pain, from all pain.

"I wish I could make it different, baby. I wish I'd have known you were looking for me back then."

Jonathan pulled back from their embrace and gazed at David.

"I don't."

David furrowed his brow and looked at Jonathan in confusion.

"Who knows what might have been, David? I wasn't happy for a long time. I felt like I was all alone, probably even before I moved to New York." He reached his trembling hand up and cupped David's cheek. "But I'm so happy now. If you can forgive what I did, then none of it matters. All the bad times brought us to this place, right now, and I don't want to be anyplace else."

Only Jonathan would take what were probably miserable years and accept them without any bitterness or resentment. The man saw nothing but silver linings. Damn, but David loved him.

"There's nothing to forgive, Jonathan. You didn't do anything wrong. Hell, I've watched my share of porn and I'm not exactly a virgin here. What kind of hypocrite would I be if I thought less of you for this?"

"Yeah?" Jonathan looked up at him with hope in his eyes.

David nodded. "Absolutely." He paused and then added, "There's just one thing, baby."

"What's that?" Jonathan worried his bottom lip between his teeth, showing his returning anxiety.

"From now on, any movies you make with your

clothes off will have a limited cast and audience consisting of two members. More specifically, the two of us. Deal?"

Jonathan beamed, picked up the disk, and snapped it in half. "Deal."

CHAPTER TWENTY-SIX

THE TALK had gone well. Jonathan was noticeably happier, more relaxed and confident. So David took the opportunity to try to expedite the moving process.

"So, I went bed shopping today."

The two men were sitting on the couch. Jonathan had his head on David's shoulder. David was petting Jonathan's hair.

"I thought you had brunch with your friends today."

"I did. After brunch I went to the gym and then hit the mall. I found a really nice furniture set that'll work well for Sam. The bed even has a trundle we can use when one of his cousins sleeps over. There's a matching dresser and nightstand. Plus, they had a madras plaid quilt that looked great with it, so I got that too. And the coordinating rug. Oh, and train sheets. Wanna see?"

Jonathan jerked his head off David's chest and stared at him.

"It's here? You mean you already went out and bought all of that?"

"You said you wouldn't move in until Sam had a bed, so I got Sam a bed. And it's not like he can sleep without bedding. Plus, he needs somewhere to put his clothes. The furniture is being delivered tomorrow, but, yeah, the rest of the stuff is here."

David got off the couch and pulled a stunned Jonathan with him.

"Come on." He led Jonathan down the hall to one of the side bedrooms. "I stashed it all in here but you can tell me which room you think he'd prefer. You know I don't use either of them."

Jonathan's eyes widened when he took in the number of bags filling the room. David pulled out the bedding and showed it to him. He was so excited, sitting on the floor and explaining how the colors in the train sheets he was holding in one hand matched the colors in the madras quilt he was holding in the other. Jonathan wiped tears from his eyes with the back of his hand and straddled David's lap.

"Hi."

"Hi, yourself." David smiled at him, little laugh lines showing at the corners of his eyes. Jonathan clasped his hands together behind David's neck.

"Thank you for doing all of this, David. You're amazing. I've never known anyone as generous as you."

David pulled Jonathan closer, sharing a tight hug.

"I had fun. I usually leave the decorating to Caleb, but this was really easy. The store wasn't very big, and they had vignettes showing the rooms all put together." He kissed Jonathan's neck. "I hope you don't mind, but I got some

Christmas presents for Sam while I was there. They had a train set that I think he'll really like, and some hand-painted wooden blocks."

Jonathan pressed his lips to David's and nibbled. He darted his tongue out for a taste. When David's head tilted to the side, Jonathan opened his mouth to make room for the tongue he knew was coming. The kiss deepened, hands clutched shirts, and moans filled the air. Eventually Jonathan pulled away and rested his forehead on David's shoulder.

"Wow. If that's the reaction I get for buying a train set, I can go back and do more shopping."

Jonathan laughed. "That's the reaction you get for being wonderful. I love you."

"Love you too, baby."

THE FURNITURE was delivered on Monday, and by Wednesday night Sam was tucked into his new bed. After turning off all the lights and locking up, David walked into the bathroom. He almost tripped at the sight that greeted him. Jonathan was standing at the sink, washing his face. He was wearing white gym socks and a white T-shirt. Nothing else. The shirt probably would've covered Jonathan past his ass, but because he was leaning over, it skated right at the edge of his cheeks, giving David an enticing view of a firm ass and swinging balls.

Jonathan raised his head and wiped his face with the

towel that was resting on the counter. He looked at David in the mirror and blinked the remaining water out of his eyes.

"What?"

David didn't say a word. He stalked toward Jonathan, his hands reaching for the button on his pants and then his zipper. By the time he reached Jonathan, his pants were open and he was freeing his dick from the confines of his boxer briefs.

"You'd better find something slick. Lotion, soap, I don't care. But I need in here and I can't wait."

David caressed Jonathan's cleft. Whether it was the touch, the words, or a combination of both wasn't clear, but suddenly Jonathan's breath quickened, his eyes widened, and his dick hardened. He pumped lotion onto his fingers from the bottle next to the sink and reached behind himself, spreading it around his pucker, and pushing some inside.

"Oh, oh, feels good." He moaned and closed his eyes.

David moved Jonathan's hands aside, cradled his right thigh and lifted it until Jonathan's knee was pushed out and up and perched on the counter, leaving him spread open and ready. Then he lined himself up with that eager opening and pushed his way in with a loud grunt.

"Damn, that's good. It's so good with you, baby."

Jonathan looked into the mirror and gasped at the reflection that met him. David was behind him, his hands gripping Jonathan's hips, his eyes closed, and his mouth open. He was pushing and pulling himself in and out of Jonathan's body; harsh sounds spilled from his mouth and passion was etched in every part of his face. He looked fierce, carnal, and sexy as hell.

"There, there! Oh, Christ, right there, David," Jonathan shouted and grunted. He kept one hand on the counter and wrapped the other around his hard cock, tugging in time with the thrusts of David's hips. It wasn't long before David's speed increased, his hips jerked and snapped, and then both men shouted out their pleasure as Jonathan saw white jets shoot from his cock while David emptied into him.

"Oh, wow," Jonathan whispered as aftershocks racked his body.

David wrapped his arms around Jonathan's chest and dropped kisses on his shoulders and neck.

"You turn me on like none other. Everything about you is so damn sexy." He closed his eyes and nuzzled Jonathan's neck. "I can't tell you how glad I am that you're here. Thanks for agreeing to move in with me, baby."

Jonathan dropped his head back against David's chest. "I'm glad too. You know, I fantasized about you for a lot of years. I never would have guessed that the real man could be better than my imagination, but you are."

"We have a real mutual admiration society here, don't we?" David laughed. "What do you say we get in the shower, then go to bed and do some more admiring under the sheets?"

Jonathan smiled at David in the mirror, then turned in his arms and gave him a squeeze.

"Good plan."

THE FIRST time anyone referred to David as a father was less than a week after Jonathan and Samuel moved in.

On Christmas Eve, David came home from work and felt, for the first time since he'd been a kid, like he was actually *home*. Upbeat children's music thumped out of the kitchen and a delicious cinnamon-vanilla smell filled the air. David slid his jacket off and draped it over his shoulder as he walked through the dining room. He reached the kitchen entryway and stopped, leaning against the wall and looking into the soon-to-be-remodeled space.

The counters were filled with cookie sheets holding dozens of holiday-shaped confections—snowmen, trees, ornaments, and snowflakes. A tree sat in the corner of the empty space adjoining the kitchen. Construction paper had been cut into strips that were glued together into connecting circles, creating a homemade garland that draped over the tree along with various ornaments made from cut-out paper. Presents wrapped in brown paper decorated with crayon drawings were stacked beneath it.

Jonathan was in the middle of the kitchen, dancing along to the music, wiggling his ass and moving his head from side to side. Samuel was on his hip, being held up by one of Jonathan's hands and clinging to his chest. Both of them were singing along to the music, using a wooden spoon Jonathan was holding in his free hand as a microphone.

When he was younger and occasionally, though less frequently, in recent years, David had gone clubbing with his friends. There had always been good-looking guys crowded on the dance floor. Some of them dressed in tight, provocative clothing, others closer to naked than clothed; all of them making their best attempt to look sexy. Hips swayed and ground, tongues darted out of mouths and licked lips sensually, hands roamed over chests and groins. But not one of those guys could compare to Jonathan, wearing sweatpants with frayed seams, a too-big T-shirt with a Dubliner logo on it, and white socks while holding his son and bebopping in the kitchen. Jonathan was breathtaking. Looking at him made David's heart soar, his skin tingle, and his cock ache.

Sam saw David in the doorway and squealed with glee.

"David!"

Jonathan shimmied over, kissed David soundly on the mouth, then wrapped the arm holding the spoon around David's waist and kept moving, bringing David into the dance. The three of them swayed around the kitchen, Samuel giggling, Jonathan singing. And just like that, David was home.

"ARE YOU up for going to my folks' house tonight or are you

too tired?"

Jonathan set Samuel down on the floor and the little boy ran out of the kitchen, holding a cookie.

"Of course I'm up for it. It's Christmas Eve and this is, like, a family tradition, right?"

"Mmm hmm. But you worked all day, so I thought you might be tired."

David sighed and drew Jonathan closer. He leaned down and kissed Jonathan's head, inhaling the fresh, clean scent of his hair.

"I'm sorry, baby. I promise I'm trying to slow down at work. It's just with me taking the rest of the week off, there were some end-of-the-year things I had to finish up."

"Don't apologize. I understand you have to work. But if you're not too tired to go to dinner, that'd be great."

"Not too tired. Looking forward to it," David replied with a kiss.

"Okay, then I'll box up these cookies and we can go. I have presents for Kaiden, Keian, Keller, and Clare stacked under the tree."

David forced himself not to laugh at the name tongue-twister.

"Yeah, I noticed those. Looks like you had a busy day. I like the decorations."

Jonathan blushed. "I know they're not fancy, but we had fun making them."

"They're perfect, baby."

After changing into jeans and a light sweater, David walked into Sam's room and found him lying on the rug, playing with the red and blue trains he carted around everywhere. He couldn't wait to see the little boy's face when he opened the new train set on Christmas morning. He squatted down next to Sam and tousled his hair.

"Ready to go to your Gram and Gramps's house, bud?"

Sam bounced up and grinned.

"Yeah, I'm ready. Can we do Superman?"

David laughed, stood up, and lifted Sam off the ground. The boy straightened his body and David rested one hand under his belly and the other around his waist as he walked down the hallway. Sam made "woosh" noises and held his hands in front of him the whole way.

"All right, Superman and I are ready to go. How about you, Jonathan?"

Jonathan picked up the box of cookies and smiled at David and Samuel. He loved how well they got along, how comfortable his son was with David, and how David seemed to genuinely enjoy playing with Sam.

"Ready Freddy."

The woosh noises followed Jonathan to the car. David buckled Samuel in while Jonathan put the box of cookies on the backseat next to him.

"Oh! The presents for the kids." David started walking back toward the house.

"I put them in the trunk, tiger. We're good to go."

"Are you ready for the Christmas madness?" Jonathan reached over and held David's hand as they made the short drive to his parents' house.

"I'm looking forward to it. I haven't had a family Christmas since I was a kid. This'll be great. I really like your family. They're warm and fun, and I like being around them."

Jonathan positively beamed. He squeezed David's hand and turned to look in the backseat.

"How about you, dumpling? You excited about going to Gram and Gramps's house?"

"Yeah, but we're coming home after, right, Papa? Because we live with David now."

"That's right, Sam."

David pulled up to the curb in front of the Doyles' house, took the key out of the ignition, and took a moment to absorb his surroundings. He'd gone from being the consummate bachelor to being Mr. Domestic Family-guy in the course of a month. After living alone for well over a decade, it should have felt strange to suddenly share his bed with another man and his house with a child. But he didn't feel strange so much as complete, whole. He felt right.

Dinner was somewhat-organized chaos. Kaiden, Keian, and Keller chased each other through the house, knocking over pictures and slamming into furniture. Keegan ignored them and sat on the couch, eating plate after plate of food from the buffet set up on the dining room table. Shannon started the night trying to keep them in line, but eventually gave up herself and sat next to her husband.

Brennan and Grace sat with Clare and made sure she ate some macaroni and cheese before they let her indulge in the colorful cookies Jonathan and Samuel made. Sam sat on David's lap while Jonathan fed him fruit and noodles. And through it all, Colleen and Brady laughed and shared stories of their three kids over the years. Someone would usually jump in and remind everyone of a missed detail that'd get the whole group laughing again. And even though he hadn't been part of those Christmases from years gone by, David felt included. They treated him like part of the family, and so that was how he felt.

"All right, we're doing something different for presents this year," Brady bellowed as his grandchildren sat on the floor surrounded by torn paper and presents from their aunts and uncles. "Instead of gettin' each of ya kids a separate gift, we got one thing that ya can all enjoy when ya come here."

Colleen held up a large picture of a wooden swing set, complete with slides, climbing ropes, a deck, and a tire swing. The kids jumped up and clamored for a turn holding the picture.

"Okay, okay. You can all look at it. We have all the parts out back, so we just need your fathers to help Gramps with the construction and it'll be ready to go."

"That's great, Ma! The kids will love it. When are your off days this week, Keeg?" Brennan asked.

"I'm off tomorrow and Wednesday and then I'm at the station for three days, back home on Sunday."

"Tomorrow would be great for me and Jon-Jon because the restaurant's closed. How about you, David? Can you make it tomorrow morning?"

David hoped the expression on his face didn't look as startled as he felt. He was taking part in the construction party? He'd never put together anything more complicated than a picture frame, but that wasn't what caught him off guard. Colleen had said the fathers were going to put the swing set together. He looked down at the little boy who had just crawled back onto his lap. Was he a father?

CHAPTER TWENTY-SEVEN

WITH THE restaurant bringing in good money, Brady was finally able to retire. Colleen had always dreamt of driving cross-country in an RV, so they decided to take the first three months of the new year to do just that. Since Jonathan had moved back to Emile City, Colleen had been watching Samuel while he worked. Her extended absence was going to make that impossible, so Jonathan and David enrolled Samuel in preschool.

"Are you nervous about Sam going to school tomorrow?"

David stroked Jonathan's hair and spoke quietly, not wanting to disrupt the intimacy of the moment. They were naked, slick with sweat, and wrapped together in their bed, recovering from yet another mind-blowing encounter. David continued to be amazed at how deep his passion for Jonathan ran, at how much he wanted him. And as they spent more time together, gained more familiarity with each other's bodies, the pleasure they found in every encounter heightened.

"Nah. It'll be good for him. He loves playing with his cousins, so I'm sure he'll really enjoy being around the other kids. And that school you found seems really great."

Alice, the associate Realtor David had hired, had told him the ins and outs of every preschool in EC West. She highly recommended one that was close to their house and had an opening. Samuel had been all smiles and giggles when they'd toured the school.

"You always have the best attitude about things. Have I mentioned how much I admire that, baby?"

David kissed the top of Jonathan's head. Jonathan had been resting on David's chest, his arm draped across David's waist. In response to the kind words and the kiss, he lifted himself up and lay on top of David. He leaned forward and pressed his lips to David's, kissing, licking, and nibbling on his lips and tongue.

Jonathan's hands stroked David's temples, his hair, his neck, and before he knew it, he could feel David's dick waking up against his thigh. When the hardening nudge became insistent, Jonathan pulled away from the kiss and reached his hand between their bodies, stroking that thick cock.

"You ready for another round, tiger?"

"Mmm, I'm always ready with you, baby. You're the most potent aphrodisiac around," David murmured against Jonathan's lips as he flipped him onto his back and draped his heavier mass over him.

"I want to suck you." Want might have been an understatement. Jonathan craved David, needed to feel the hardness press into his mouth, forcing his lips to spread wide, feeding him heat and strength and David's seed.

David took one more deep, penetrating kiss, then flipped his body around. He remained perched over Jonathan, but he scooted his knees onto the pillow where Jonathan's head rested and held himself up on his hands and knees so the tip of his cock brushed over Jonathan's face. Jonathan whimpered and opened his mouth wide, tilting his head back slightly to align that sought-after appendage with his throat. When Jonathan's hands reached up and cradled David's ass, pulling him down, David moaned and pushed into the wet warmth of Jonathan's mouth.

"Mmmm." Jonathan made the whimper-moan noises that drove David wild as he slurped and sucked on the thick cock penetrating his mouth.

David raised his body up and down, slowly at first, but then increasing his pace when he realized Jonathan could take a harder thrust, that he wanted it. With the increased speed, Jonathan was no longer able to concentrate on technique. He simply held his mouth open, his head tilted back, and accepted the assault from David's body. Moans left his lips in a steady stream as his arousal heightened with every push of that thick cock against his tongue.

"Oh fuck, Jonathan. Those noises… Makes me crazy how much you enjoy this."

David's hips snapped and his passion grew, taking Jonathan with him. Jonathan's cock leaked against his firm, flat stomach. David bent his face down and licked the nectar then took the rod into his mouth and sucked hard.

Jonathan cried out, the sound muffled by the hard dick filling his mouth. David reached under Jonathan's body and cupped his ass, pulling Jonathan up and deeper into his mouth as he pushed his own cock in and out of Jonathan's throat. The animal noises that came from both men matched their ferocious lovemaking, each of them digging fingers into the other's backside, pulling the other's hardness into a willing, eager mouth. All too soon, they reached the pinnacle, moaning and crying out their pleasure as they emptied into each other's throats.

David rolled to his side, so he wouldn't squish Jonathan with his weight, but he kept that softening member in his mouth, kept stroking Jonathan's ass. They nuzzled and licked, letting their heart rates return to normal. Eventually, Jonathan pulled on David's arm in a silent request for him to rejoin Jonathan at the top of the bed. David turned around, pulled Jonathan flush against him, chest to chest, and wrapped his arm around Jonathan's waist. With a final, silent kiss, they drifted off to sleep, sated and happy in each other's arms.

THE SECOND time someone referred to David as a father, it was more overt.

David was able to finish up his work early, so he decided to pick Samuel up from school. He called Jonathan to let him know that they'd meet at home when he was done at the restaurant, then made the five-minute drive from his office to the preschool. He approached the gray-haired woman at the front desk and handed her his driver's license.

"I'm David Miller and I'm here to pick up Samuel Doyle. Today's his first day, so I'm not sure which classroom he's in."

"Oh sure. Sam's had a great day today," she said as she compared David's license to some documents she had in her drawer. "I'll walk you to his room."

She rolled back her chair and got to her feet, then walked around the counter, handed David his license, and led him down the hall, chattering about a petting zoo that was coming to the school the following month and a fundraiser they were planning for the spring.

"Sam, your daddy's here," the woman called out as she opened a bright red door covered with papers that had been finger-painted by the children.

David wasn't sure what to say. Should he correct the woman? Was there a point? He and Jonathan were both listed on all the paperwork, and he didn't want to confuse things. Sam was in the corner of the room, playing blocks with his friends. He looked up when he heard his name, saw David standing at the door, and a smile covered his face. He hopped to his feet and ran over to David, who was crouched down and ready for the bundle that jumped into his arms.

"Did you have a good day?"

"Uh-huh. It's fun here. Wanna see what I made?"

THE WEEKS turned into months, and David continued to share childcare drop-off and pickup duties with Jonathan, so he spent quite a bit of time at the preschool. As a result, he got accustomed to being called "Sam's daddy."

"Sam's daddy, will you get my cup?" From a little girl with black hair and brown eyes when David was opening the refrigerator and placing Sam's lunch and sippy cup inside.

"Oh, there's Sam's daddy, maybe he can help us tack this up." From one of the petite classroom teachers who was perched on a chair, trying to hang a poster high on the wall.

And eventually, the one that tugged at his heart: "My daddy's here, I gotta go." From Sam when he saw David enter the room at the end of the day.

But the time when being referred to as a father mattered most took place a few days later. Sam had fallen asleep in front of the television. As soon as David hit the remote to turn off the cartoon the little boy had been watching, Sam started to whine.

"No! I was watching my show."

"It's bedtime, buddy." David lifted Sam into his arms and began walking toward the bedroom.

"Not tired, Daddy." The little head dropped onto David's chest, the eyes closed, and the body went limp.

He called me Daddy. David blinked back tears.

"Not tired, huh? Well, let's read a story and see how you feel."

David settled Sam into his bed and picked up a book off the shelf next to it.

"I like that one, Daddy!"

It came out so naturally, like he'd always been saying it.

"I know you do." David looked at Sam's happy face. "You know you have your papa's smile, Sam? You're very lucky."

"Uh-huh," Sam said as he wiggled under the blanket. "I have Papa's smile and your blue eyes, and we all have black hair."

They weren't the exact same shade, but they did both have blue eyes. The realization that Sam noticed the similarity and thought his eyes came from David made his voice thick with emotion. He cleared his throat, flipped the book open, and started reading.

When Sam's heavy eyes closed, David kissed the tiny forehead, turned off the light, and walked through the living room. The once-pristine designer space had warmed up since Jonathan and Sam had moved in. Pictures with smiling faces sat on the console and end tables, a basket holding a few of Sam's toys, DVDs, and books rested next to the armchair, and a blanket that David and Jonathan cuddled under most evenings was draped over the back of the sofa. The dining room had also been slightly "redecorated"—Sam's artwork now adorned the wall holding the original oil painting. David liked to call it the gallery, and whenever Sam brought home a particularly nice picture from school, he'd place it in a simple black frame and add it to the collection.

He entered the newly remodeled kitchen, where Jonathan was washing dishes. They'd been living together for months, but he was still occasionally hit with pangs of awareness over how much his life had changed. It was so much richer since Jonathan had walked in, claimed his heart, and turned his house into a home.

He wrapped his arms around Jonathan's trim waist, his chest pressing against Jonathan's back as he wiped down the sink. He rested his chin on Jonathan's head and kissed his neck.

"Sam called me Daddy."

David shared the information in a whisper. Jonathan turned off the water, dried his hands on a towel, turned around, and pushed a lock of hair off David's forehead.

"It's not the first time."

"It isn't?"

"Nope. I listen to him talking to his cousins when they're playing. The things they say crack me up. Anyway, the other day he was telling Kaiden about how his Daddy played football with him. Last week he told Clare that his Papa's favorite cookies were oatmeal raisin but that he and his Daddy both loved chocolate chip. And when you're working late, he asks me when Daddy's coming home."

Tears glistened in David's eyes. His chest constricted with overwhelming emotion. Jonathan wrapped his arms around David's waist and clung to him. He looked up at the beautiful face and fell in love all over again.

"You're okay with that?"

"Okay with it? Are you kidding? It's great. I never thought I'd have a child. Do you have any idea how much it means to me that he thinks of me this way? That he thinks of me as family?"

"I do have an idea because it means as much to me that you feel that way about him and me."

David leaned down for a kiss. He murmured against those sweet, red lips, "We are a family. You and me and Sam."

THE END

(BUT WAIT…THERE'S MORE—BONUS CHAPTER AHEAD.)

BONUS CHAPTER

When the U.S. Supreme Court released their historic marriage decision, I wanted to celebrate so I wrote a bonus chapter with Jonathan and David's reaction to the wonderful news. I hope you enjoy it. –CC

WHEN DAVID was eight years old, he rode his bike to school. He distinctly remembered doing jumps off curbs into puddles and racing with his friends. And other than a few scrapes and bruises, he hadn't gotten into any trouble during those bike rides.

But when he looked down at his son, he still saw Sam as the almost-three-year-old who had walked into a pizza parlor, asked him for ice cream, and found a permanent spot in his heart. Right next to the one owned by the boy's papa. And no matter how old either Sam or Jonathan got, David wanted to keep them close and protect them from the world.

"Please, Dad," Sam begged. "I'll be really careful."

And just like the first day he'd met his son, David could deny him nothing. "How about a compromise, Sam?" he said.

Sam chewed on his bottom lip and, for a second, he looked so much like his father that David almost gave in to his request and said he could do anything, have anything he wanted, just to see him smile. It was all he could do to remain seated on the couch and not hug his little boy.

"What do you mean?" Sam asked.

"Well, how about we put your bike in the back of my car and I drive you close to school? Then you can ride your bike the rest of the way."

Sam seemed to consider the proposal. "What about after school?" he asked. "Do I get to ride my bike home?"

"You can ride your bike over to the same spot, and either Papa or I will be waiting there for you."

And David would make sure to choose a spot with a direct line of sight to the school so they would be able to see Sam every single second.

"That sounds okay," Sam said and smiled brightly. "Thanks, Dad." He ran off, and David breathed a sigh of relief at the averted crisis.

"Nicely done."

David turned toward the doorway and grinned at Jonathan. "Thanks. It was touch and go there for a minute."

Jonathan walked over and straddled David's lap. "You're a great father," he said, his tone and expression adoring.

"You don't think I'm too strict with him?" David asked.

"You're stricter than my parents were, probably stricter than I would have been if I'd been raising him alone. But you do it because you care about him, and Sam knows it. That's why he never argues with you." Jonathan wrapped his arms around David's shoulders and melted against him, resting his face in the crook of David's neck. "He loves you just as much as you love him. We're so lucky to have you in our lives."

David pushed his hands underneath the back of Jonathan's shirt and ran them over his smooth, hot skin. "I'm glad I get to do this with you, baby. I wouldn't give up our family or our life together for anything. I hope you know that."

Jonathan nodded. "I do."

"Good."

They sat together a little longer, enjoying the closeness, and then Jonathan sighed and climbed off David's lap.

"Where are you going?" David asked as he grasped Jonathan's hand. Even after all the years they had spent together, he still hated being separated from his silver-eyed beauty for any length of time.

"It's getting late," Jonathan said. "I'm going to get dinner finished."

"We can go out if you want."

"Nope. The food is almost done. Just give me ten minutes and we'll be ready to sit down to eat."

David kissed the back of Jonathan's hand. "I'll just go get changed, round up Sam, and then meet you in the kitchen."

"ARE YOU sure he'll like this?" Sam asked Jonathan for what felt like the hundredth time.

"Yes, I'm sure," Jonathan said with a sigh. He continued cutting up tomatoes for the salad while he spoke. "You've seen Dad eat steak lots of times. You know he loves it."

"I know." Sam was quiet for a few minutes, so Jonathan hoped they had moved on from the menu inquisition. The hope was short-lived. "But shouldn't we make something more special?"

Jonathan stopped chopping and looked at Sam over his shoulder. "We're making filet mignon, Sam. This counts as a special meal."

He had moved on to peeling cucumbers when Sam spoke up again. "What about the potatoes?" he asked.

"Uh, they'll be ready in a few minutes."

"But they're just regular potatoes. There's nothing special about them. How do we know Daddy will like them?"

Jonathan gave up on cooking and sat down at the table with his son. "Your dad loves potatoes in any form, honey. Now, how about you tell me what has you so nervous."

Sam looked down at the table, his black hair flopping in his face. "I don't know." He shrugged.

"Sammy," Jonathan said, putting a warning note into his tone.

"I want him to say yes, that's all." Sam traced unknown shapes on the kitchen table. After a few seconds, he looked up at Jonathan. "This is really important, Papa."

Jonathan dropped to his knees next to his son and hugged the boy tightly. "He's going to say yes, Sam. David…

Daddy loves us both very much. You never, ever have to worry about that, okay?"

Loving David came easily, which was no surprise. Who wouldn't love a man who was beautiful, strong, and successful? What was surprising, though, was how secure David made Jonathan feel about those feelings being returned in full. Almost from the moment they got together, Jonathan knew that David wanted him, that the intense desire Jonathan felt was wholeheartedly reciprocated.

"Okay," Sam said.

Jonathan ruffled his hair as he stood up. "You go set the table and I'll finish this salad. Then everything will be ready."

He was plating the last steak when he heard the front door open, and David called out, "I'm home."

Sam came rushing into the kitchen. "Dad's here!" he whispered frantically.

"Dad lives here," Jonathan whispered back with a smile.

"How are my guys doing?" David said as he walked in. He kissed the top of Sam's head and then pulled Jonathan into his arms. "Hey, baby," he said hoarsely. "I missed you today."

No matter how many times Jonathan heard those words at the end of a workday, they still made his body tremble and his chest ache. "Missed you too," he said as he tipped his chin up and puckered his lips expectantly.

David gave him a tender kiss; then he took a deep

breath, and his eyes widened. "It smells great in here." He darted his gaze around the kitchen. "What's for dinner?"

"Filet, baked potatoes, roasted carrots, and salad."

"Mmm, that sounds amazing," David said. He reached around Jonathan and popped a piece of cucumber into his mouth. "What's the special occasion?"

Jonathan had plans for a fancy meal followed by heartfelt words and a romantic proposal. But Sam was eight and patience was not his virtue, so the plan changed when the boy said, "We're asking you to get married."

David jerked his head toward Sam and then back to Jonathan. He gulped. "What?"

Oh well. Time to go with the new plan.

"Sam's right." Jonathan gazed into David's beautiful navy-blue eyes. "You already know I fell in love with you the first moment I saw you. And when we started dating, I think I told you the reality of being with you was even better than the fantasy I'd been living with for years." Jonathan took a deep breath. "But after all this time being together, sharing our lives, raising our son, I learned something. Love grows. What I feel for you now is so much more, so very much better, than I ever could have imagined when I first saw you in that hospital." Jonathan dropped to one knee. He glanced at Sam, and after a second, the boy remembered this part of the plan and joined his father. Jonathan smiled and grasped Sam's hand. Then he looked up at David. "David Miller, will you marry us?"

With his eyes decidedly shiny, David joined his family on the kitchen floor, wrapped them in his arms, and gathered them close. "Yes," he said, his voice thick with emotion. "Of course I'll marry you."

Jonathan was caught in David's heated gaze. His heart felt full enough to burst.

David dipped his face down and brushed a kiss over Jonathan's lips. "Love you," he whispered.

"You see, Papa?" Sam said, sounding as smug as possible for an eight-year-old. "I told you Dad would like the steak."

IT WAS a special occasion, so they let Sam stay up late. After dinner, all three of them changed into their pajamas and sat around the coffee table, playing Uno. When Sam's eyelids started drooping but he continued to insist he wasn't tired, they put on a movie. Five minutes later, he was out like a light.

"I'll carry him into his room," David said. He scooped Sam up and then looked meaningfully at Jonathan. "Meet me in our room so we can start the adult portion of this celebration."

Jonathan trembled and David smiled smugly as he strutted out of the room. After all these years, he still had the ability to turn his man on with nothing more than a vague promise of what was to come. The plumping flesh in David's pants reminded him that thoughts of being alone with Jonathan ramped him up just as quickly.

At twenty-two, Jonathan had been strikingly beautiful. He had captured David's attention at first sight. And with each passing year, the man had somehow managed to get even sexier. He hadn't outgrown the innocence David had found so appealing, but there was a confidence in Jonathan now that showed when he stood tall and smiled widely. During their time together, he had found his place in the world, and he never failed to let David know that that place was by his side.

David tucked Sam into bed, kissed his forehead, and took a moment to be thankful for being a father. Finding a man like Jonathan to share his life had been a miracle, and adding an adorable child who looked at him like he knew the answers to all the questions in the universe was more than he ever could have hoped for. But he'd been blessed with both. And they wanted to make it legal. He thought maybe he'd split his lip from smiling so widely.

Knowing Sam didn't like waking up in the dark, David left the bedroom door cracked open just enough to let some light in. Then he walked down the hall, opened his bedroom door, and said, "Hey, baby."

The room was dark and empty, but the door to the adjoining bathroom was ajar, and he could hear water running. His dick went ramrod hard at the thought of his partner, now fiancé, naked and wet in the next room. He stripped off his clothes, hurried into the steamy room, and joined Jonathan in the shower.

"Hi." Jonathan blinked water out of his eyes and looked up at David, a shy smile on his perfect face.

David pushed his wet hair back and met his gaze. "Hi." He bent down and pressed his lips to Jonathan's.

"I'm all done washing. You get under the spray, and I'll get you all cleaned up."

David did as he was told and stepped under the hot water while Jonathan lathered his hands. He pressed his body to David's and nuzzled his neck while he caressed and soaped every inch of his skin, ending with his dick.

The feeling of warm, skilled fingers stroking and tugging had David arching his neck and moaning in pleasure. He wasn't surprised when Jonathan dropped to his knees—his desire to suck dick was exceeded only by his need to have his ass filled. Damn, but was David ever lucky. He looked down to see Jonathan at his feet, leaning back on his haunches while he jacked David's dick.

"Will you step back just a little?" Jonathan asked. "I want to wash the soap off so I can suck you."

David moved under the water, cupped the back of Jonathan's head, and lovingly caressed him. When all the suds were gone, he stepped out of the spray and gave himself over to Jonathan.

A warm tongue lapping at his crown, sure fingers rolling his balls, and the sound of those arousing whimper-moan noises Jonathan made combined into an erotic pleasure

David had grown to crave. Living with Jonathan and sharing a bed every night hadn't diminished the heat between them. If anything, familiarity had bred a deeper connection and more fulfilling sex life.

"Suck me, baby," David moaned, and Jonathan did. He pulled David's erection between his lips and sucked hard, taking his thick length down to the root right from the start. David rocked forward and back, in and out of the welcome heat, his arousal ramping up further. "You want me to come like this?" he asked, knowing he was close to the point of no return.

Jonathan increased the strength of his suction and then pulled off David's dick with a pop. "I love tasting you," he said breathlessly. "But I want to feel you inside tonight."

It was the response David had expected, which was why he'd asked the question instead of falling into his orgasm and spending himself down Jonathan's throat. He gripped the handle and turned off the water, then reached down for Jonathan. "Come on, baby," he said. "Let's finish this in bed."

They were mostly dry by the time they slid between the sheets. David lay on his back with Jonathan on top of him. They touched—hands wandering over all available body parts—and kissed—lips meeting and tongues tangling. Making out with this man was something David adored. Jonathan craved affection and David loved giving it to him.

"I love your muscles," Jonathan said as he skated his fingers over David's well-defined arms and chest. "So strong."

David flexed, showing off a little; then he cupped Jonathan's ass and squeezed it, making him buck and groan. Jonathan spread his legs and dropped his knees on either side of David, leaving his cheeks spread wide and his pink hole exposed. David rubbed his fingertips over that puckered skin.

"Ungh," Jonathan groaned. "Feels so good when you touch me." He pushed back against those digits, clearly trying to take them into his body.

David loved how responsive and eager Jonathan was in bed. The man still fucked like the porn star he had been once upon a time. But Jonathan's energy and positive attitude weren't limited to the bedroom. He carried that zest for life with him everywhere, glowing from within and lighting up everything and everyone around him, David included.

"You ready for more?" David asked, his voice husky with arousal.

Jonathan nodded and reached for the lube. He coated David's cock and rubbed his slick fingers over his own hole; then he pushed himself back until David's erection pressed against hot skin. Their eyes met.

"I love you," David whispered as he gripped Jonathan's waist and tilted his own hips up, pushing through the ring of muscle and making Jonathan gasp in pleasure.

"Love you too," Jonathan said. He pushed back against David's dick, not stopping until he had taken David completely inside. "God!" He shuddered. "You feel so good inside me."

David bent his knees and planted his feet flat on the bed, giving himself leverage; then he started a steady thrust up and down, fucking himself up into Jonathan. Not one to stay still during sex, Jonathan flattened his hands on David's chest and bounced, moaning and crying out as he was speared and stretched.

With their eyes locked on each other's faces, they moved together, enjoying the connection and the friction. David raised his arm, twined his hand around Jonathan's nape, and pulled him down for a deep kiss. Jonathan sucked on David's tongue, increasing the pace of his lower body as his orgasm neared.

"You close?" David asked, sounding breathless.

"Uh-huh." Jonathan's eyes rolled back. "So close, so good."

With one hand on Jonathan's hip and the other on his back, David held Jonathan in place as he flipped them over. Once he had Jonathan beneath him, he held onto Jonathan's shoulders and started fucking him in earnest, his fast, hard pace designed to take them both over the edge.

It didn't take long before Jonathan shouted David's name, scratched his nails down his back, and filled the space between them with the evidence of his pleasure. David buried his face in Jonathan's neck and grunted as he came deep inside the most gorgeous ass he had ever seen.

"Mmm," David moaned and went in for more kisses. He felt sated and happy. After a few minutes, he pulled back just enough to be able to look into Jonathan's eyes. "So you want to be my husband?" he asked.

Jonathan's expression turned serious. He grasped David's hips and said, "I want that more than anything."

The feeling was mutual. "Me too, baby," David said. He gazed at those incredible silver eyes and fell even deeper. "Thank you for asking me."

THE END

ABOUT THE AUTHOR

Cardeno C.—CC to friends—is a hopeless romantic who wants to add a lot of happiness and a few *awwws* into a reader's day. Writing is a nice break from real life as a corporate type and volunteer work with gay rights organizations. Cardeno's stories range from sweet to intense, contemporary to paranormal, long to short, but they always include strong relationships and walks into the happily-ever-after sunset.

Email: cardenoc@gmail.com

Website: www.cardenoc.com

Twitter: https://twitter.com/cardenoc

Facebook: http://www.facebook.com/CardenoC

Pinterest: http://www.pinterest.com/cardenoC

Blog: http://caferisque.blogspot.com

OTHER BOOKS BY CARDENO C.

AVAILABLE NOW

He Completes Me
(2nd Edition)

Not even his mother's funeral can convince self-proclaimed party boy Zach Johnson to tone down his snark or think about settling down. He is who he is, and he refuses to change for anyone. When straight-laced, compassionate Aaron Paulson claims he's falling for him, Zach is certain Aaron sees him as another project, one more lost soul for the idealistic Aaron to save. But Zach doesn't need to be fixed and he refuses to be with someone who sees him as broken.

Patience is one of Aaron's many virtues. He has waited years for a man who can share his heart and complete his life and he insists Zach is the one. Pride, fear, and old hurts wither in the wake of Aaron's adoring loyalty and as Zach reevaluates his perceptions of love and family, he finds himself tempted to believe in the impossible: a happily-ever-after.

Home Again
(2nd Edition)

Imposing, temperamental Noah Forman wakes up in a hospital and can't remember how he got there. He holds it together, taking comfort in the fact that the man he has loved since childhood is on the way. But when his one and only finally arrives, Noah is horrified to discover that he doesn't remember anything from the past three years.

Loyal, serious Clark Lehman built a life around the person who insisted from their first meeting that they were meant to be together. Now, years later, two men whose love has never faltered must relive their most treasured and most painful moments in order to recover lost memories and secure their future.

Just What the Truth Is
(2nd Edition)

People-pleaser Ben Forman has been in the closet so long he has almost convinced himself he is straight, but his denial train gets derailed when hotshot lawyer Micah Trains walks into his life. Micah is brilliant, funny, driven...and he assumes Ben is gay and starts dating him. Finding himself truly happy for the first time, Ben doesn't have the willpower to resist Micah's affection.

When his relationship with Micah heats up, Ben realizes has a problem: his parents won't tolerate a gay son and self-confident Micah isn't the type to hide. If Ben wants to maintain his hold on his happiness, he'll have to decide what's important and own up to the truth of who he is. The trouble is figuring out just what that truth is.

The One Who Saves Me
(2nd Edition)

At fourteen, Andrew Thompson and Caleb Lakes become best friends. As the years pass, they stand by each other through family trauma, school, and the start of their careers. They share their first sexual experiences, learning and experimenting, and they talk each other through countless dates and breakups.

Decades of trust and loyalty build a deep and abiding friendship, one that surpasses any relationship in their lives. But when the parameters of their unique friendship change, neither man knows how to break out of their established roles to build something new. After all, boyfriends come and go, but best friends are forever.

Where He Ends and I Begin
(2nd Edition)

Aggressive, physical, and brave, Jake Owens is a small town football hero turned big city cop who passes his time with meaningless encounters believing he can't have who he really wants: Nate Richardson, his best friend since before forever.

Thoughtful, quiet, and kind, Nate is a brilliant doctor who has always known who he is and has never been able to shake his crush on loyal, courageous, *straight* Jake.

After a passionate night together, Nate realizes Jake isn't as straight as he assumed, but he worries that what they shared was a fluke, a result of too much closeness for too long. For Jake, the question isn't how they ended up in bed together because he has always known that Nate holds his heart, it's how he'll convince Nate that he wants and needs to stay there.

Walk With Me
(2nd Edition)

When Eli Block steps into his parents' living room and sees his childhood crush sitting on the couch, he starts a shameless campaign to seduce the young rabbi. Unfortunately, Seth Cohen barely remembers Eli and he resolutely shuts down all his advances. As a tenuous and then binding friendship forms between the two men, Eli must find a way to move past his unrequited love while still keeping his best friend in his life. Not an easy feat when the same person occupies both roles.

Professional, proper Seth is shocked by Eli's brashness, overt sexuality, and easy defiance of societal norms. But he's also drawn to the happy, funny, light-filled man. As their friendship deepens over the years, Seth watches Eli mature into a man he admires and respects. When Seth finds himself longing for what Eli had so easily offered, he has to decide whether he's willing to veer from his safe life-plan to build a future with Eli.